Death Comes Around

A McCall / Malone Mystery

Glenn Harris

Death Comes Around is a work of fiction. Names, characters, places and incidents either are the product of the author's imagination or are used fictitiously. Any resemblance to actual persons, living or dead, or events is entirely coincidental. Portland, Oregon, actually exists of course. Major landmarks like Pioneer Courthouse Square and the Justice Center are where they belong, as are the streets and neighborhoods, but I have moved a few buildings around, put restaurants where none exist, erased houses that do exist, and wreaked other minor havoc with Portland's reality for the purposes of my story.

Copyright © 2017 by Glenn Harris

ISBN 978-0-9969155-5-7

First Edition 2017

First Paperback Edition 2017

www.glennharris.us

Cover design: Cathleen Rehfeld

Death Comes Around

SATURDAY, FEBRUARY 16

Shit, piss, and a faint whiff of putrescence. The stark combination of odors was unmistakable. Somewhere within this overheated, dimly lit apartment something was dead. I could only hope it wasn't human.

I hoped with all my heart it wasn't who I feared it might be.

I drew my gun and took a step further inside, pushing the door flat against the wall to my right to make certain no one was concealed behind it. The *thunk* of the knob hitting the wall fell heavily into a silence broken only by a low hum from the direction of the open kitchen doorway across the room. Sounded like a refrigerator trying to stay cool.

And no wonder it was having to work hard; the air felt like someone had turned the thermostat as high as it would go. Morning sunlight glowed faintly through drawn shades in the modest living room. The furniture seemed well-cared-for but a little shabby: several plush chairs with side tables and small frilly lamps, along with a big overstuffed sofa angled across the left rear corner, a skinny floor lamp standing behind it. A diminutive dining table was to the right of the sofa with four plain wooden chairs tucked into it. A couple of five-shelf bookcases contained no books but rather stacks of CDs or DVDs along with a variety of knickknacks. The walls were decorated with what looked like generic motel art. Besides the open kitchen doorway, I could see one other interior door and it was closed. Probably a bedroom.

No dead animals or people in this room.

I cautiously crossed the carpet toward the kitchen.

The entire room was visible from the doorway. I could see the normal appliances, none too modern. Cabinets. The counter was bare as was the small, centered table. The smell was stronger here, but nothing suspicious otherwise.

1

I stepped a few paces to my right, opened the bedroom door, and looked inside.

She was on the bed—and it appeared she'd probably been there for a number of hours. An almost overwhelming sense of despair seized my chest and shortened my breath.

There appeared to be no point in checking her pulse, but I was about to step to the side of the bed to do it anyway. Suddenly I heard a slight noise behind me in the living room, a whisper of motion. The hairs on the back of my neck stood at attention and a chill darted down my spine.

Crap. There'd been no one in the corridor, no one visible in the living room. I'd thought that space next to the floor lamp behind the big couch was too small for someone to have been crouched back there. Maybe I was wrong. I'd missed something and I was an idiot.

My body was tensing to turn when I heard a familiar voice, not more than four feet from my back.

"Goodbye, Clint," it said.

CHAPTER ONE
Eight days earlier...

In Portland, Oregon, February is the cruelest month. It's dreary, it's wet, it's cold.... It's the winter of my fifty-second year and I am surrounded by intimations of mortality, or at least mutability.

I'm a private investigator. My full name is Clinton Nicodemus McCall, after my father and (for reasons I never understood) a fallen-away-Catholic great-grandfather. As a journalist my by-line was Clinton N. McCall. When I was an academic I'd sometimes, just for fun, style myself as C. Nicodemus McCall. And my ex-wife, who met me when I was a college professor and left me when I stopped being one, took to calling me "Nico" near the end of our marriage, which made me sound like an Italian gangster—I guess to signify her view that I was associating too much with the criminal element.

For the past eleven years, I've been simply Clint McCall, sole owner and proprietor of the McCall Detective Agency located here on the second floor of an old two-story commercial building on the northwest edge of downtown, above Previously Owned Books. Besides my office, the second floor houses the Witkowsky Insurance Agency, the law firm of Bitterly and Barclay, Eleanor Ivory Accountancy, and Pacific Northwest Research, a small firm that does telephone surveys.

The two elderly detectives who've always provided my backup are slowing down and thinking seriously about quitting the game entirely. My daughter is a drama major, in many more ways than one. I haven't had a woman in my life for quite some time. And my best friend's career may be in serious trouble because of a new homophobic boss.

On the other hand, my agency is going well and I have good friends. I'm in fine shape for my age, primarily thanks to the taekwondo training space (dojang) that I lease along with six other black belts.

And fifty-one is the new thirty-one, right? Or is it forty-one? Or could it be true that you're as old as you feel, which would mean that I sometimes totter out of the dojang at the age of sixty-five.

At least I have a new case, thanks to my insurance agent Ray Witkowsky across the hall; to wit, investigation of one Marvin Montgomery, professional student and suspected insurance scammer.

On this particular late Friday afternoon, my new case was my *only* current case and I planned to devote most of my weekend to surveillance of Marvin Montgomery. The man claimed to be unable to work because of a back injury sustained in a minor car accident. Ray Witkowsky suspected he was faking it, not least because 47-year-old Marv had apparently never worked a day in his life prior to said accident. All I had to do was get a photo of Montgomery lifting something heavy, playing tennis, having wild tempestuous sex, or doing anything else that would preclude a debilitating back injury. Should be easy enough.

I had decided to go on home and get my surveillance kit together when someone knocked on the frosted glass that constituted the upper half of my office door.

"Come in," I called after a quick glance around to make sure the office looked presentable. Who knew? It might actually be a potential client.

A woman poked her head hesitantly around the partly open door. "Mr. McCall?"

"That's me." I waved her on in. "Have a seat."

Her eyes took in the office as she slowly stepped inside and closed the door behind her. A single big room, my office is dominated by a large wooden desk in front of a pair of slightly dirty windows. Computer table next to the desk. A couple of beige metal file cabinets along one wall, next to storage shelves badly in need of organization. On a somewhat rickety corner table by the door sits a compact fridge, microwave, and coffee maker. No plants, no decorations of any kind except a framed license from the Oregon Board of Investigators and my black belt certificate hanging on the wall.

I was dressed as usual in chinos and short-sleeve knit shirt, despite the miserable February weather. I always keep the office thermostat set in the mid 70's. I don't like cold.

My visitor crossed to the nearest chair in front of my desk. I put her at around thirty years old, about five-foot-five, a little chunky, with short-cropped brown hair and glasses. Cute upturned nose with freckles. Dressed conservatively but not inexpensively under a beige wool coat and scarf. She carried a small purse in her left hand.

She shrugged off the coat and scarf, settled them over the arm of the other visitor's chair, and then stiffly sat down. She took another glance around the office, smoothed her skirt with a series of short, jerky motions, and faced in my general direction.

"My name is Samantha Quiller," she said. Her voice was soft, reedy, as if her throat were almost too tight to allow speech.

"What can I do for you, Miss Quiller?"

"Mrs. Quiller," she corrected me. Her eyes traveled from me around the office once again, stopped for a moment on the framed documents.

"You're a black belt?" She blinked and gave me a once-over the way people usually do when they find out about my training, wondering why I look like a short, stocky old guy with thinning hair, pug nose and big ears instead of a young hunk like the ones they've seen in martial arts movies.

"Yes, a fourth degree in taekwondo." Never hurts to try to impress the potential client. "What can I do for you?" I asked again.

She took a deep breath, seemed to steady herself, and looked me in the eye. "I want you to find my husband." She pulled a photograph out of her purse. "This is what he looks like."

Aha. Missing spouse. No sweat. I opened a notebook and picked up a pen. "What is your husband's name?"

"George. George Quiller."

Duly noted. "And when did you see him last?"

"I saw him downtown, here in Portland, yesterday afternoon. He was crossing Broadway and then disappeared into the crowd in Pioneer Courthouse Square. I honked at him and he saw me. He *recognized* me and then hurried away. I know it was him!"

Missing spouse who doesn't want to be found. Still not a problem. "Okay. And when was the last time you saw him before that?"

She suddenly seemed oddly hesitant. "Last March."

Nearly a year. Could make it a little more difficult. "That's when he disappeared?"

She looked down at her nice smooth skirt and began toying with it. Her hands were trembling. "Well...he didn't exactly disappear."

Faint alarm bells going off. "Hmmm. What exactly did he do, then?"

"He was killed by a car bomb."

CHAPTER TWO

Whoops. Those bells were clanging now. Never assume, I reminded myself as I uttered a lame "oh" and put down the pen.

"You must have heard about it. It blew up right in our driveway."

"I'm afraid I don't recall anything like that off-hand."

"He kissed me and Kinsey goodbye, walked out the door, and a minute later I heard this horrible explosion in front of the house. It shattered the living room window. Thank God we were in the kitchen."

"Kinsey...?"

"Our daughter. She's two, now."

"It must have been a terrible experience for both of you."

"God, yes. I ran out front and all I could see was smoke and parts of the car on fire and pieces...." Her words stumbled to a stop at that point.

"Would you like a glass of water?"

She waved that off. "No, no, I'm okay. I haven't had to describe it out loud since the police talked to me that day."

"I don't need those details anyway, so that's okay. But...I gather that you now believe it wasn't your husband in the car."

"How could it have been?" Her eyes flashed and she began to sound angry. "I saw him downtown yesterday! We looked at each other, for God's sake. I know he recognized me when I recognized him!"

I picked up the pen again. "I understand this is difficult, but wasn't your husband identified at the time of the...incident?"

"Yes. No. I don't know. There were just.... Nothing *looked* like him, if that's what you mean, but I was sure it was him and so was everyone else. He went out to get in the car and then it blew up. It was only a minute, less than a minute. It had to be him! But, some-

7

how, it must not have been." She gazed fiercely at me, her eyes glistening with tears. "I want you to find him."

I sat back and tried to gauge whether there might be a sensible alternative to her perception. I looked again at the photo she'd handed me. Solidly built guy, burr-cut blond hair, sharp facial features but nothing really distinguishing. "They say that everybody has a double somewhere."

"That's what they say...but I saw the recognition in his eyes. That was my husband looking at me. I would *swear* it. And yet.... If so, who got in his car that day? Why did he leave us?" She suddenly sagged. "Maybe I'm going crazy."

The thought had crossed my mind as well, but it seemed the better part of discretion not to agree. The lady clearly didn't think there was an alternative. If I took the case, all I'd have to do was determine whether her husband was alive after he'd presumably been dead and buried for nearly a year *and* track down a man she'd glimpsed yesterday about whom she could provide absolutely no information other than that he resembled said husband.

Well, first I'd have to determine if she was in fact nuts. If not, then all that other.

I told her my fee, noted that expenses were additional, and cautioned her that what she was talking about could take a *lot* of hours.

She reached over to her coat on the neighboring chair and pulled a checkbook out of the pocket. "I have enough money," she said. "Would a thousand dollar advance be sufficient?"

I agreed with barely tempered enthusiasm that it would do quite nicely.

After an exchange of check and receipt, the rest of the interview went smoothly. It turned out that Mrs. Quiller was a fairly successful real estate agent and George had been a very successful traveling salesman for a company manufacturing large farming equipment. Thus the thousand-dollar retainer without blinking an eye.

She said there had been no arrests in the car bombing, that in fact she knew of no leads or suspects. If true, it meant the job had probably been a professional hit. I'd be checking with my friend and fellow black belt Mike Whitehall in the Portland Homicide Detail to see if the cops had more than she knew.

We went over all the details she could think of concerning her husband—friends, co-workers, enemies, habits, faults, virtues, etc. It wasn't odd that she could think of no enemies. It was somewhat odd that she could think of few friends or co-workers. Apparently George had been quite the loner, which I guess wouldn't be unusual for a traveling salesman.

When I asked if anything had seemed to be troubling him before the day of the bombing, she admitted that she'd suspected "mental problems" as she called them. Most of the time, she said, he was a loving and even-tempered man but now and then he would become noticeably distant for a few days; he'd forget where things were and get very irritable when he couldn't find them. Then he'd go back to normal as if nothing had happened. She said she tried to talk to him about it, but he wouldn't admit to any concerns. She'd begun to wonder if he was using drugs or had some kind of personality disorder. Sounded like simple moodiness to me.

I asked her if there'd been any specific evidence that the victim of the bombing was her husband, if they'd found his wedding ring or if DNA testing had been done on the remains from the bombing. She said he didn't wear a wedding ring, which was interesting, and she didn't know about DNA testing. She didn't think there had been any testing since, at the time, there'd been no question about who was in the car. I decided that was a good place to start and wrapped up the interview a little after five. Samantha Quiller left with my promise that I'd report regularly on my progress (or, as I didn't say, lack thereof).

CHAPTER THREE

I skimmed over my notes once more and could think of nothing I'd left out, so I stashed the notebook in my top left hand drawer, retrieved my Smith and Wesson from the top right hand drawer, clipped the holster to my belt, and got up to retrieve my jacket from the hall tree near the door. My hand had just touched the doorknob when the phone rang. I glanced at my watch. Five twenty-five. My office hours were over.

Still, a third client wouldn't hurt. I strode back over to the desk and picked up the phone. "McCall Detective Agency."

"Dad?" It was my daughter Colleen. She sounded tense, maybe afraid.

"What's up, kiddo?"

Silence.

"Colleen? What's the matter?"

"I saw Mom."

It was my turn to be struck silent. Colleen's mother Sarah, my ex-wife, had disappeared four years ago. No note, no apparent explanation, no evidence of a crime. Just gone one day. It had driven a wedge between me and Colleen for a long time as she blamed me--because I'd somehow driven her mother away, or failed to find out what happened to her, or maybe both. We'd grown close again over the past year or so and I'm ashamed to admit that a large part of my initial reaction was fear that this would bring up the old estrangement again.

A thousand questions buzzed around my head. I chose "Where?" as the first one to voice.

"I was at the mall, Clackamas Town Center, up on the second level, and I saw her in the crowd down below. I called out but she didn't seem to hear me. She didn't look up. And by the time I got down there she was gone. I couldn't find her again." Her voice went up at least a register. "Dad, it was her! She's back! Have you heard from her?"

"No. Nothing. Honey, you're absolutely sure it was her? Not someone who looked like her?" Talk about déjà vu; I'd been asking Samantha Quiller the same questions just minutes ago.

Colleen answered with even more certainty than Mrs. Quiller had. "It was Mom. No question. Dad, we've got to find her! Maybe she has amnesia!"

It was as good an explanation as any. "We will," I said. "I want you to write down every detail. Exactly where you were and when, where she was in relation to you, what she was wearing, hairstyle, everything. We'll go over it later this evening. Come by the house."

"Okay. This is big, you know? See you then." She hung up and I slowly put my own phone back in the cradle.

I don't like coincidence; it's hardly ever coincidental. This time, though.... I get a client who's seen her dead husband at almost exactly the same time my daughter spots her missing and feared-dead mother. Barring the extremely unlikely event that George Quiller had disappeared in order to run around with my ex-wife, this coincidence was probably genuine.

It still left me with two very mysterious people to find. Not to mention more emotional land mines than I cared to count.

CHAPTER FOUR

It was nearly six when I pulled into the driveway of my little house three doors south of Hawthorne on 37th. I retrieved my mail from the box by the steps—all junk, it looked like—and unlocked the front door.

I opened it to see Stella, one of my two tortoiseshell cats, waiting as she always does in the middle of the living room carpet. Her sister Maxine would be somewhere in the bedroom, cautiously assuring herself that it was me before making an appearance.

"Hello, Stella," I said. She trotted over to bump my leg as I closed the door behind me. Maxine's head appeared around the bedroom doorframe at about the same time. Strictly indoor cats, Stella is a short-hair and the extremely fluffy Maxine could be a Maine Coon. They don't look like sisters, but I was assured by the cat rescue group two years ago that they were from the same litter and would be best kept together. I'd always been a one-cat-at-a-time man myself, but I hadn't regretted the adoption of these two for a moment.

I fed them dry food in two bowls and then microwaved a frozen dinner for myself. It's fortunate that we all three have simple tastes.

I didn't know when my daughter would be dropping by, so after dinner I busied myself putting together the surveillance kit for the weekend. There was nothing I could do for Samantha Quiller until Monday and I'd have to see Colleen before I had any idea what I could do for her. So I'd probably spend the weekend doing what I had assumed I'd be doing: watching Marvin Montgomery.

The kit consisted of snacks, bottled water, a selection of music and recorded-book CDs to help keep me awake, a clean urine bottle to help keep me in the car, and backup batteries and memory cards for my cameras. I always have binoculars and a simple point-

and-shoot digital camera in the glove compartment. For a formal surveillance like this, I bring along a much more sophisticated digital camera with a long-range lens.

It was mid-evening by the time I was satisfied with my preparations. I settled down on the couch with a paperback novel to await Colleen's arrival. As usual, Stella curled up in my lap and Maxine took up her station on the other end of the couch.

Also as usual, when we heard someone knocking Stella headed for the front door to greet whoever it was and Maxine for the bedroom to hide under the bed.

It was my daughter. She moved into the hug I offered without a word; it felt like embracing a tangle of vibrating wires. Colleen has always had an aura of unrelenting intensity about her, but it was rarely so close to the surface that I could literally feel it.

I stepped back and ushered her into the house.

Colleen is twenty-four, a small woman with long reddish-blonde hair. She wears wire-rim glasses and the slightly flamboyant outfits typical of a college drama major. This evening it was loose red satin pants with an orange blousy top and white sandals.

At the moment she was so keyed-up that even the normally friendly Stella skittered a few feet away. Maxine, who usually considers Colleen one of the few acceptable human beings besides me, chose to stay out of sight.

My daughter dropped onto the couch hard enough to bounce a little, then sat forward looking down at the floor past her two hands gripped tightly together. Whatever she'd seen at Clackamas Town Center mall had shaken her deeply—and if she was right about what she'd seen, it was going to have no small impact on me as well.

She looked up, her glasses glinting in the lamplight. "You've got to find her this time," she said.

Ah, yes: this time. There it was already, the old resentment. Colleen's version of events at the time of the divorce was that her mother had left me because I became a private detective and then I'd failed as a private detective because I couldn't find her mother.

Which was actually a pretty accurate version of events.

CHAPTER FIVE

Sarah and I had married when I was a Portland State University professor on the faculty of the Department of Communications. She liked the fact that I'd gotten the job because I'd been an award-winning journalist with the *Oregonian*. While she took vicarious pleasure in my many past adventures as an investigative reporter, she loved being a professor's wife—not least, I think, because she believed all the adventures were in the past.

She managed to ignore the fact that I was always a little uncomfortable at PSU, somewhat a fish out of water given the department's emphasis on spoken communication rather than written. She was dubious when I began taekwondo training at the age of 38--and even more dubious when soon after that I began my part-time apprenticeship with the private detective agency belonging to Johnny Crew and Hap Harbaugh. About the time I got my first degree black belt she decided that I was caught up in some kind of mid-life crisis. At least I didn't buy a Porsche.

But Sarah couldn't find the cure for what she came to view as a kind of mental illness (again, shades of Samantha Quiller). When I finally left my position with the university eleven years ago to start my own agency, she decided that was it; she said she didn't want to be married to a tough-guy black-belt private detective. It was not what she'd signed up for.

After the divorce she started an interior design business with a friend of hers, which seemed to make her very happy, and embarked on quite a number of adventures of her own—mostly involving men who didn't make her very happy. Which really, I guess, just continued the trend that she had started with me.

Then, after seven years of that life, one day she was gone. And with all my resources I hadn't discovered a single clue as to how or why.

I looked down at those glasses glinting as if with anger in the light, unable to see my daughter's eyes behind them. What I *wanted* to say was, I still don't have a clue. I don't know if it was your mother you saw and, even if it was, how can I track down someone glimpsed hours ago in passing at the mall? It sounds like my new case for Samantha Quiller but it's not; I've already done all the background on this one, years ago.

What I did say was, "I'll do my best."

And I would, too. What the hell. I could retrace the steps of my old investigation. If Sarah really was in town, maybe something new would turn up.

CHAPTER SIX

Sixty hours later, nothing had. I mounted the steps to my office at eight a.m. Monday morning, still a little woozy from a long weekend of watching Marvin Montgomery live a life that seemed unlikely to strain his back, his brain, or pretty much anything else.

My surveillance subject was short, overweight, balding...generally a total schlump in addition to being a geek. A long-time professional student, he had doctorates in English and sociology and apparently was working—if you want to call it that—toward a Master's in psychology.

He spent most of his time at home, a small apartment just off the intersection of southwest Broadway and Jackson, close to both the Stadium Freeway and the Portland State University campus. He stayed up late and slept in even later. When he did go out, so far it was to the library, to the grocery, or to simply stand on some downtown corner watching the girls go by—which none of them seemed to notice.

I couldn't guarantee that that was all he'd done with his weekend because there was always the possibility, however unlikely, that he'd gotten up in the middle of the night and gone out after I went home to sleep. Also because I'd taken some time off from the surveillance to stop by Clackamas Town Center Sunday afternoon.

Friday evening I'd promised Colleen that over the weekend I would at least scope out the scene where she thought she'd spotted her mother. That calmed her down enough that Maxine finally came out from under the bed.

So, for a few minutes I stood on the upper level where Colleen had stood, looking down at the crowd as she had. Not surprisingly, I saw no one familiar down there. I did, however, make a list of the nearby stores on the first level. Early this week I'd go back with a photo of Sarah and check with the weekday retail personnel to see if anyone remembered her. As long as I was going to do it, might as well do it right.

Meanwhile here in the office I got the coffeemaker going, settled in behind my desk and typed up a report of Montgomery's weekend activities for Ray Witkowsky. That took only about twenty minutes and then I sat for a few minutes sipping coffee and watching the Monday morning traffic on Stark while I decided on my priorities for what promised to be a busy couple of days.

Most important, I needed to get some background on George and Samantha Quiller. She hadn't made a big deal out of the fact that her husband wore no wedding ring, but I might. Plus I wanted to confirm whether DNA tests had been done. Second, I had to recruit a backup for the Montgomery surveillance since it was going to take longer than I'd hoped; I had too many demands on my time during the workweek to do a good job of watching him. He could be doing some heavy lifting right this moment, for instance, if he'd gotten up early. Then, moving on to activities that weren't going to bring in any money, I wanted to keep my promise to Colleen and try to determine who she'd seen at the mall.

And, darn it, as always when I got really busy I would have to neglect my evening workouts at the dojang. Somehow, sitting in my car watching Marvin Montgomery waste his life wasn't as invigorating as a good sparring session.

Finishing my cup of coffee and noting that it was now quarter to nine, I swung back to the desk and picked up the phone.

My first call was to the Portland Homicide Detail, where I found Mike Whitehall at his desk as I'd hoped.

My good friend Mike is a veteran homicide detective, a lieutenant who's probably doomed to languish without further promotion because he's gay. Mike's heyday had been a decade or so ago, when the then-Chief's daughter was an openly lesbian officer. The homophobes in the department went *way* underground during that period, but since that Chief retired they'd crept back out again—and some of them were in positions of substantial authority.

Nevertheless, he answered the phone with enthusiasm. "Homicide. Our day begins when yours ends. Mike Whitehall at your service." Clearly he'd seen on his Caller ID that it was me.

"That's a very old joke," I said by way of hello.

"It never fails to get a chuckle over here. What can I do for you this dreary and wet February morning?"

"Looking for some background. You remember anything about a car bomb last March, guy named George Quiller in the Beaumont-Wilshire neighborhood?"

"Hmmm. Rings a bell. Why?"

"His wife just hired me. She thinks he might not be dead after all. In fact, she says she saw him downtown last Thursday."

"Really? That must have been a shocker. She didn't confront him?"

"She was in a moving vehicle and he was on foot entering Pioneer Courthouse Square."

"Tough. So what do you need from me? You don't have nearly enough for a court order to exhume the body."

"I'd appreciate it if you'd check the file to see how the remains were identified. Dental records? DNA? How sure were they that it was George Quiller in the car when it blew up?"

"Okay, I'll check...but I imagine they were pretty sure. I wasn't on the case myself, but I don't usually proceed without being as certain as I can who the victim is."

"I understand. It's likely this lady is mistaken. Just let me know, okay?"

"Will do. See you be at the dojang this evening?"

"Maybe, but I've got a surveillance and all kinds of stuff going on."

"Okay. If you aren't there I'll call you tomorrow."

We hung up and I was about to punch in Johnny Crew's number when the phone rang.

"Clint McCall."

"This is Samantha Quiller." She sounded tense, her soft voice almost raspy.

"Mrs. Quiller. Is something wrong?"

"I'm being stalked."

It was a categorical statement. One thing you could say for my new client: she never doubted her perceptions.

CHAPTER SEVEN

I figured I might as well skip the are-you-sure part. "Do you know who it is? It's not your husband, is it?

"No! I don't know who it is."

"Well..." Slight exasperation. "What does the stalker look like?"

"I haven't seen his face, not very clearly. He's short, about my height, kind of thin, wearing a parka kind of thing with a hood. I think he might be young."

"And I gather you've seen him more than once."

"I noticed him first in a grocery store parking lot, then outside my dry cleaners, and then sitting in a car down the street from my house."

Good enough. If that was really all the same person, it did indeed qualify as stalking—or surveillance. I opened my notebook to a blank page. "Give me the details," I said. "Exactly when and where you saw him, make and model of the car, everything you can think of."

When she was done reeling off all the particulars, I assured her that I'd look into it and cautioned her to keep an eye out in the meantime. She said she'd let me know of any further sightings.

Then I called Johnny Crew, whom I needed more with every passing moment.

Johnny and his partner Hap Harbaugh started their own agency after a full career at the Portland Police Bureau, where they had also been partners in the Detective Division.

Hap is sixty-nine, I think, a completely bald and massive man who even when he was younger and on the force thought nothing of wearing the same clothes a week at a time. No wife. Never had one. Now that he's older, he complains constantly about his back, bunions, knees, neck, and all the other parts of his body he can no longer reach. His nickname on the force was "Hap the Hulk" and everybody loved him, as do I.

Johnny is a couple of years younger than Hap, short and burly but very well-groomed with a full head of luxurious gray hair. At the Bureau he'd been known as "Dapper John." His voice, like his ex-partner, is about twice his size and—did I mention—he has an incredibly foul mouth.

"How the fuck are you, Clint?" he inquired as soon as I'd identified myself.

"In need of a little backup," I replied, getting straight to the point.

Which did me no good at all, since Johnny went right on with his news of the day; it was how he started every phone conversation no matter what his caller said. I suppose he even did it with cold-callers.

"I was just readin' about this old fart in England who digs tunnels for a hobby," he announced dramatically. "Ain't that fuckin' weird?"

Did I mention that his news of the day was always "fuckin' weird"?

"Yes, it is," I agreed with a grin of resignation that he of course couldn't see. There was no point in trying to get on with my end of the conversation until he'd gotten this news item out of his system.

"The ground collapsed in front of his house, this huge fuckin' hole, and they found out the old dickhead had been diggin' tunnels under and around his house for more than forty fuckin' years? Can you believe that?"

"Sounds unbelievable all right."

"And you know what he said when they asked him about it?"

"What did he say?"

"He said, 'I just have a big basement.' Can you fuckin' believe that?"

"That's amazing, Johnny."

He cackled. "It sure as fuck is! So...what kind of backup you need?"

Ah. At last. The workaday world appears on the horizon. "Keeping an eye on a 47-year-old unemployed nerd until he does something to prove he doesn't have a bad back."

"Insurance, huh. He live in Portland?"

"Right off Broadway on Jackson."

"Hap and I can do that. Hope it don't take too long, though."

"You got intestinal problems again?"

"Yeah," he said morosely, "but it ain't the runs this time. I'm so constipated lately I feel like I get butt-fucked by every turd."

I was not totally thrilled to contemplate that image. "All the more reason to stay in the car and watch my client," I replied as helpfully as I could. "It doesn't have to be 24/7. No overnights." I rattled off the more specific details and hung up after wishing them luck.

Meanwhile, I was free to get on with my other cases. First thing, I wanted to interview some of the friends whose names Samantha Quiller had given me so I could ask them about the quality of her marriage. I wanted to know why her husband didn't wear a ring. Then I was going to have to find out whether she really had a stalker or was just displaying more symptoms of mental instability.

The life of a private investigator is just one excitement after another.

CHAPTER EIGHT

My entire body reverberated as I blocked the spinning heel kick with both forearms. Retired Army Colonel Roger Arbuckle had a couple of years and more than a few inches on me, plus being by far the most intense of the black belts who shared our training space. He didn't back off even when sparring the much smaller women, which I think they actually appreciated, but taking him on was no picnic for any of us.

I landed a good solid sidekick to his chest, somewhat like kicking a stump, and he came right back at me with a combination of straight punches and elbow strikes.

Well, this is what I was here for.

All seven of us were in the dojang this Tuesday evening. "Dojo" is the more familiar term to Americans, but that's Japanese and taekwondo is a Korean martial art. Thus "dojang."

We'd pooled our resources to lease this space after the teacher of our original dojang retired. We were his six most advanced black belts, plus Eleanor, and we decided to continue training together rather than take over all his classes.

Our practice space is one large room with attached office that comprises the second floor of an old warehouse at the corner of Second and Pine. We'd sanded and polished the wood floor, hung some heavy canvas bags along one side, brought the plumbing in the single bathroom up to code, and installed lockers in the office space to create a dressing room.

Portland Homicide Detective Mike Whitehall and I were fourth-degree black belts. Roger, Daisy Mansfield, Carmen Gonzales, and Bobby Brewster were third degree black belts. By my special request, second-degree black belt Eleanor Ivory had been included in our group; I'd been her teacher even before she became my accountant and resident hacker and she was very skilled for her belt level.

We didn't advertise, we didn't take students, we didn't even have a name for the dojang. The space was strictly for our own training and workouts. Whenever more than one of us was present, which was most evenings, the senior black belt led the workout. And this evening that would be me because I'd been promoted to fourth degree six months ahead of Mike.

The fact that I was the senior belt motivated my current opponent even more, of course, making me grateful that the end of the session was almost upon us.

While I took on Roger, Mike was sparring with his life partner, corporate lawyer Bobby, and the three women were going two-on-one, Eleanor and veterinarian Carmen against the independently wealthy—and fastest of us all—Daisy.

I took one last bone-crunching straight kick to my own chest and called everyone to attention.

After a moment or two of everyone catching their breath and getting reoriented, we all sank to our knees in the "seiza" position, in which you sit upright resting your weight on your heels, hands together in your lap with thumbs touching. We traditionally begin a session with five minutes of meditation and end with ten minutes, even when only one of us is working out. You need the time to initially get relaxed and then to dissipate all that adrenaline when you're done.

I chose not to simply clear my mind this time, but instead to contemplate recent events. I'd had a busy couple of days, topped off by some new but not entirely unexpected information late this afternoon. I hoped that two hours of distraction by sweaty combat might give rise to some kind of sensible conclusion from it all. So, time to review rather than meditate:

I'd spent most of the previous two days interviewing Samantha Quiller's friends, who had been of little help. For one thing, they were all very much *her* friends and not his. More evidence that he had been a loner.

Several of them testified that the marriage wasn't the best and that George had been "odd," but only on the basis of what they'd been told by Samantha herself. None of them had seen first-hand examples. The only new information—rumor, innuendo, whatever—I heard was that George might have been "moody" about sex as well as other aspects of their home life. Samantha had shared with a couple of her closest friends that he was mostly indifferent except on rare occasions when he couldn't seem to get enough. I wasn't sure what to make of that. Chemical or hormonal imbalance maybe, natural or artificially induced.

None of the friends had heard anything about a stalker, by the way, nor did I hear any hint of why there would be one.

I came away from the interviews thinking that I still needed to find someone who had known them both intimately—and afraid that, if none of her close friends qualified, I probably was not going to find such a person.

Then this afternoon Mike Whitehall called to tell me that there *had* been DNA testing of the remains from the explosion and the tested sample had proved a match to George Quiller. After hearing the details, I could understand that Mrs. Quiller might not have known. It had been a pro forma testing, there being no other way to confirm the identity of the victim, and the results hadn't come back until more than a month after the funeral. Since the results were as expected, there'd been no notification to the surviving spouse. No record of whether she'd originally been asked for a reference sample or if someone on the scene had simply obtained one.

It nevertheless meant that I was not looking for her husband, but rather someone who looked like her husband. Sensible conclusion: there was no particular point in finding someone who looked like her husband.

Now all I had to do was get Samantha Quiller to accept the idea that she'd been mistaken about seeing George. As for the stalker? Yet to be determined, but probably in the same delusional ballpark.

The remainder of the past two days was not really worth meditating upon. I'd checked in with Johnny and Hap several times to learn only that Marvin Montgomery had yet to do anything that required a strong back. I'd diligently put off looking any further into Colleen's supposed sighting of her mother. Part of me didn't want to know, at least not any sooner than I had to, and so far that part was winning.

Having blown my meditation time on cogitation, I brought my fellow black belts back to their feet and dismissed the session for the evening.

CHAPTER NINE

My first stop Thursday morning was Samantha Quiller's big old home on a shady block near the corner of Knott and 35th and just north of Grant Park.

I'd called her as soon as I arrived home the previous evening. She wasn't happy that I wouldn't share much about my "progress" over the phone, but at least it got me an early morning appointment.

I parked in the driveway of her brown two-story home nestled among ancient oak trees and hedges. It appeared to be relatively modest given her financial resources, probably three thousand square feet and worth no more than a million dollars or so.

My client answered the doorbell in a gingham dress and fuzzy slippers, continuing the informal I'm-not-really-wealthy look she'd brought to my office. Her short brown hair was damp and she carried a delicate china cup of coffee in her left hand. Neither the bathing nor the caffeine had apparently done much to calm her anxiety; behind her glasses, her eyes were wide and underlined with dark semicircles.

She shook my hand in greeting and led me from the foyer into a large bi-level living room with a picture window that looked out over the spacious front yard. There were several different seating clusters in the room and she directed me to the most intimate— two well-stuffed leather chairs angled toward each other on either side of a low marble table. She set her cup carefully on the gleaming surface and inquired if I wanted any coffee.

I couldn't bring myself to make her wait any longer, so I said no as I settled into my chair. She dropped into her own with a barely suppressed sigh of relief.

"What news do you have?" she asked with obvious trepidation.

I went straight to the point. "The police did do DNA testing and confirmed that the victim of the explosion was a match to your husband."

She pulled back, her face twisting into an expression of dismay. "Really? How can that be?"

"Well," I replied with some exasperation, "it can only *be* if it was indeed your husband in the car—unless he had an identical twin. Did your husband have a twin brother, Mrs. Quiller?"

She made a dismissive sound through pursed lips. "No. No, of course he didn't have a twin brother, but...."

I interrupted with conviction. "Then it could not possibly have been your husband you saw downtown. The DNA match is definitive."

"But...but I'm sure...." Her eyes were darting around the big room as if seeking the certainty she wanted to claim.

"I'm sorry, Mrs. Quiller," I said as gently as I could, "but you're wasting your money. There's no point in my looking for a man who happens to resemble your husband."

She looked down into her lap for a long moment, biting her lip, and then looked up to meet my eyes, her own brimming with tears. "Please," she said simply.

Then it was my turn to chew on my lip for a moment. "Well," I finally said, "it's your money—but what are you going to do if I'm able to track down this gentleman? He probably won't have a clue who you are or what you want."

She took a moment to straighten her back and firm up her expression. "That's my point, Mr. McCall. He *did* know who I was! I would swear it. And I'm going to ask him how he knew."

I was about to grudgingly concede the point when I heard a melodious ringing across the room. Samantha Quiller started, then rose and walked quickly to the far wall where a phone set rested on another, taller table.

I could just hear her voice as she answered. "Hello?" Short pause, then again: "Hello? Who's there? Hello?"

After another pause she hung up the phone and walked slowly back to me. She was trembling a little as she approached.

"What was that?" I asked. "A hang-up call?"

"Yes," she said as she carefully sat down again. "And not the first. And I saw that *person* once more late yesterday."

This woman just wasn't going to let me go. "The stalker?"

"Yes. It was a warm evening and I took Kinsey for a walk around the neighborhood in her stroller. Suddenly I saw that same car I'd seen before. It was parked a little way down the street again and there was someone sitting in it. I'm sure it was the stalker and he was looking at us! I turned around and got my daughter back home as quickly as I could." She looked at me pitiably as she twisted her hands together in her lap. "Please don't abandon us, Mr. McCall. Even if you can't find the man I saw, you have to find out who's watching us. What if it's some monster who wants to hurt me or Kinsey? *Please!*"

What could I say? I'm sorry, madam, but I think you're crazy as a loon and I'm not going to waste any more of my time or your money? Yes, theoretically I could have said that—but not to that face. I agreed to stay on the case. We shook hands and she escorted me to the front door. I promised again that I'd keep her apprised of any developments.

CHAPTER TEN

I arrived back in my office a little before nine-thirty to find a voicemail from my daughter. Of course she wanted to know how I was doing in the search for *her* possibly phantom sighting. I swung my chair around to check the street below my window, just to make sure Kafka wasn't out there directing my life. It was getting just about that surreal. Having confirmed there were no dead existentialists hanging around, I decided to seek a fresh point of view from my combination accountant, fellow black belt, and information services consultant down the hall.

I locked my office and headed for Eleanor Ivory Accountancy, the third door on the other side of the corridor. Yes, Eleanor is my accountant just as Ray Witkowsky is my insurance agent—and Sam Bitterly is my attorney. It's pretty damned convenient to have so many of my resources right here, though I've yet to need a telephone survey.

Her contralto voice responded immediately to my knock. "Come in!"

Eleanor's single-room office is about the same size as mine, but there are four more file cabinets and many more decorations, including a whole shelf of collectible dolls. A few plants. Probably no gun.

She sat behind her big metal desk in front of windows that looked out on Third Avenue and the lot where we have our parking spaces. The desktop was piled with file folders and CDs that were no doubt data disks rather than music. On a side table to her right her PC and printer, the latter currently spewing sheets of paper. Next to the printer, somewhat oddly, a big Valentine's Day card was propped upright. Which reminded me that today was February 14. And I had no one to send a Valentine's Day card to.

She smiled and pointed at one of her visitors' chairs as she gathered up the accumulating printed pages.

Eleanor Ivory has long been one of my favorite people, though she's never been a candidate for romantic interest. She's fourteen years younger but, more importantly, of a *very* different lifestyle. A woman with all the right curves and lots of unexpected muscle, a full mouth and wide violet eyes, Eleanor goes for young, extremely good-looking, and even more extremely rich guys. This week—at least as of yesterday—she was dating a tall Hispanic playboy with a claim to some obscure relation to Spain's royal family, elegant movie star looks, and a silver Ferrari.

She'd apparently been an overweight nerd in high school and most of college, but at some point grew tired of men being put off by her intelligence, aggressiveness, and weight. She lost the weight and made herself incredibly fit, which would have been sufficient, but then she also made a conscious decision "to become a sex object," as she put it. As in most other things, she did an excellent job of implementation.

I could keep up with her in the dojang but I seriously doubted if I'd stand a chance on the party circuit.

At this moment she was dressed sedately in earth tones that spoke of her abilities as a first-rate tax accountant and computer expert. She placed the stack of newly printed pages neatly on the one clear corner of the desk and gave me an inquiring look.

"You've got that worried expression," she said. "New clients or new financial problems?"

"The former, fortunately. *Un*fortunately, one of them is a woman named Samantha Quiller who's seeing both her dead husband and a stalker—and another is Colleen who's seeing her missing mother."

Eleanor sat back with a moue of surprise. "Well. Gee. Welcome to the twilight zone."

"No kidding."

"Do you think Sarah might actually be back?"

Eleanor had never met my ex-wife but had heard enough about her over the years to be on a first name basis.

I shrugged. "Who knows? Colleen is certain she saw her. Of course, Mrs. Quiller is equally certain about deceased hubby."

"That does sound a bit less likely than a missing wife. You think this Quiller woman is nuts?"

I shook my head, not so much in denial as in bewilderment. "I just don't know."

"What does your gut tell you?"

"If it weren't for the purported stalker, I'd say I probably had a client who simply saw what she wanted to see downtown. As it is...she doesn't strike me as crazy enough to have manufactured the stalker as well as the walking dead husband. The two of them showing up at the same time is one hell of a coincidence. My gut tells me something's going on."

Eleanor grinned. "And you always listen to your gut."

"Yup."

"So you need me to...?"

Since I am a relative amateur at Internet searches and don't have the time to learn more, all my investment—and it is substantial—in the databases available to private investigators has gone into sign-ups for Eleanor's PC rather than my own. Thus, my assignments for her today were to do further background on the Quillers and track down where Sarah's closest friends from back in the day are now; I hadn't talked to any of them since the initial investigation of her disappearance.

Eleanor agreed that she'd get on it and I returned to my office. I was just finishing a good hour of paperwork when the phone rang. Caller ID said it was incoming from Mike Whitehall's cell phone.

"Hey Mike. What's going on?"

I could tell from the quality of the signal and the traffic sounds in the background that he was out in the field somewhere. He did not usually call me from a scene—unless it was bad news.

"Your client's name is Samantha Quiller, right?"

Oh shit. "Yeah."

"Somebody just took a shot at her and her daughter in a deli parking lot on Broadway. I think you better get down here."

CHAPTER ELEVEN

"Are they okay?" I asked Mike as I got to my feet and reached for my jacket.

"Pretty shook up, but otherwise fine. The shooter missed. It was a drive-by."

I had jacket in hand and was eager to hang up and get going, but I had to ask: "You're sure Samantha Quiller was the target?"

"There was no one else nearby. Of course, that doesn't mean it wasn't random. The weapon was a .45; we already dug the bullet out of the front of the deli. That makes our shooter a little unusual. Probably not a gang member."

"Where exactly is this deli?"

"Corner of Broadway and 33rd."

"I'm on my way," I said, and hung up the phone.

They were still in the midst of the on-scene investigation when I got there. All of the small parking lot was marked off by yellow tape. An ambulance, a CSU van, and two patrol cars were parked nearby. Further down the street were at least three news vans and quite a number of spectators.

I eased my car through the congestion and finally found a parking spot just off Broadway on 32nd. From there I hiked back to the scene.

One of the uniforms stepped up as soon as I reached the tape and I showed him my ID. "Detective Whitehall requested my presence," I told him and he in turn asked another officer to go confirm that.

He took the occasion to tell several other people to step back while we stood waiting, me stomping with impatience, but soon the other cop returned with word that I was legit. I ducked under the tape. The cop who'd brought the okay told me Whitehall was over by the ambulance.

Samantha Quiller sat on the rear tailgate of what I presumed was her SUV, clutching to her chest a bundle that was no doubt her daughter Kinsey. One of the EMTs was just walking away, toward the ambulance. Quiller was pale and trembling. As I approached I saw a spilled grocery bag on the ground beside the vehicle. Mike Whitehall wasn't in sight.

I stopped and crouched down to look in my client's eyes; she stared at me as if she were trying to place who I was. The little girl appeared to be asleep. Finally I saw recognition in the mother's eyes and her face twisted with some combination of grief and residual terror.

"Why?" she asked me very softly. Just that one word.

"I don't know, Mrs. Quiller," I replied equally softly, "but I promise you I'll find out."

"Thank you."

"You and Kinsey all right?"

"Yes. Yes, we're fine. I just need to sit down for a while."

"No problem. The medics are here and I'll be nearby if you need anything. Okay?"

She looked around as if surprised that there would be medics in the vicinity. "Yes," she said absently. "That's okay."

I patted her knee with as much reassurance as I could and stood up. Now I saw Whitehall just in front of the deli entrance, deep in conversation with one of the CSU techs. He caught my eye and held a palm out to keep me at a distance until he was done.

A minute later the tech who'd been conferring with Mike walked away and we met about halfway between the storefront and Quiller's vehicle. My friend was scowling. "Your client tells me she has a stalker."

I shrugged. "That's what she tells me, too."

"You don't believe her?"

"I just don't know. She also says there's a guy identical to her husband walking around—and that he recognized her when she saw him downtown."

"Well, given that someone just tried to shoot her I guess we have to take her concerns seriously."

"Agreed. Any description of the vehicle or shooter?"

"Nada. Quiller certainly didn't see who or what it was. Apparently she reacted pretty fast, hitting the ground and covering up her daughter. We haven't found any other witnesses yet. I've put out a BOLO for a man with her husband's description. I'm going to put one out on her stalker, too, if we can drag a few more descriptive details from her."

I gave him a look and he made a *humph* sound back at me. "Maybe she's nuts," he said, "but she's now a nut who's been shot at. It's all we've got."

I realized he was right. And realized my gut was now telling me my client wasn't crazy after all. I had no idea yet what was really going on, but very likely all her "sightings" were related--to each other and to the shooting. It was up to me to find out how. The cops would be working on it too, of course, but I had the extra obligation of earning the money Samantha Quiller was paying me.

Not to mention the fact that I just plain don't like people who shoot at women and little girls.

41

CHAPTER TWELVE

It didn't seem like a good idea to let Samantha Quiller drive when she was still shaky, so as soon as they were cleared by the EMTs I gave her and her daughter a ride home. She said she could ask one of her friends to pick up her SUV later. I escorted her and Kinsey inside, took a quick look around just for my own peace of mind, and then headed back to the office.

This time I picked up my mail on the way upstairs. A quick sort after I sat down revealed that it was all junk again. There were no voicemail messages waiting for me, so my first priority was to re-assign Johnny Crew and Hap Harbaugh. I called Johnny's cell phone and he answered on the first ring.

"Crew."

"Johnny, it's Clint. Where are you right now?"

"Sitting in my car just down the street from tub-of-lard's house, waiting for him to do something besides fucking bore me to death."

"Then you're in luck," I said, "because I need you to switch your surveillance to another client of mine who's just been shot at. Protecting her might be a little more exciting than waiting for Montgomery to move. Is Hap free to cover for you there?" I wanted ed the more mobile of the two old detectives on my client.

"Hot shit! I'll get him on the phone right away. What's the address of the woman?"

Happy to have cheered him up so much, I provided Johnny with a quick summary of Samantha Quiller's situation as well as location and he confirmed that he'd be on his way as soon as Hap relieved him. Then later, of course, I was going to have to figure out who could relieve both Johnny and Hap. They were way too old for all-day surveillance jobs with no relief, not for more than a day or two anyway.

I gave Quiller a call to describe Johnny and his vehicle so she wouldn't think she had yet another stalker. Then I settled back to try to get a grip on recent events.

Obviously, Mrs. Quiller was going to be my priority—which gave rise to a couple of thoughts.

The first was more a question: What the *hell* was I going to do about my daughter's very real need to have some answers about whether she had seen her mother or not? I couldn't very well hire a back-up detective to handle Colleen.

My second thought was that I needed to adjust Eleanor's priorities as well. If she'd come up with anything on my ex-wife's old friends, that was fine; then I could at least assure Colleen I was on the case—sort of. But what I needed most was anything Eleanor could give me on the Quillers.

CHAPTER THIRTEEN

I had provided Eleanor a list of six of Sarah's friends and her first words to me as I entered her office were that she'd found five of them. She handed over a printout of the search results as I took a seat in front of her desk. "I'm afraid," she said with a grimace, "that tracking down a particular woman named Mary Smith has defeated even my incredible skills with a search engine. Do you have any idea how many there are just within Portland city limits, much less in the rest of the world?"

I had to laugh. I didn't really expect you to find Mary," I said. "She was on her fourth marriage when we knew her, anyway, and at the rate she was going there might have been a couple more name changes by now. Five out of six is good."

"Only three of them are still local. Ariel Hilton lives in Eastern Washington and Willamina Standard, now Willamina Harvey, moved to Delaware with her new husband."

"I see that," I agreed as I looked over the list. "So Dorothy Ogden, Patty Samuels, and Nancy DeFazio are still here."

"Ogden's an attorney and DeFazio a homemaker. Samuels has a graphics design business out of her home."

"No big changes, then. Patty and Sarah started that design business together; it was downtown at the time. I guess Patty let the storefront go after it was just her." I put the printout aside for the moment. "Anything on the Quillers?"

"Not yet. I focused on your ex-wife first."

"Well, since we last talked the Quiller case has taken on some urgency."

Eleanor's eyebrows shot up inquiringly.

"As in somebody tried to kill her and her daughter this morning."

Her eyebrows went significantly higher. "Oh wow. I guess I'll get right on that."

"I appreciate it," I said as I picked up the printout again and rose to leave. "Call me if you come up with anything interesting at all."

"No problem."

CHAPTER FOURTEEN

I headed back down the hall to my office and opened the door just as my phone began to ring. I hurried across the room and picked it up. There was no name on the Caller ID and I didn't recognize the number.

"McCall Detective Agency."

"Are you working for Samantha Quiller?" It was a deep, strong, but female voice. I imagined a physically imposing corporate executive of some sort.

"Who is this?" I countered, not one to answer abrupt questions from unknown inquisitors.

"I'm a friend of Samantha's and I thought I might hire you myself, depending on what you're doing for her."

The answer came smoothly enough, but I didn't believe a word of it. "And your name is?"

"Not important unless I decide to hire you. You are working for Samantha, aren't you? Does she have you looking for someone? I have a missing person I might want you to find."

Yeah, sure you do. "I'm afraid I can't share information about who's a client and who isn't. If you're a friend of this Samantha person, you can ask her whether she's hired a private detective or not. If you want to hire me, I'll be happy to discuss *your* case."

There was a long pause. "You really should be more helpful, Mr. McCall." The voice had gone even deeper, making the statement sound like a threat. What the hell was going on with this person?

"Gee, and most people say I'm a real boy scout."

A snort. "I'm surprised more people don't say you're an asshole." Sounding less like a corporate type all the time.

"Look," I said, "I don't have time to trade insults with un-known callers. Either tell me who you are and what you want or I'm hanging up."

The only reply was a click followed by dial-tone. She beat me to it. So I hung up and sat down to contemplate this latest weirdness.

Who the hell could that have been? Not a good buddy of my client's, I was willing to bet. She—the caller—asked if I was looking for someone.... Could it connect with the man Quiller saw down-town? How would the caller know about that...and yet *not* know for sure that I was involved? Samantha and I were going to have anoth-er talk very soon.

I copied the incoming number off my Caller-ID and called Eleanor to see if one of our fancy search engines could track it down. It took her about thirty seconds to tell me that it was a burn-er cell phone purchased today here in Portland. Other than that, all she could tell me was that she was just beginning her background work on the Quillers and had nothing yet.

I thanked her and hung up. So the mysterious caller had gone to some trouble to make sure she stayed mysterious. The plot was thickening rather than clarifying.

Meanwhile I had to take care of my daughter while I figured out what was happening with my client. It seemed unlikely that my disappearing ex-wife would be back in the area, casually mall-shop-ping, without having contacted Colleen. It seemed even more un-likely that Samantha Quiller's husband had returned from the dead and hired a hit man.

I was going to need some better theories in a hurry.

CHAPTER FIFTEEN

A leisurely late lunch at the Home Run Sports Bar across the street from my office provided me with an excellent hamburger and the opportunity to watch most of a women's tennis match on the three TVs visible from my table...but not a single new theory about Quiller, Sarah, or anything else.

I ambled back across Third Avenue and down Stark Street to my entrance leading to the second floor. I decided as I climbed the stairs that I'd go straight back to Eleanor's office to see if she had any of that Quiller background yet.

That plan changed when I heard my phone ringing as I started to pass my office door. I unlocked the door and hurried across to my desk to pick up the receiver. The Caller ID said it was from the Pen and Pastry.

Expecting Colleen's voice, I was a little surprised to hear Veronica Fortune's instead. I suppose I shouldn't have been; she does own the Pen and Pastry, after all.

Veronica had been one of my first clients twelve years ago, soon after my break-up with Sarah; she was a sex worker (as prostitutes prefer to be called) at the time and hired me to help her and her pimp Reuben Keys deal with a new gang that wanted to take over Reuben's territory and abuse the girls. Oddly enough, Reuben was considered a good guy—by Portland street standards, anyway. He treated the women who worked for him pretty decently, not only refusing to control them with drugs but refusing to let them *take* drugs.

I'd basically been hired to offer tactical advice and provide extra muscle. Not my usual kind of case, but Veronica was—and is—a beautiful woman with long dark hair and an exquisite figure; that combined with her intelligence and vulnerability easily persuaded me to take the job. It paid well and Reuben and I were effective in

49

persuading the gang members to consider a different part of town, becoming sort-of friends along the way. He likes to play detective, gets a kick out of being on the "right" side of the law now and then, and of course enjoys the standard fee I pay contractors—even Johnny and Hap—to provide backup.

Also along the way, Veronica decided it was time for her to leave that life. With a little encouragement from me, Reuben agreed.

And she certainly had moved on since then, writing a bestseller about her life on the street and using the money from the book to open the Pen and Pastry, where she employed and mentored other women who had left the street life.

I'd kept in touch with her all along and she'd become good friends with my daughter who spent a lot of her free time hanging out at the café.

"Clint, how are you?" Veronica asked in her soft voice.

"I'm doing good. What's going on? Colleen okay?"

"Not really. She told me she saw Sarah."

Aha. Well, I hadn't asked her not to tell anyone else. So now I had to deal with it, while wondering how many other people she'd told.

"She really needs you right now, Clint," Veronica went on. "Whether she truly saw her mother or not, she's depending on you to find out—and very frightened that you won't."

"I know she is," I replied, still not sure where this conversation was leading.

There was a long pause. "And you're going to...?" She let the sentence hang.

"I'm going to do what I can," I filled in as firmly as I could.

"But you have a more important case. She told me."

"Well, I have a young mother and her two-year-old child who were shot at just this morning if that's what you mean."

I heard a very quiet inhalation. "Someone's trying to kill them?"

50

"So it would appear."

"So you'll protect them and that same someone will then go after you."

"There's no reason to believe that."

"No reason but history and experience."

I sighed, deeply. "I'm sorry, Veronica. I'll do everything I can to find the person that Colleen saw. I'm not going to ignore her feelings. You know that."

"I do know it. You should come by the café soon, though, just to check in with her. She's here right now."

"I'll do that, as soon as I get the chance. But probably not this minute. Tell her I'm doing my best."

"Okay. Take care."

"I will—and thanks for calling. You're a good friend, to her and to me."

CHAPTER SIXTEEN

While Veronica and I had never had a romantic or sexual relationship, she did serve as a mother figure for Colleen and that could bleed over into spousal-type nagging at me, reminding me that my work sometimes put my daughter in jeopardy and other times distracted me from what she considered my fatherly duties. She was usually right, of course, but meanwhile I had to get on with my business.

I picked up the phone and punched in Eleanor's number.

She picked up on the first ring. "Hey Clint."

"Anything interesting on the Quillers?"

"Hard to tell what's interesting and what isn't. I'm running every kind of search I can think of. What's most unusual, really, is how negative the results are. As far as I can tell, George Quiller didn't belong to any organizations, subscribe to any magazines, or have any treatable health problems. About all I could find was a minor police record."

That caught my attention. "Really? What?"

"A couple of DUIs. One arrest, no conviction, for drunk and disorderly. Another for 'riot,' apparently an occasion when several other drunks were disorderly along with him. Sounds like he was pretty good buddies with the bottle."

"That might be interesting. This was all during the time he was married?"

"Looks like it."

"I'll see what the wife has to say about that. Anything else?"

"Nothing so far."

"Well, keep at it—and thanks."

"I will, as time allows, and you're welcome." She hung up.

Okay, I thought to myself as I swiveled around to contemplate the afternoon traffic on Stark, so I need to have another chat with Samantha Quiller. I want to see how she's doing anyway. And maybe I can combine that with some work on Colleen's "case."

Checking the addresses of Nancy DeFazio, Patty Samuels, and Dorothy Ogden, I saw that I could indeed make a fairly reasonable loop starting with Quiller's house, stopping by DeFazio's and Samuels' homes, and finally hitting Ogden's downtown law office when I got back.

A quick call confirmed that Quiller was home and willing to see me. I would try to catch the others without advance warning; they weren't that far out of the way and I've found that initial interviews are almost always more productive when the interviewee has no time for preparation.

I was just retrieving my Smith and Wesson from the drawer when my office door opened abruptly after a quick knock.

CHAPTER SEVENTEEN

There being very few people who feel they have the right to enter my office unannounced and without permission, I wasn't surprised to see Mrs. Myrtle Prendergast standing in the doorway. Mrs. Prendergast is Ray Witkowsky's secretary, receptionist, and general factotum. I'd always guessed her to be in her sixties, but she could have been a healthy eighty-five for all I knew.

As far as Mrs. Prendergast is concerned, her boss is God and she is his Prophet. I, apparently, am assigned the role of Chief Sinner.

Tall, lean, slate-gray hair pulled severely back in a bun, the sharp features of her thin face pulled just as tight, the woman glared at me and then at the gun in my hand.

"Have you finally decided to shoot me, too, Mr. McCall," she inquired dryly, "or do you greet all your visitors with weapon in hand? It wouldn't surprise me, of course, if you did." She took another step into the office and closed the door behind her.

There had been one, just one, incident near the building, but none of the occupants of the building were wounded or killed. Mrs. Prendergast had repeatedly made it clear that she disapproved anyway.

"I was on my way out," I said by way of explanation, then stashed the gun back in the drawer and closed it. "What can I do for you, Mrs. Prendergast?"

She didn't approach further, but spoke to me ex *cathedra* from across the office. "Mr. Witkowsky requires a report on your progress vis-à-vis the Montgomery matter."

"Mr. Montgomery remains under surveillance and there is nothing yet to report."

Her tiny smile reminded me of a second-grade teacher I once had who adopted the identical expression right before rapping my knuckles with a ruler. "So I gather you can see Mr. Montgomery from here?"

"No, Mrs. Prendergast, of course not. The surveillance is being handled by one of my operatives." The woman always made me start to imitate her formal, prissy speech.

"So Mr. Witkowsky's concerns are not important enough for your own attention. Perhaps we should just hire this 'operative' of yours."

I shrugged. "You are certainly welcome to do so. His name is Hap Harbaugh. Would you like his cell phone number?"

She harrumphed with great dignity. "You'll not escape your responsibilities so easily as that, Mr. McCall. Please get in touch with this...operative...and provide us with an updated report forthwith."

"I'll do that very thing, Mrs. Prendergast, and you'll be hearing from me soon." I reopened my gun drawer suggestively.

Another harrumph. "We will await your call," she said and departed as stiffly as she'd arrived.

I'd often speculated that her less-than-cheerful demeanor arose from her parents naming her Myrtle. Even sixty-some years ago, Myrtle must not have been high on the popular-first-names-for-girls list. She was still paying the rest of us back for the misery she'd endured in grade school.

I pulled the Smith and Wesson back out of the drawer, stuffed it in its holster and headed across the street to retrieve my vehicle.

CHAPTER EIGHTEEN

I drive a Subaru Outback, which is basically a small SUV. Since half the vehicles on the road in the Pacific Northwest seem to be SUVs, it's the perfect surveillance vehicle. You could hang behind somebody all day and they'd never notice you.

As I drove out Burnside toward 39th, I called Hap to confirm he was on Montgomery now. He reported no new developments as expected. I called Mrs. Prendergast to report same and, as hoped, got her voicemail.

I was thinking as I turned north on 39th that it was fortunate I'd been making a good income this past year since I was currently spending so much money on subcontractors and time on a non-paying case. In the last twelve months there had been a steady stream of clients despite the fact that I'm no real competition to the large, high-tech detective firms. I attributed this success primarily to media coverage, particularly from my sometimes-buddy and sometimes-nemesis Alison Roberts.

She was only in her mid-twenties and her news segment was on the least-watched local channel, an independent with no network affiliations, but still she managed to generate a lot of water cooler buzz. Which was *why* she had her own time slot at such a young age. And I—for better and worse—was one of her very favorite subjects.

Think of the Devil, my cell phone rang as I was crossing Sandy Boulevard and the display said the call was from Channel 11. I thumbed the talk button and put the phone to my ear. "Clint McCall."

"You don't call. You don't write. Even when one of your clients is the victim of a drive-by. What kind of friend are you, anyway?"

"And I don't comment, either. Hello, Alison. How did you get onto that so fast?"

"I watched some of the coverage that the *other* channels got and saw you talking to Detective Whitehall. Since you rarely drop by crime scenes that have nothing to do with you, I leapt to the conclusion that you had some reason to be there."

"We were setting up a lunch date."

"Yeah, right. Come on, McCall. Give."

I thought about the mysterious female caller who wanted to know if I was working for Samantha Quiller. "Did any of the other channels mention my name?"

"No. I'll be the first to have that privilege."

The caller could find out any number of other ways, but they might take longer than an announcement on TV. "Not yet," I said firmly. "Tell you what. I'll be the friend you've always wanted for once. I'll promise you first dibs on the story when there is one, but it's important that my name not be associated right now with the woman who was shot at. It could put us both in a passel of trouble."

"*Passel?* You going cowboy on me?"

"Just call me Tex. But don't call me Clint McCall in any stories you do on that drive-by. Trust me, I'll make it up to you."

"Oh, all right. Grump, grump. You better make good on this."

"I keep my word."

"I guess. When you have one."

"Talk to you soon," I said and cut off the call—a little abruptly because I'd been keeping my eye on the rear view mirror the last few blocks and had just decided that there was a possibility I had a tail.

CHAPTER NINETEEN

I remembered seeing a green Toyota Highlander behind me downtown, then again on Burnside. Now the same vehicle, or one just like it, was four cars back as I approached Knott Avenue. Just like Subaru Outbacks, there were a lot of Toyota Highlanders on the Pacific Northwest streets, so even three sightings in a row weren't conclusive. I pulled over to the first available curb to see what would happen.

The Highlander braked for a split second and then went on past me as if minding its own business. I couldn't make out the driver through the tinted windows, but that hesitation had been enough to convince me I was not mistaken about being followed.

So maybe I had myself a lead at last. I pulled out three cars behind the Highlander, pulse picking up in anticipation. I could at least spook the son of a bitch. If I were really lucky I could stay with him long enough to get a sense of where he—or she—was going.

No such luck, as it turned out. I'm pretty good at following someone without being detected—but in a case like this, of course, my subject is likely to notice the vehicle that was in front of him is now behind him—and take off like Roadrunner being chased by Coyote.

The driver of the Highlander poked along for another block or so, across Knott to the corner of 39th and Stanton, then turned right on Stanton and floored it. By the time the three cars ahead of me had crossed the intersection, my quarry was already more than two blocks away and still accelerating. I made the turn and sped up, but I already knew I'd blown it. Even the cops are restricted from high-speed chases through residential neighborhoods; no way a lowly private investigator could get away with it. I waved bye-bye as the Highlander made a hard left in the distance and disappeared.

Well, okay. I didn't have the driver but I certainly *had* spooked him and I did have the make and model of the vehicle as well as the license number. It was still a lead, damn it, though maybe not much of a one; chances were the SUV was either stolen or rented under a false name. Perhaps the when and where would tell me something.

CHAPTER TWENTY

Speaking of when and where, my watch said 3:22. Plenty of time yet today to interview Samantha Quiller and check on Sarah's three friends. I turned the car back toward Knott and 35th, pulling up in front of the Quiller residence just a few minutes later. On the way I left a voicemail for Mike Whitehall with the tail's vehicle info. Cross fingers.

I waved at Johnny Crew parked across the street as I pulled into the Quiller driveway. My client answered the door promptly, leading me to the living room and the same seating cluster as before, where we took the same two comfortable leather chairs.

After assuring myself that she and Kinsey were well, I got right to the point. "Were you aware that your husband had been arrested several times when he was drinking?"

Her startled expression said no and her verbal response agreed. "When was this?" she went on to ask. "When he was very young?"

"No. Apparently all the arrests were during the time you were married to him."

"That's impossible. I would have known." She frowned. "Wouldn't I?"

"Apparently not. Did your husband have a drinking problem that you knew of?"

The frown grew deeper. "There were times he would drink a fair amount, but most of the time he didn't at all. It was certainly never a problem. It wasn't like he got drunk and abused us or anything."

"Well, he did get arrested for driving under the influence as well as drunk and disorderly a couple of times. He must have spent at least a few hours in jail and probably more than that in court."

She leaned forward, elbows on knees and head in hands. "I can't believe this," she said to her lap. "Did I not know who I was married to?"

Which struck me as a very interesting question. Either Samantha Quiller was lying or she had had a remarkably distant relationship with her spouse. I understand there are women who neither know nor care much about their husband's drinking habits. Surely, though, there are very few who are unaware of their husbands spending time in jail.

"I'm going to figure this out," I said finally. *Including whether you're lying*, I didn't say. "Just hang in there and be careful. My guy is still across the street, watching the house, and he'll stay with you if you go anywhere. But don't rely on him to keep you safe. Keep an eye out for yourself."

She looked up, eyes red-rimmed but clear. "I will. I know this all sounds completely crazy, Mr. McCall, and I appreciate your taking me seriously."

"I'm not the only one taking it seriously, believe me. That's why you need to be careful."

"I understand."

We talked a few minutes more about what life is like when you have a bodyguard because someone is shooting at you. (It's not much like regular life.) Then Mrs. Quiller escorted me back to the front door and we said goodbye.

CHAPTER TWENTY-ONE

Before getting in my own car, I walked across the street to visit with Johnny. He was sitting there with the windows rolled up and bundled in a heavy down jacket, drinking something steaming hot from a polystyrene cup, and looking bored—which is pretty much how everybody on stake-out looks.

He gave me a hopeful eye as I walked up to the driver's side window. "You coming over to tell me I can go home? I'm freezing my balls off out here."

I shook my head and grinned. "Sorry, no. I'll get you some relief this evening, though—me or someone else. Meanwhile, be on the lookout for a green late-model Highlander. It was following me earlier."

"Driver?"

"Didn't see."

He sighed. "Okay. I'll watch for it."

"If it stops in front of the house, give the cops a call and be ready for some action."

"Gotcha."

Johnny looked old and tired, scrunched down in his parka as he was. I leaned in. "You all right?"

He straightened up some. "Yeah, yeah, I'm fine. Bit of a headache. Looking forward to the end of the day. It's tough for an old fuck like me to sit in the car all day." He shrugged as he straightened even more. "Gettin' old is no fun. I'm not sayin' I can't do it—but my bones are sayin' it. Loud and achy."

I reached in and patted him on the shoulder. "I understand. I promise I'll get you some relief as soon as I can. Meanwhile, you can always go in the house if you need a change of scenery. I'm sure Mrs. Quiller wouldn't mind."

"I already been in there to use the john, but if I'm gonna keep watch I gotta be out here. You know that."

I was the one who sighed this time. "I know."

It was tough to walk back to my own vehicle with so much weight on my shoulders. Johnny certainly couldn't handle protecting Samantha Quiller twenty-four hours a day—and, for that matter Hap would have a hard time staying on Marvin Montgomery every waking hour.

I considered having one of my fellow black belts take a shift for Hap. Several had been making noises about helping me out; I think they entertained some unrealistic fantasies about the life of a private eye. But I wasn't quite ready to try them out, even on something so simple as surveilling Marvin Montgomery. So I didn't know what I was going to do for backup. Hiring somebody from a local security firm or another detective agency was a possibility, but not an attractive or inexpensive one.

The fact was, I had *too frigging much going on*!

Bigger sigh. I got in and started up the Outback. Nothing to do but the next thing next. I backed out of the Quiller driveway and headed for Nancy DeFazio's address.

CHAPTER TWENTY-TWO

DeFazio lived on Dyer in a little area of residential cul-de-sacs just beyond 82nd, a matter of simply going north to Fremont and then straight west. Her driveway was already occupied by a large camper, so I parked on the street in front.

The house was a single-story with a neatly kept front yard just like all the other houses in sight. I walked up the sidewalk and used the knocker on the front door. Tacked up next to the door was one of those "Welcome" signs, this one decorated with two impossibly cute puppies.

Even though I had often heard her name from Sarah after our divorce, I didn't remember having met this particular friend nor did I recognize the woman who opened the door—smiling, matronly, gray-haired, and wearing an apron. They could well have been her real-life puppies.

"May I help you?" she asked.

I held up my I.D. so she could see it. "Nancy DeFazio?"

She peered at the card. "Yes, I'm Mrs. DeFazio."

"My name's Clint McCall. I'm a private investigator. I'd like to ask you a few questions about an old friend of yours."

A slight crinkling of the brow was added to the smile. "My goodness. A private investigator." She started to take a step back. "I suppose you'd better come...." Sudden stop. I could see the wheels spinning behind the crinkle—which was edging toward a frown. "McCall. McCall. I have a dear old friend named McCall, a friend I haven't heard from for a long time. She was married to a detective." She squinted hard at me, smile entirely gone. "You're her ex-husband," she said in the same tone she'd probably use to say, "You're a child molester."

I began to wonder if I'd even make it in the door, much less get any useful information. "Sarah was my wife, yes."

"Where did she go? What did you do with her?"

That was a little startling; I'd never before been accused of being responsible for her disappearance. "Me? I don't know where she went—or why." I hurried on as it looked like she might be about to close the door. "But my daughter thinks she saw her at a mall just a couple of days ago. I'm trying to find out if she's back in town and I thought you...."

The formerly cherubic homemaker interrupted, looking now like she probably owned attack dogs rather than puppies. "I just told you I haven't heard from her. If she's back and wants to talk to you, I'm sure she'll get in touch."

"Mrs. Winter...."

"Good day." Slam.

Well, I thought as I contemplated the door, whatever Sarah told this friend about our marriage had obviously not included what a great guy I am.

I got back in my car. At least it appeared that these interviews weren't going to take long.

CHAPTER TWENTY-THREE

Patty Samuels, next on the list, had her combined home and design business on Burnside near 60th. It was a mostly commercial area with only a few homes. Samuels' building was a two-story box with brick front, several parking slots in place of a front yard, and a small but attention-getting sign: S-Mac Design. So she hadn't changed the name of the business.

Patty I knew well, or had at one time, when she and Sarah were operating out of a storefront not far from my office.

All the parking slots were empty, so I pulled in next to the front door—which opened before I was fully out of my car.

I'd remembered Patty Samuels as being every bit as attractive as Sarah. Framed in the doorway, she was still a beauty. Red hair in contrast to my ex-wife's blonde, standing a little shorter and looking perhaps a few years younger. Her pale, narrow face at the moment featured a big smile.

"Clint! How good to see you!"

Relieved to find myself back in the good-guy category, I stepped up to give her a hug—and discovered that, smile or not, her body felt keyed up enough to set off nearby ammunition. I stepped back and saw that the smile didn't make it anywhere near her eyes. Hmmm. Maybe not so good after all.

"Come in, come in!" She motioned me inside a small foyer, from which I followed her into a larger but homey office space. Frilly curtains, old wooden desk with several upholstered chairs in front of it, walls covered with samples of Patty's (and perhaps Sarah's) design work.

"This is a very nice space," I said as I took one of the comfy seats and Patty went around the desk to sit in a well-worn swivel chair.

She sat, placed her hands carefully together on the desktop, and glanced around the office as if seeing it for the first time. That initial smile hadn't wavered yet. "Yes," she said, "it's quite comfortable." She looked at me with what might have passed for pleasant curiosity. "What can I do for you, Clint?"

I went for it. "Colleen tells me Sarah's back in town."

Talk about pupil dilation. But the smile hung in there. "Really? That's wonderful. I'm surprised I haven't heard from her."

"Don't feel bad. I haven't either."

She leaned forward almost imperceptibly; otherwise, I might as well have been talking to a mannequin. "But she has talked to Colleen?"

"No. Colleen believes she saw her at the Clackamas Mall a few days ago. I've been trying to verify that it really was Sarah but I haven't found anyone who's been in touch with her. You say you haven't?"

Finally she moved, sitting back a little and spreading her hands as the smile dissolved into an expression of perfect innocence. "No, of course I haven't. I would have told you. You're not sure it was her, then." Too perfect, that expression, but all I could do was play along.

"No, not sure at all."

The hands rejoined and the smile returned. "It probably wasn't, you know. Why in the world would she come back without contacting you or her daughter? Or me? I don't think she would."

I sighed appropriately. "Probably you're right," I said. "Just in case, though, keep an eye out and let me know if you see or hear anything."

"Of course."

We got quickly to our goodbyes after that exchange and Patty Samuels showed me to the door with smile in place, betrayed this time by a barely repressed urgency.

My mind was racing as I got back in the Outback but I had no time to process because my cell phone rang just as I backed out onto the street and pointed the car downtown. Fortunately there was a space right across the street where I could pull in for a moment.

I saw on the phone's display that the number was blocked. I answered anyway and it was Mike Whitehall.

"I've got the info on that plate—and even better," he said.

"Yeah?"

"It comes back to a vehicle reported stolen yesterday morning. Highlander, right? Late model green?"

"That's it."

"Well, check this out: we've come up with a witness to the Quiller drive-by and guess how they describe the shooter's vehicle."

"Late model green Toyota Highlander."

"Got it in one. What is going on with your client, my friend?"

"Hah. When I figure that out, I'll let you know."

"I look forward to it. We've issued a BOLO for the Highlander and if we find it I'll let *you* know. Meanwhile, be careful out there."

"Thanks. I will."

I punched the phone off and dropped it in my jacket pocket. Glancing over at Patty Samuels' building as I pulled into traffic, I noticed a window curtain falling back into place. No doubt she'd been wondering—and probably worrying—about why I'd stopped again before driving away.

Actually, I didn't blame her. I had a lot to wonder and worry about myself.

CHAPTER TWENTY-FOUR

Among the most recent entries on my ever-growing list of questions was: *Why* did Patty Samuels appear to be so uneasy?

Also: Who the hell was driving that Highlander? Why were they shooting at Samantha Quiller? Not to mention following me?

The real difficulty lay in the fact that these questions arose from two entirely different cases. Not that I never take on more than one case at a time; neither I nor the cats would be able to eat if I restricted myself that way. But normally I wouldn't take on two complex, labor-intensive investigations like these at the same time, mainly because I don't have the resources to pull it off. I am the sole permanent staff of my detective agency, after all, with only a couple of contractors I normally use as backup.

In this instance, however, I was going to have to find a way to pull it off. I could not allow Colleen to feel once more that I was neglecting the mystery of her mother's disappearance, no matter how much Samantha Quiller also needed my attention.

I was still hoping I could quickly determine that it wasn't Sarah that Colleen saw in the mall; then I could devote all my efforts to earning my paycheck. Honestly, though, my hope was wearing a little thin.

In any event, I had plenty to think about on my way back downtown. I pulled into the parking lot across from my office at quarter to five, hopped out and headed up the block to 4th Street. With luck, Sarah's third and final friend would still be in her office, which was just a couple of blocks over.

The young brunette receptionist was on her feet, purse in hand, when I opened the door to Dorothy Ogden's law firm on the third floor of a small office building.

"May I help you?" she asked politely, retaining her hold on the purse.

"Is Dorothy Ogden in?"

She glanced at the clock on the wall with a slight frown. "Do you have an appointment?"

"No, I'm sorry, I don't. My name's Clint McCall and I'm a private investigator looking into the disappearance of a friend of Miss Ogden's." Which was not literally a lie. "I only need a moment of her time." Which could be true.

She set the purse down. "Oh." Picked up the phone. "Let me see if she's available."

After quickly repeating what I'd said to whoever answered, presumably Dorothy Ogden, she hung up the phone and indicated a door to her right. "Miss Ogden will see you."

I noted the receptionist picking up her purse again as I turned the knob of the inner door; apparently Dorothy Ogden felt secure enough to let the help go on home while she met with me. She might have recognized my name, of course, despite my not putting it in context.

Ogden stood behind her desk as I entered, a small compact woman with short dark hair, in her late forties I'd guess. She held out her hand, very business-like. "Mr. McCall. This friend you're investigating wouldn't be your ex-wife, now, would it?"

Yes, indeed. She had recognized my name.

"It would," I conceded as I took her hand.

She motioned to one of her comfortable visitor's chairs and eased down into her own. "You're running a little late if you're only beginning an investigation now. As far as I know, Sarah has been missing for four years."

"Then you haven't heard from her recently?" Might as well get straight to the point.

Her eyebrows went up. "No. Is there some reason to believe I should have?"

"My daughter Colleen thinks she saw her mother at Clackamas Town Center Mall a few days ago."

"They didn't speak?"

"Colleen was on the second level and saw Sarah—or someone she thought looked like Sarah—in the crowd below. By the time she got down there the person wasn't to be found."

She mulled that over for a moment. "Interesting. I'm sorry that I can't help you—though I hope Colleen was correct. It would mean that Sarah is still alive, at least, however mysteriously she may be acting."

"Agreed. Do you have any theories as to why she might be acting mysteriously?"

A shrug. "Sorry. Not a one. We were good friends but not the best of friends. I'm sure she'd call me if she needed a lawyer, but not necessarily if she needed a confidant—possibly *because* I'm a lawyer."

Hmmm. "You think she might be in trouble with the law?"

The shrug was somewhat impatient this time. "I have no idea, Mr. McCall. If Colleen did see her mother, though, that means Sarah is in the area but not getting in touch—at least not with me, nor with you, or your daughter. Either she has amnesia, which is quite unlikely, or she has some reason to remain incognito."

I had to agree with that as well. There being little else to say, I thanked Dorothy Ogden for her time and let myself out the hall door.

Since it was after five, I stopped in my own office just to check for messages (none of any interest) and then went on home.

CHAPTER TWENTY-FIVE

As I collected my mail and opened my front door, it felt like I had been away from the house for days. Stella and Maxine seemed to agree; they both came galloping through the living room to meet me as I entered.

I set the mail on the nearest side table and bent down to give them both a good head scratch, one head under each hand. "I hope you girls had a more relaxing day than I did," I said as Maxine rolled over for a belly rub—her own personal preference. After a minute or so they both had enough of petting and pulled away from me to head for the kitchen. "Okay," I said as I stood up to follow, "let's go check on your food."

People who don't have cats can't understand what a relief it sometimes is to come home and simply be told what to do.

By the time I'd provided food for everyone, including a frozen dinner for myself, it was nearing six p.m. and I had to do something about the fact that Johnny Crew also needed relief. It was bad enough he was having to do the surveillance alone; I couldn't ask him to try to continue all night. Which left only one option right now: me. It meant going without sleep myself, but it was the best I could do.

Thus it was that I found myself sitting in the Outback across the street from Samantha Quiller's home, struggling to stay awake at one the following morning. I'd relieved Johnny at seven after checking in with Mrs. Quiller to tell her what was going on. He was planning to come back in only six more hours. Whoopee. Clearly I was going to have to make another arrangement before his next shift was over.

I was on my second thermos of coffee already, buzzed to the gills, but not exactly feeling sharp. Besides keeping an eye on the steadily decreasing traffic flow and the Quiller house, I'd spent most of the last six hours trying to make some constructive sense out of my interviews with Sarah's friends and Mike Whitehall's revelation that the vehicle following me might well be the same as the one involved in Samantha Quiller's drive-by.

What could I conclude from my interviews? One: Nancy DeFazio really didn't like me and probably knew nothing about Sarah's disappearance or purported reappearance. Two: Patty Samuels was hiding something. It might simply be that she also thought I was a louse—or it might be the truth about where Sarah was right now. Three: Dorothy Ogden was a smart lady and, being a lawyer, probably a good enough liar to conceal any information she might have —though that didn't mean she actually knew anything relevant.

Action item: Look again more closely at Patty Samuels.

Switching my attention to the case I was actually being paid to investigate, what could I conclude from Whitehall's information?

Samantha Quiller comes to me saying that she's seen her supposedly dead husband downtown. Dead hubby supposedly also saw her, but avoided contact. All available information so far, including DNA evidence, indicates that dead hubby is indeed dead. But all of a sudden someone is shooting at her. At about the same time I get a mysterious female caller wanting to know if I'm working for Quiller—and a mysterious tail that probably is Quiller's drive-by shooter.

Conclusion? Somehow Samantha Quiller and I had kicked a hornet's nest wide open.

Action item: Other than to keep poking the damned nest, I had no good ideas on this one—except that we should try to avoid getting stung.

I watched a late model pickup truck slowly drive by, weaving just a little, the first vehicle I'd seen in more than a half-hour, and thought to myself that I'd much rather have gone to the black belt training and then home to nurse my latest bruises. I took another long sip of coffee.

About five minutes later I was wondering if a good sex fantasy might help keep me awake when I saw another set of headlights coming in my direction from the front. Not a pickup this time, but not a sedan either. I looked more carefully as the vehicle continued to approach, perhaps moving a little faster now. Well, golly, it was an SUV—and it was definitely speeding up.

There is no question that the sudden appearance of a possible shooter is even better than a sex fantasy for clearing the cobwebs.

In the middle of the night with few streetlights to help out, it was impossible to know at this distance if I was looking at a green Highlander—much less *the* green Highlander. Even if I were, the shooter might be only reconnoitering; a random shot at a dark house couldn't accomplish more than frightening the occupants.

Which could be the point. That vehicle was still accelerating—a little more than a block away now.

I drew my gun and moved over to open the passenger side door, planning to use the door for cover as I eased out onto the street.

I'd just started to slide off the seat in a semi-crouch when my front windshield *cracked* explosively. Out of the corner of my eye I saw the driver's side headrest jolt from the bullet's impact. I fell forward onto the street, curled up so as not to extend into the path of the oncoming vehicle. I landed facing in that direction and put a bullet in the grill of the SUV that was now right on top of me. Didn't slow it down at all. I could see at least one muzzle flash from the driver's side as it roared by. I rolled over and took a couple more shots at the retreating rear-end.

Then its tail lights were fading into the distance. It squealed around a corner several blocks down and was gone.

Meanwhile porch lights were going on all over the neighborhood. Clearly it would not be necessary for me to find my cell phone—and who knew where it was after all my tumbling around —to call the cops.

CHAPTER TWENTY-SIX

As time began to speed up again, my first thought was that every inch of my body seemed to have some kind of ache or pain. My second was that it had been really stupid to take those last two shots; if they hadn't hit the fleeing vehicle they might have hit someone's house—or even someone. Never a good idea to have a shootout in a residential neighborhood.

I groaned, more from the second thought than the first, as I slowly pushed myself to my feet and noted that the lights were also now on in Samantha Quiller's house. I probably had a very frightened client in there. I couldn't go reassure her quite yet, however; it would be best if I held my position until the police arrived. It wouldn't be long; I could hear the sirens already.

I didn't know any of the uniformed officers who were first on the scene—and they didn't know me, so it took a few minutes to establish that I was the victim. Cops with adrenaline running high are always reluctant to concede that a stranger in possession of a weapon might be innocent. And none of us knew that I *was* entirely innocent until it became clear, to my great relief, that those last two bullets had done no harm down the street.

Meanwhile I had asked one of the uniforms to contact Mike Whitehall and he arrived just fifteen minutes later; either he sleeps with his clothes on or had already been up for some reason. I'd also had a chance to briefly tell Samantha Quiller what just happened in front of her house. Neither she nor Mike was thrilled.

Quiller was safely back in her house with an officer posted by the front door as Mike and I stood by my Subaru looking at the nice starburst pattern around the bullet hole in the windshield.

"I'll tell you what," he finally said. "I'll keep that guy posted up there and increase patrols in the neighborhood, at least until Johnny shows up to start his shift, if you'll just get the hell out of here before my boss asks me why you haven't been arrested for endangering the public. Okay?"

"He shot first!" I protested jokingly.

Whitehall didn't seem to find any humor in the situation. "Or I could actually arrest you and then my boss wouldn't have any questions."

I held up both hands in resignation. He was right. It would be better if I took off before all the cops who were questioning the neighbors got together to compare notes. The media would be arriving soon, as well, which was another good reason to disappear. And, what the hell, I could get a couple hours of sleep if I left now.

I agreed that I'd head home as soon as I had another word with my client. Mike told me to hurry it up, which I did. All I wanted to do was reassure her that there'd be a police presence until Johnny Crew was on scene again and that I'd be back in touch soon.

The drive home gave me time to realize that my body was really not happy. I'd twisted my left knee pushing myself out of the car and badly bruised my shoulder landing in the street. Investigating a sharp pain just in front of my right ear, I found a small shard from the windshield (so much for shatterproof glass). I pulled it out and felt a trickle of blood running down my cheek. Great.

I limped in my front door just after two-thirty, found an adhesive bandage to staunch the bleeding from my tiny wound, and barely managed to get undressed before sprawling on the bed. I hadn't checked to see if I had any mail (voice, electronic, or snail); if there were any more developments this night, I didn't want to know about them. My last awareness was of Stella and Maxine snuggling up against me as I fell into a restless sleep.

To my groggy dismay, the phone woke me just three and a half hours later. Glancing at the clock, I couldn't believe I was hearing my daughter's voice at such an hour.

"Colleen? What are you doing up at six in the morning? Is something wrong?"

"That's what I was going to ask you. I just saw on the early morning news that somebody tried to shoot you last night. Are *you* okay?"

"I'm fine. They missed." But the media hadn't missed my name. That was going to make the new day even worse. "Jesus, you're not only up but watching TV? What happened to the girl I used to know who slept in until nearly noon?"

"Earth calling Dad. She grew up and became a morning person." Pause, deep breath. "Do you think that shooting had anything to do with Mom?"

I was still shaking my head trying to fully wake up and for a moment her question completely threw me. "What? Oh, no. No, of course not. I was staked out in front a client's house and I'm sure it had to do with her rather than your mother."

"That's good. Have you found out anything?"

The cats scattered as I sat up and got my legs over the side of the bed. That left knee was *not* feeling good. And I badly needed about six cups of coffee. "I've been talking to some of her old friends but I don't have anything concrete yet."

She was silent for a long moment. "You're not going to have much time to work on it, are you? You've got that client and people shooting at you...."

"Sweetie, I always have clients and often have people shooting at me. If your mother has come back, I will find her. Guaranteed." I noticed my mouth go dry on that last word.

But I could feel her smile over the phone, so it was worth it. "Okay," she said. "I hear you. I'll stop nagging. For a little while."

"I'll let you know as soon as I know anything."

"Good enough. You take care, Pops."

"I will. Talk to you soon."

We hung up and I sat there on the bed looking down at Stella and Maxine sitting on the floor looking up at me. They were hungry. I was not.

CHAPTER TWENTY-SEVEN

I wasn't feeling much better by seven, but at least I could then confirm that Johnny was back on station in front of Samantha Quiller's house. He'd already heard something about the night's events from the officer Mike Whitehall left on duty until he arrived. I provided the remaining details and Johnny assured me with somewhat more than the average obscenity that he would be watching his back—and front, and sides.

Before heading to the office I finally forced myself to consume some toast spread lightly with peanut butter, liberally washed down with coffee. Still dealing with that dry mouth. And contemplating the absolute impossibility of my relieving Johnny again this evening. I desperately needed some more backup.

At least the limp wasn't so bad this morning and my shoulder felt slightly numb rather than painful. All in all, not much worse than the day after a vigorous taekwondo sparring session.

There had been no mail of interest at home when I finally checked, but when I arrived at the office the message light on my phone was blinking busily.

Somewhat to my dismay, the first voicemail was from Hap Harbaugh, who apparently was already back on the job this morning, announcing that there were "things happening" in the Marvin Montgomery case and I should call him right away. No hint what the things might be, though I hoped they involved Montgomery single-handedly lifting the front end of a semi.

Before dealing with Hap, however, I wanted to follow up on my second voicemail, from Alison Roberts. Her message was simple: "I'll trade what I've learned for an exclusive."

I called her extension at the TV station and she picked up on the first ring. "Channel 11 News. Alison Roberts."

"Too soon for an exclusive. Clint McCall."

"Humph. What do you mean, 'too soon'? Then I guess it's too soon to report what I've found out about George Quiller."

I did my best to repress a sigh of exasperation. "Alison, you can have your story when there's a story to tell. Right now I don't know what the hell is going on and publishing any speculation will only make finding out even tougher. We've had this conversation plenty of times before."

"You could at least give me a first-person on the shooting last night."

"I could."

She tried to wait me out. Finally: "But you won't."

"I *will*—as part of your exclusive when the time comes."

"Oh, damn you. All right, here it is: I think this George Quiller of yours was a little too perfect."

Well, that wasn't what I expected to hear. "What do you mean?"

"I got curious after we talked and did some research on Quiller. Everything looks normal enough going back about eight years but before that the record's just too clean."

"I'm still not following you. You mean he was never in trouble with the law before he married Samantha?"

"No, I mean he had what must have been an incredibly humdrum life before then. No deviations. No blemishes. Nothing." She rushed on before I could express my confusion again. "According to the few records I can find, up until around fifteen years ago George Quiller's life is a simple straight line. Really simple. Very little childhood schooling, with whatever records there were apparently lost. Once he came of age, a series of low-level jobs in obscure locations with no known associates or associations. Nothing that can easily be confirmed. Nothing that I've been *able* to confirm, in fact. Then suddenly he's a married, successful whatever salesman."

"Hmmm," I said. "Are you trying to say what I think you're try-ing to say?"

"It's subtle and I have nothing more than my gut to back it up, but the contrast between pre-Samantha and post-Samantha looks very clear to me. I think there's a real possibility 'George Quiller' was a manufactured identity, one acquired not long before he met his wife."

That's what I thought she was trying to say, but it sounded pretty flimsy to me. "On the other hand," I pointed out, "he wouldn't be the first guy to lead a totally boring life before he met the right woman."

"True—though I have to tell you, it's my experience that the boring guys mostly remain boring even *after* they meet the right woman."

"The cops surely investigated Quiller's background when he got blown all to shit in front of his house. And I just had Eleanor Ivory checking him out as well. How come you're the only person to see this pattern?"

"I don't know. I'm smarter than they are? Maybe they didn't go back far enough. Or maybe they were looking for a clue rather than the absence of clues. What can I say? I think I'm right about this."

My mind was beginning to wrap around the possibilities even as she spoke. After all, this would be just one more weird aspect of an already very weird case. "Okay," I finally said, "I'll run with that for a while and see if it takes me anywhere. Eleanor did pick up on the fact that Quiller seemed to have no close friends or associations during his marriage and probably no cop would have put such speculation into a written report even if it had occurred to him or her. Not without something concrete to back it up, anyway."

"I appreciate your confidence," Alison said, sounding relieved. "I'm betting that if you dig deep enough you're going to hit con-crete—and then you owe me that exclusive."

"I won't forget," I assured her, and at that we hung up.

CHAPTER TWENTY-EIGHT

My remaining voicemails were from various other media people, none of whom were friends of mine and none of whom offered any juicy info as a trade for the requested interview. So I simply erased all the messages and called Hap.

"You're on the case early," I said as soon as he answered.

"Ah, I couldn't sleep anyway. The lumbago was actin' up. You know I get that bad."

Given that Hap was in the habit of complaining about every manner of illness, ache, and pain, this didn't surprise me too much. It did remind me once again that I was using two very old retired cops as my backup and would have to think of something else (besides black belts who wanted to play detective) one of these days.

"So what's the big development so early in the morning?"

"Well, I got here about six and guess where our guy went about fifteen minutes later?"

"Where?"

"To a sports club!"

All right, I thought to myself. And of course he'd go at some off time, to make it less likely he'd be caught at it. "That is good news," I said. "I hope you got some nice, clear photos of him lifting heavy weights or something similar."

"Ah. No. No, I didn't."

"Why not?"

"I couldn't get into the damned club."

"Why not?"

"They wouldn't let me in."

"They wouldn't let you in?" I was beginning to sound like a parrot.

"I wasn't a member."

"Did you ask if they had something like a one-time visitor's pass?"

"I did. They got one, all right, one that cost fifty bucks. It was one of those really fancy places, probably with lots of frou-frou drinks and guys in spandex."

I took a deep breath, frustrated but also amused. Marvin Montgomery in spandex. Now, *that* would be a photo for the ages.

"You could have charged it to me, you know. You are working for me right now."

"My card's about maxed out and they wouldn't let me charge it to someone else. And I sure didn't have fifty bucks on me. Really sorry, Clint."

"That's okay, man. Just stay on him. At least we know now there will be more opportunities. Where is he now?"

"Back home. I'm parked just down the street."

"Good enough."

We hung up and I swiveled my chair around so I could contemplate the traffic down on Stark. It was too bad Hap couldn't get photos at the club, but it was just a matter of time.

CHAPTER TWENTY-NINE

Meanwhile I had to resolve the dilemma of keeping my promise to my daughter while also fulfilling my responsibility to my client. Neither my lack of sleep nor my various aches and pains could be allowed to stand in the way.

The top three items on my priority list (two items too many, given my resources) were to follow up on Alison Roberts' theory that George Quiller was a fake identity, find out more about Patty Samuels, and find a relief besides me for Johnny Crew.

Taking number three first: I still didn't want to hire another contractor or use one of the black belts. Much as I hated the idea, I was going to have to call Reuben Keys. I needed somebody who could handle a gun to help with protecting Samantha Quiller, and Reuben certainly met that qualification.

Veronica's former pimp had given me a hand on a number of cases—though usually just as muscle, a particular expertise of his. Reuben most often intimidated possible opponents into surrender before the fight even started, which was particularly handy for a licensed private detective who didn't want his backup arrested for assault or worse.

The problem was that he wouldn't last a quarter hour parked in Samantha Quiller's neighborhood, sitting in his bright pink pimp car dressed in chartreuse or whatever, without somebody calling the cops. I would have to convince him to keep it a bit more muted. If I could convince him to help me at all. Probably enough money would do the trick. Damn it.

Shit. This was going to get *very* complicated and expensive. And staring down at the traffic on Stark wasn't going to simplify it.

I checked my watch as I swiveled back to my desk. Nine twenty-five in the morning. Reuben would have been in bed no more than three or four hours and his phones would all be shut off. If I

89

wanted him today, I'd have to go roust him out in person. No problem. Why should *he* get a lot of sleep?

I grabbed my jacket, hooked my holstered Smith and Wesson onto my belt, and headed out.

He currently lived about a mile east of the Burnside Bridge in a dilapidated two-story apartment building near the corner of 21st and Ash. I parked on the street a couple of doors down and took the outside metal stairway up to the second floor balcony that ran the length of the building. I knocked on the door of Apartment 2B.

And knocked. And knocked. Eventually I heard some faint noises from within and then Reuben's voice, sounding even lower and rougher than usual: "What the fuck!"

"It's Clint McCall. I know you probably just went to bed, but I need to talk to you."

"Fuck. Gimme a minute. It better be good."

It was more like five minutes, which gave me plenty of time to calculate how much money would constitute "good" under the cir-cumstances. Probably more than I had planned to offer—but still less than hiring real backup from another agency.

Finally the door opened and he stood there in all his menacing glory.

Reuben Keys is about my size, 5' 10" and stocky, quite possibly the last living pimp to dress like the late-night-movie stereotype. The colorful outfits contrast sharply with the coal black of his skin, the salt-and-pepper hair, and a face scarred by cuts, burns, and God knows what other misadventures. The bright, cheery accouter-ments end up making him look even more scary and, believe me, he knows it.

Before opening the door he'd taken time to don a relatively conservative outfit: dark pants, expensive athletic shoes, white tee shirt, heavy gold chain, and a Magnum the size of a small cannon. Like I said, guns were not a problem for Reuben.

He glared at me and poked his head beyond the doorframe to look both ways down the balcony—at which point he took his hand off the holstered weapon and gestured me inside.

I said he sometimes provided backup, not that we were trusting friends.

There were only two rooms visible, the small living room with a fold-out couch and a kitchen that barely qualified as a nook. Clothes, magazines, discarded fast food packaging and a number of unidentifiable items littered every square foot. The odors of unwashed clothing and pot hung in the air.

"What the fuck do you want this time of day, McCall?" he inquired sourly as I followed him toward the couch. He plopped onto it and swung his feet up as he pointed at the ratty armchair nearby. "There," he said.

So I sat there.

"I need you to keep an eye on someone for me," I said, "a client who might have a stalker or worse. Johnny Crew is watching them during the day and I relieved him last night, but I need somebody else tonight. Maybe for a few more nights."

Reuben sat staring at me for so long that I thought maybe he'd gone back to sleep with his eyes open. "You got me the fuck out of bed to watch some lady who might have a stalker? And you want me to do it at night, when I got my own business to do?"

"Don't you do most of your *business* on your cell phone, anyway? You don't actually hang out on the street corners with the women, do you?"

He huffed. "I do sometimes. Gotta keep an eye on the merchandise, you know. Enforce good business practices. All that shit."

"Well, I'll pay you good money for keeping an eye on this woman and her kid. Somebody's already taken a shot at her. I need a gun on this one. And you need to use a different vehicle."

"I got a fuckin' gun, all right. But what the fuck about a different car? Why do I gotta use a different car?"

91

"This woman lives in a respectable white neighborhood. You park your pimpmobile there and people see you sitting in it dressed in your usual fancy duds.... How long before somebody calls the cops?"

"You sounding downright racist here."

"Not me. Them. That's the point."

He grimaced. "Why the fuck do you need *me* to do this? I ain't no fuckin' private eye. I'm a fuckin' entrepreneur."

I gave him a very brief summary of everything I had going on. I apologized for expecting him to do something besides provide muscle, him being an entrepreneur of fucking and all. I explained, as best I could without sounding totally lame, that I was in a real jam here. I offered him even more money than I had calculated while waiting outside the door. Damn it. He finally agreed. He even agreed to dress down and use another vehicle.

Then, to my surprise, he circled back around to the news that Sarah might have returned, which I'd included in my summary. He'd never met her even though he'd been a client of mine before she disappeared. "That's real interesting about your ex," he said.

"Yeah? What's so interesting—to you—that my ex-wife might be back in town?"

"Got to do with somethin' I heard last night."

"What did you hear?"

"I heard somebody was lookin' to kill you."

"Really? Were you planning to let me know about this any time soon?"

He shrugged. "Probably after I got me some sleep."

"Thanks a bunch. Who's looking to kill me and what do you think it has to do with Sarah?"

"I don't know who it is." Slight grin. "Nobody told me her name."

My spine went cold. "Her?"

"A woman. Who just got into town."

Crap.

CHAPTER THIRTY

In addition to no name, there was no description that Reuben had heard. Just that it was a woman, new in town, out to kill me.

To which my second response (after "Crap!") was *What the fuck?*

It couldn't be Sarah. I mean, a lot can happen in four years and people change, but she'd never been *that* pissed off at me. There was the mysterious female who'd called my office to ask if I was working for Samantha Quiller. Maybe that's who it was. But why? Why would some woman show up in town wanting to do murder because I was supposed to look for Quiller's already-dead husband? And what kind of woman would be hanging around and dropping hints among Reuben's likely informants?

Well, the answer to that was: a really dangerous woman.

As I left Reuben's apartment, my thought processes were more than a little chaotic. I'd managed to give him the necessary details about the surveillance job and urged him to stay alert for any further details about potential female assassins, but that was about the most sustained coherence I could achieve.

I stopped at the bottom of the outside stairway, catching my breath and trying to think of something, anything, I could constructively do with this new information.

Couldn't think of a damned thing.

When I finally turned toward my car I saw that it was not alone. I didn't recognize the very large white guy leaning against it with his arms crossed, but his glare certainly seemed to recognize me.

I ambled in that direction to see what he wanted. Everything about him said tough guy: close-cropped dark hair, slightly shaggy moustache, bulging biceps in a thin tee shirt that disregarded the sharp February chill in the air. He didn't move even one of his many muscles as I approached, nor did his glare waver.

I stopped about four feet away. "Can I help you?"

He actually sneered as he straightened up to face me. "You can leave my wife alone. That's what you can do, motherfucker."

For one insane moment I thought I was looking at George Quiller telling me to leave Samantha alone. Then I realized he didn't match the description. And wasn't dead.

"If I'm going to do that," I said as reality returned, "you're going to have to tell me who your wife is."

He dropped his arms to his sides and took a step closer, his expression twisting into an even more belligerent expression. "Don't fuck with me, old man. If you bother Patty again, I'm going to stomp you."

Aha. Patty Samuels. What was her husband's name? Fred? Frank? That was it: Frank. And I was determined to stay cool despite the "old man" reference.

"I'm a private investigator. I had to talk to your wife as part of an ongoing investigation. There was nothing inappropriate about it. I'm sorry if it upset her."

"I don't give a fuck if it upset her. I don't want anybody messing with my wife—and what the fuck investigation is it?"

Hmmm. She hadn't told him what I was asking about. So why did she tell him I was there at all?

Might as well try to find out, seeing as how this was getting so interesting. "What did Patty tell you about my visit?"

"She didn't *tell* me about your *visit*." There was that really irritating sneer again and he was stepping in closer, too. "I got my own ways of finding out when a guy *visits*. And where he is when I want to find him. What the fuck were you asking her about?"

Now I was imagining some kind of jealous-husband-cam trained on the front door. And apparently he was into following people. No wonder the woman seemed nervous.

Whatever, no way I was going to share with this asshole if she didn't. "The investigation is confidential. There's nothing I can tell you about it."

Another step forward. His steadily reddening countenance was definitely getting into my personal space. "Fuck confidential, old man. You're gonna tell me or I'm gonna kick your ass."

Well, gee, there he went being ageist again. I shifted my left foot back and settled just a little into a fighting stance, but with my hands still open. "I'm not actually required to tell you that I'm a fourth-degree black belt," I said softly, "but I will give you that courtesy. Now: if you don't give *me* the courtesy of backing off, Frank, we're going to find out real quick whose ass gets kicked."

His eyebrows went up at that and his face darkened even more —but he didn't make a move. We held our little tableau for probably twenty seconds and then he took a step back.

"I ain't gonna violate my parole for an old fart like you. Black belt, my ass."

I very subtly bit my lip. If he called me old one more time, I might put him down anyway.

He took another step back and a half-turn as if to leave. Then glared back at me. He seemed to glare a lot. "I'll find out from Patty what you wanted," he growled. "Then maybe we'll talk again."

I looked him right in the eye. "If she wants to tell you, fine. If she doesn't and you lay a hand on her, I guarantee we'll be talking very soon."

He blinked. "Fuck you," was all he said, and walked away.

CHAPTER THIRTY-ONE

As my newest less-than-articulate acquaintance got into his vehicle down the street, my mind continued urgently circling around everything I'd just learned.

Which was what, exactly? One: Someone, supposedly an unidentified female who'd just arrived in town, wanted me dead. Two: For some unknown reason, Patty Samuel's husband didn't want me or apparently anyone else talking to his wife. Given the unidentified and the unknown, I hadn't really learned much.

At the very least, however, I needed to find out who my female caller had been, follow up on Alison's theory that George Quiller was a fake identity, *and* try to keep an eye on Patty Samuels in case her husband intended to get violent with her.

That was a lot for the very least. I checked my watch as I got into my car. It was only ten thirty in the morning. How many further wonders might the day bring?

I pulled away from the curb and headed for Samantha Quiller's house.

Before going in, I again trotted across the street to see how Johnny was doing. He assured me, with typical surrounding obscenities, that he was fine. I thought he looked a little glassy-eyed, but probably no more than I did. The obscenities only multiplied when I told him that Reuben would be his relief.

"What the fuck are you going to do when Hap and me *really* retire?" he asked with some exasperation. "Your regular backup's gonna be a pimp? Talk about your business going down the fuckin' toilet!"

I had a hunch that Johnny and Hap would never really retire, but I conceded the point that I was not utilizing the best resources at the moment. Then I headed back across the street to talk to my client.

She didn't look all that great, either. Her freckles stood out against a complexion that was noticeably more pale than when we'd first met; her short-cropped brown hair was somewhat awry and her glasses needed cleaning. She managed a tiny smile of greeting, however, and as usual offered me some coffee as I took my seat in the living room. I thought we both could probably use some and she soon produced a pot with two cups.

We dispensed with the small talk within a couple of sips and she sat looking at me inquiringly. "No," I responded to the unspoken question, "there's no real news. A couple more mysteries, maybe."

The corners of her mouth turned down. "*More* mysteries? What is going on, Mr. McCall? I never dreamed when I went to see you that people would be trying to kill us within a few days. I just thought I saw my husband downtown!" She took a deep breath and another sip of the coffee. "Maybe I should never have said anything about it."

"Let's find out what's going on before you go blaming yourself," I said.

She sipped again. "All right," she said finally. "What are the new mysteries?"

It was my turn to take a deep breath before I plunged in. "It's beginning to look like your husband's identity might have been a fake."

She didn't even say anything; she just looked at me with her mouth slightly open. I would have sworn, though, that I could hear her coffee cup vibrating slightly in its saucer.

"If you look carefully at his history," I went on, "the records are characteristic of someone who has had an identity constructed."

She was squinting at me, now, as if the effort to understand what I was saying might be too much for her. "You mean," she said finally, "like someone in witness protection?"

"Exactly."

"First you tell me George had a police record I didn't know about and now you tell me he might not have been George at all." She gulped the coffee this time. "Is there any more news?"

"There's a possibility the person who's doing the shooting is a woman." This was my own shot in the dark. It did appear that the same vehicle had been involved in the drive-bys of Samantha Quiller at the grocery and me in front of her house, but why would a woman who wants to kill me shoot at Quiller?

In response, meanwhile, my client carefully set her coffee cup and saucer down on the table beside her chair and began to softly laugh. I, in turn, began to fear for her sanity. "Is the idea of a woman shooter funny to you?" I asked.

"It's all just so totally insane," she replied between dying chuckles. "A woman from George's past? What is that? An affair? Another *wife*? This is beyond crazy. I don't know what to think. To do."

Thinking of Johnny looking so tired and Reuben being...Reuben, I did have a suggestion: "How about moving to a hotel for the interim? You'd be much less exposed and easier to protect."

That finished sobering her up. She thought about it. "I suppose you have no idea how long the 'interim' would be," she finally said.

"Not a clue," I agreed.

She grimaced. "I'll think about it, for Kinsey's sake. Let's give it one more day. I don't want to leave our home."

"I understand. Maybe by tomorrow I'll have some better information."

I explained to her that there would be a different protector in front of the house during the night, a black man, and that I'd used him before. She took me at my word, still somewhat in shock I think.

I left her sitting in her living room; she didn't even offer to get up and escort me to the door. My sincerest hope as I drove away was that by tomorrow I would have something, anything, I could offer that would bring her back from the edge. My client was teetering, for sure, and she had a little girl to take care of.

I needed to take care of them both.

CHAPTER THIRTY-TWO

But first I had to go see Patty Samuels again. Even if her husband were simply a jealous jerk, she might still be in some jeopardy because of my last visit.

Again all the parking slots were empty; the design business did not appear to be thriving. As I got out of my car, I looked around to see if I could see a surveillance camera or a stake-out of some kind. Nothing in sight. There was no welcoming smile this time when she opened the door.

"Clint, I really can't talk right now," she announced with a slightly shrill edge to her voice before I could even open my mouth to say hello. Which pretty much guaranteed that I was going to stick around until I found out what was going on.

"I understand that you're busy," I said politely, "but this will take just a minute—and it's important. Can I come in?"

She chewed on her lower lip and fluttered her hands, probably trying to think of some way to say no. Apparently she couldn't think of one. "Just for a minute," she said, and stepped back.

I followed her through the foyer and into the cozy office space. She perched on the very front edge of her chair behind the desk and placed her hands, twisted together, on the desk. She was trying so hard to stay focused on me that her expression was essentially blank, but I could see that her eyes wanted to bounce around the room anyway. Something was very definitely not right. Could her husband have beaten me here after all?

"What do you want?" she asked.

I decided to check theory number one right off. "Frank came to see me today."

The way she jerked back with eyes widening told me that Frank had *not* already arrived to give her that news. Unfortunately, I didn't have a theory number two yet.

She licked her lips and her eyes flicked around again. They seemed to be going to her right more than anywhere else.

"Frank...? Frank talked to you? Why? Did you tell him you were here?"

"I didn't have to. He already knew. That's why he came to see me."

There went the eyes to the right again. On that side of the room was a second door. I'd assumed when I was here before that it led to the other portion of the living space. What was so interesting—or scary—back there? Maybe theory number one was partially correct after all: Frank was here but hadn't told her he'd been to see me.

Meanwhile I would swear that I saw the woman's skin ripple when I told her he already knew. She certainly blanched. "He knew? How? How could he know?"

"My guess is that he has some kind of surveillance on the front door or"—I gestured around—"in here."

This time her eyes riveted for a moment on the door to her right. "My God."

"So," I asked casually as I eased out of my chair and stepped in that direction, "what's behind door number two?"

I was looking back at Patty Samuels as my hand grasped the knob. She started to rise, her mouth open to protest, and then she sank back down resignedly.

I turned the knob and opened the door, tensed to confront husband Frank or whoever.

Well, maybe not whoever.

There in the middle of a spacious tastefully decorated living room stood a small, lean woman with strong familiar features and shoulder-length blonde hair. I think my own skin might have rippled.

"Hello, Clint," Sarah said with a wry little smile.

CHAPTER THIRTY-THREE

Talk about a rush of conflicting emotions.

I took a moment—maybe longer than a moment—to get the shards of my composure together and finally said, with admirable calm if little originality, "Hello, Sarah. Fancy meeting you here."

Patty Samuels' voice came over my right shoulder. "I'm sorry, Sarah. I tried."

"It's okay, Patty," my ex-wife said. "He would have figured it out pretty soon." She was looking at me, not at her friend. "Clint's a smart guy."

Wow. This woman had been my ex-wife for twelve years and had been completely out of my life and my daughter's life, gone from the face of the earth as far as we knew, for four years. Now here she stood, eight feet in front of me, looking not that different from the last time I'd seen her. Right down to that little smile. There was a time I'd been very fond of that smile.

In fact, I had loved her like life itself. I'd hated her for abandoning me—as I usually thought of it. I'd feared for her, wondering if she'd been abducted or worse. I'd resented her, suspecting that she'd disappeared of her own volition. There was, to say the least, a full cauldron of feelings as my eyes held Sarah's gaze.

"Where the hell have you been?" was all I could say.

She crossed the distance between us and touched me on the arm. Didn't take me by the arm, just touched me lightly as she moved on past toward the office. "Let's all sit down," she said.

So we did, Patty Samuels behind her desk and Sarah and I in the two visitor's chairs. As if we were finally getting around to that marriage counseling we never had. I could still feel her light touch.

"How did you know I was back?" Sarah asked as soon as we were settled.

"Colleen saw you at Clackamas Town Center."

Her face twisted up with concern. "Colleen? Oh dear."

"Yeah," I responded dryly. "She was more than a little upset."

"Why didn't she say anything to me?"

"She saw you from the upper level and by the time she got downstairs she couldn't find you."

"So she told you about it and asked you to find me."

"I am a private detective, after all—not that that helped me find you four years ago. I repeat: Where the hell have you been? And why?"

She took a deep breath, seeming to gather herself. "I've been mostly on the move, not more than six months in any one place. Boulder, San Francisco, Tucson, most recently Los Angeles."

"Sounds like you were running from something."

"Someone."

"Who?"

Again that pause for a breath. "His name is Brad Winters." She exchanged a look with Patty Samuels. "Actually he's a friend of Patty's husband, Frank."

At last a few connections were beginning to appear. "Why were you running from him?"

She sat back. "He was one of a number of bad choices I made after you and I split up," she said. "The worst of the choices, it turned out. I met him through Patty. She and I both thought at the time that he was a perfectly charming fellow. We started dating. He started to get controlling. I tried to break it off...." She paused. "To make a long story short, he turned out to be your basic psychotic stalker type."

"Why didn't you come to me?"

She actually grinned at that, a kind of sickly grin.

"Go to my private eye ex-husband whom I'd divorced because he became a private eye? I don't think so. I wanted to handle it on my own."

"And how is that working out?"

105

The grin faded fast as she gestured vaguely around the cramped office space.

"Well," she said, "here we are."

I took in the space myself. "Indeed. And why, exactly, are we here? Is this Brad Winters guy around here too?"

She frowned as she answered the second question first. "I'm afraid so. He and Frank are still tight, I guess." She looked over at her friend again. "I had to come back because Patty was in trouble."

"You kept in touch with Patty but not with your own daughter?" I couldn't keep the anger out of my voice.

She heard it. "Brad is really crazy. I knew that if he thought I was in touch with Colleen he'd go after her to try to find out where I was. The only person I felt I could safely keep in touch with was Patty—because Brad was confident she had Frank to keep her in line. Neither one of them would believe we'd have the nerve to keep in touch." She grimaced. "They don't think much of women."

"They're both fucking sexist pigs," interjected Patty.

"There's that, too," agreed Sarah.

I looked at Patty. "What trouble are you in?"

She stared down at her lap for a moment and her lower lip was trembling as she raised her head. "Really the same old trouble," she said, "but it's getting worse. Frank. I think he's going to kill me."

Which brought my attention back to my ex-wife. "You came back to stop Frank from murdering Patty?"

That little smile again. "No, I'm not that brave. I came back to help Patty get out, to hide on the road the same as I've been doing." She paused. "I was sure I could pull it off without you or Colleen ever knowing I was in town."

"The best laid plans," I said dryly.

"Yes. That was very bad luck, that Colleen saw me."

"Or very good luck, since it means your private eye ex-husband is now on the case whether you like it or not."

She gave me another look I was familiar with, the you-are-probably-bullshitting-me-but-I'll-go-along-with-it-for-now look. "I guess."

Patty Samuels finally spoke up. "What do we do now? Do you think Frank knows Sarah is here?"

"That depends," I replied. "Has she visited you here before?"

"Yes. A number of times, but she hasn't come in the front. There's a back door you can access from the next street over."

"Then it still depends, on how smart he was about setting up the surveillance. Give me a moment." I got up and stepped back into the foyer. Bare walls and ceiling. A single over-head lighting fixture. No place to secrete a camera. Back in Patty's office I did another more careful survey. No vents, no lighting fixtures that would have served. "Nothing in here," I said. "I'll do some checking outside when we're through talking."

Patty was practically bouncing up and down in her chair. "Please, could you check out back right now? If he knows Sarah is in town, then Brad knows—and that wouldn't be good. That would be very bad."

I said I would and she showed me to the back door. I felt an odd hesitation before I actually went outside, as if Sarah might disappear again while left alone in Patty's office. I shrugged it off, went out and looked around. Very small unfenced back yard, a couple of scraggly little trees. Several residential properties were directly behind Patty's building and I could see the path running from Patty's property between two houses to the next street. A careful scan revealed nothing in the trees or along the rooftops. I doubted that Frank Samuels would have involved one of the neighbors in keeping an eye on his wife. I went back inside. Patty had retaken her chair and Sarah was still there.

"Is Frank friendly with the neighbors behind your house?" I asked as I sat down again.

"Frank isn't friendly with anybody but Brad and a few other sexist assholes. I doubt he knows the people back there at all. I don't myself."

"Then I think you're clear on that side."

She breathed a sigh of relief. "Good."

"It doesn't mean you're entirely clear, though," I cautioned. "Colleen saw Sarah. Someone else could have. And, also, there's the fact that I've been going around town asking people if she might be back. That could be a big hint if Frank or Brad Winters heard of it."

"God, this is such a mess," averred my ex-wife.

I agreed.

Over the next half-hour or so, I heard the details of the two abusive relationships. Frank Samuels had in the course of their eight-year marriage gone from somewhat controlling to insanely jealous, from irritable through verbally abusive to the occasional drunken beating. As far as Brad Winters was concerned, thankfully his abuse had not gone beyond verbal threats and some extremely sinister stalking. However, he'd made clear before Sarah fled that he was determined no one would have her if he couldn't. She believed him.

So, they asked me again, what do we do now? I could see no point in going to the police. Even Mike Whitehall would be hard-pressed to find any resources to protect them when no provable crime had been committed. The mere accusation of spousal abuse could theoretically serve, but as a practical matter it was too far down the spectrum of law enforcement urgency.

I asked Sarah where she was holed up and she said she was registered at a hotel downtown under a false name. I inquired if her room had a second bed and she said it did. So I told them to get whatever they needed together, go out the back door and meet me on the next street over. Whereupon I took them to Sarah's hotel and we registered Patty under a false name in the same room.

I did finally hug Sarah as we said goodbye, she having made the first move. Then I hugged Patty as well to make it clear that these were detective-client hugs rather than reconciliation-of-exes hugs. Why try to simplify life when it's so wonderfully complicated?

CHAPTER THIRTY-FOUR

It was nearly three by the time I got back to my office. The message light was blinking ominously—it seemed ominous at the time—and I chose to ignore it for a few minutes while I sat at my desk and tried to mentally and emotionally catch my breath.

One of my top priorities was to talk to Samantha Quiller again about getting out of the house. If I could get her and Kinsey a room right next to Sarah and Patty, that would certainly make it easier to keep them all covered.

Meanwhile that light was blinking and blinking. I punched up the first message.

It was Colleen. "Hey, Dad, just checking in to see if you've found out anything. Give me a call if you have."

Oh, talk about timing. Had I found out anything? That would be a big yes, but telling my daughter that I'd found her mother wasn't on my to-do list until I'd somehow taken care of the threats from Frank Samuels and Brad Winters.

I had one other voicemail and it was an interesting one, from my mysterious female caller of last Wednesday, the strong deep voice who wanted to know if I was working for Samantha Quiller. At least she was no longer pretending she wanted to hire me.

"George Quiller is dead, Mr. McCall. You can take my word for it. You should drop your investigation now before somebody else gets hurt. I'm watching. I'll know if you don't."

That was it.

I swiveled around and examined the building across the street. Watching me? Watching Mrs. Quiller? Nothing suspicious in the windows over there. I'd have to caution Johnny and Reuben to keep a particular eye out the rest of today. I gave Johnny a quick call and he said he'd pass the word when relieved—*if* he was relieved. He doesn't share my confidence in Reuben Keys.

"You can take my word for it," the woman had said. Because she killed George Quiller herself? Or knew who had?

So, what to do next? It was certainly hopeless to try to confirm that George Quiller was in witness protection. The federal marshals wouldn't share that information with Mike Whitehall, much less me. I looked at my watch. Nearly four. I hadn't eaten since breakfast. Definitely not a day to knock off early and go home, so a big hamburger, maybe two, at the Home Run Sports Bar was next.

It was only after I got settled in a booth that I realized I wasn't very hungry. If it hadn't been so many hours since my last meal, I'm sure I wouldn't have had an appetite at all. As it was, I settled for one hamburger, a small side of fries, and a beer.

Sarah and Patty should be safe enough in their hotel suite with room service. Watching my waitress move on to another table reminded me to ask Sarah how she financed all these years on the road. It couldn't have been easy, but she'd worked her way through school working in local restaurants. That could be it. Or maybe she wouldn't want to share.

Samantha Quiller had Johnny Crew watching over her—I checked my watch between sips of beer—for another two hours or so. After that it was Reuben—and I hoped he would stay focused rather than spending all his time on his cell.

Before six, I would definitely try one more time to persuade her to abandon the house for the time being; I probably should have called her before now.

And what about Marvin Montgomery? I had an obligation to my client, Ray Witkowsky, but no question that Marv's probably fraudulent back problem had slid almost all the way off my to-do list. Hopefully Hap would come up with something. I had a client and an ex-wife in jeopardy, after all. Not to mention my own sorry ass.

CHAPTER THIRTY-FIVE

I got back to the office a little before five and put in the call to Samantha Quiller. No answer. That was a little worrisome, so I called Johnny. He answered after a couple of rings and said he could see her on her front porch talking to a neighbor; she was just going back inside. No worries then. About her, at least. Johnny sounded downright groggy and I was glad Reuben would be relieving him soon. I called Quiller again and, as expected, she insisted on remaining in her home.

Feeling uneasy about literally everything, I decided to remain in my office. There was some paperwork I could do, a few bills to catch up on, and lots of notes on two different cases to shuffle around.

It was full dark outside and just past six thirty when my cell phone rang. "McCall."

Reuben's voice rang in my ear. "The old guy is down, McCall. Johnny's down!"

That brought me to my feet. "What do you mean? What's happened?"

"I don't know what the fuck happened. I got here a couple of minutes ago and found him slumped over the steering wheel. I don't see any blood, so don't the fuck ask me. He's got a pulse; I can tell you that much. I called the medics already."

Oh God. Did he have a heart attack or something? I should have paid more attention to the fact that he didn't look or sound good. "What about Quiller?"

"The woman in the house? What about her?"

"Goddamn it! Have you seen her?"

"Fuck no. I told you, I just got here and found this old fart unconscious."

"Get in there and make sure she's all right!"

"You want me to leave this old guy alone here?"

"There's nothing you can do to help him right this second. Get your ass over to the house and check on Mrs. Quiller and the kid! Now! I'm on my way."

I shoved the phone in my pocket, grabbed my gun and jacket, and dashed for the door. I made it across to the parking lot in probably less than a minute, backed the Subaru out of my slot, and was ready to pull out onto Stark when the cell phone rang again.

With a curse I suppressed the urge to punch the accelerator. I punched the phone on instead. "Yes."

"Nobody's answerin' the door here, McCall. Maybe they ain't home?"

Oh crap. Oh God. "They're supposed to be home, Reuben. Get inside that house and find out what's going on. Break in if you have to. Call the cops if you find anything that doesn't look good. Don't call me again. I'll be there soon."

I cut the connection without waiting for his response and punched that accelerator, cutting off a couple of cars as I squealed into the street hoping that the traffic light gods would be with me on the way.

"Anything that doesn't look good," I'd said? Fuck. Like dead bodies? And what was going to happen if the cops arrived and found Reuben Keys inside the house with dead bodies? *That* wasn't going to be pretty. I focused on weaving through the vehicles ahead as quickly as I could. Might as well still be rush hour, for Christ's sake. At least the first light was green.

CHAPTER THIRTY-SIX

An ambulance was pulling away as I arrived in front of Samantha Quiller's house and there were two patrol cars at the curb. I suppressed the urge to follow it. I needed to find out what had happened first. I didn't even know for sure who was *in* the damned ambulance, after all.

It wasn't Reuben; he was standing spread-eagled with his hands on one of the patrol cars that still had all its lights going. One cop was patting him down while another held a gun on him. If he hadn't ditched it somewhere already, they were going to come up with his gun and that would not be good for him. In the brightly strobing illumination, I could see that he was really pissed off. Not my biggest problem at the moment.

But he apparently thought it was. "McCall! Get your white honky ass over here!"

I slammed the door of the Subaru and strode over to the three of them. I didn't know either of the cops but I showed the one with the gun my ID and stopped where he indicated I should, maybe three feet out. The other cop had finished his pat down and apparently the gun had been ditched. His hands were empty. "I can't rescue you right now, Reuben," I said. "Where's Mrs. Quiller?"

He glared at me. "How should I know? She ain't inside. Tell these fuckers I'm one of the good guys."

Right. "Who was in the ambulance?"

"That was the old man. He had some kinda attack, I guess."

"He was attacked?"

"Nah, he *had* an attack or somethin'. No injuries. Just passed out, is all I know."

"Did the medics say anything? Is he okay?"

Still glaring. "He was breathin' last time I saw him. They're takin' him to Providence downtown. That's all I can tell you." He transferred his ire to the cop still holding the gun. "I'm with this private detective here. No need to be pointing that thing at me."

The cops looked at me. Shit, I was going to have to resolve this before I could move on. "It's true," I said. "The woman who owns this house hired me to protect her and Reuben here was supposed to take the night shift. He broke in after finding Johnny Crew because those were my instructions. He's done nothing wrong that I know of." A qualification that I wouldn't have needed if it weren't Reuben.

Finally the gun lowered and the other cop gestured that Reuben could stand upright.

"Okay," I said, then focusing on him. "You say the house is empty?"

"Nobody home."

"You looked for the baby?"

"I looked in every room, closets, even under the damned beds. There ain't nobody home."

"Any signs of a struggle?"

"Nah. Looks like they probably left in a hurry, but that's all. Some baby stuff scattered on one of the beds, but nothin' broken or turned over or like that."

"What kind of baby stuff?"

"You know. Little clothes, some kinda suck-on thing. Pumpers or whatever they're called. Baby stuff."

I looked at the other patrol car beside us, which was empty. "There are cops inside now?"

"Yeah, they're checkin' around too. I heard one of them call for a supervisor, so we'll have more company in a minute."

Even as he spoke the words, I saw headlights come around the corner down the street. As they approached they resolved themselves into an unmarked Portland police car that pulled up with a

116

screech. The door opened and a plainclothes female got out. Black denim pants with leather jacket and matching boots. Apparently the department had decided to send a detective rather than the shift lieutenant.

I didn't recognize her. Early thirties, athletic-looking, short dark hair, slightly sharp features pleasantly arranged, and all business as she strode over to where we were standing.

"Detective Sergeant Malone," she announced briskly, "and you are?"

CHAPTER THIRTY-SEVEN

I introduced myself and Reuben. She gave him a long look and then focused on me. "Mike Whitehall said you'd probably be on scene. He asked me to come by as a favor, said it might be a missing person's case. So, is that what we've got?"

"I thought I knew everyone in Missing Persons," I said.

"I guess not. I've been here in Portland nearly a year. Tigard PD before that."

"Oh, okay. Good to meet you."

"Glad to be here," she responded dryly. "If you're satisfied with my bona fides now, how about letting me in on *why* I'm here."

I laid it out for her as briefly as I could. The patrolman came out in the meantime and reported to her pretty much the same information Reuben had reported to me. By the time we were all done, Detective Sergeant Malone was looking skeptical.

"Let me see if I understand this. What we've got is your theory, hunch—whatever you want to call it—that your client and her kid have been abducted, but we have no actual evidence a crime has been committed. Your stake-out got sick and the woman took her kid and left; that's all we know for sure."

"Maybe I can't prove it, but what I have is certain knowledge that she's been abducted."

She stood for a moment gazing at the house and then looked at me askance. "I think we have different definitions of 'certain knowledge,' Mr. McCall, *but*"—she held up a hand to stave off my further protests—"I'm going to open a case file and pursue it, at least for now. Mike said your judgment can be trusted, so I'll trust it —for now. And let me make it clear," she emphasized as she stepped in closer to my face, "that I don't like to be left out of any loops when I'm working a case. You savvy?"

"I'll keep you posted on anything I find out," I agreed firmly. I'd decide later whether I was telling the truth or not.

I turned to Reuben, who was looking like he'd rather be anywhere else. "It just occurred to me," I said, "that your call came in right around six-thirty. You were supposed to relieve Johnny at six."

He stuck his scarred chin out at me, looking typically mean and belligerent, which didn't faze me at all. "I had business," he grated. "I needed to make some arrangements before I could get over here. You know I got business that time of day."

"And if you'd been here on time, Johnny might not be on his way to the hospital and we might not have a missing mother and child."

He hunched his shoulders. "I had business," he repeated.

I sensed motion to my left and realized that Sergeant Malone was still standing there, all her attention on my unreliable backup now. "Who are you and what exactly is your business?" she inquired of Reuben.

Now he *really* looked like he wanted to be someplace else. "Keys," he muttered. "My name's Reuben Keys and I'm an independent businessman."

"I thought you were working for the private investigator here."

"I was doin' him a favor. But I had to finish my business first."

"So let's try that again. What business, exactly, are we talking about?"

"I'm...a talent agent."

I'm afraid I snorted rather loudly at this point. Malone glanced at me and then stared at Reuben. "How about I take a guess what talents you represent, Mr. Keys. You think I might get it right the first time?"

"Don't know. How would I know?"

"So you were supposed to be here at six, but you conveniently arrive a half-hour late, after everything has gone down. That wouldn't have been part of the plan, would it? Maybe you know some-

120

thing about what happened here, something you don't want to tell us?" She pulled out her notebook and looked at him expectantly.

At that Reuben jerked a step back and looked from her to me and back again. "What the fuck? First McCall gets on my case about being late and now you want to pin the whole fucking thing on me? I don't know nothing about it. I was fucking late. Thirty fucking minutes, maybe less. That's all."

Even though I was pissed at him, I had to speak up. "You're wasting your time thinking that Reuben was involved in whatever happened here," I said to Sergeant Malone. "Your guess about the talent is right, but he wouldn't be involved in a kidnapping, at least not this one. We've known each other a long time and I've used him as backup before. I trust him." I gave Reuben a quick glance. "Usually."

Now they were both glaring at me.

"Thanks all to fuck for standing up for me, McCall."

"You're welcome all to fuck," I said right back. "Be on time next time. If there is a next time." I was still pissed—and worried about Johnny.

"And I'll be seeing you around, Mr. Keys," Malone said.

He again looked from one of us to the other, clearly with something to say...but he didn't say it. He grunted, then turned and walked away.

Malone looked at me. "That's the kind of low-life you employ, McCall? Makes me wonder if Whitehall was right about you."

"Like I said, I've known him a long time," I said. "It's complicated. Reuben's been reliable in the past and I feel like shit that he blew it this time. Probably he does, too, believe it or not. We need to find Samantha Quiller and her daughter."

She carefully put her notebook away. "*We* don't need to find them—*if* they are missing. That's my job. Your job is to tell me anything you learn so I can do my job. Got that?"

"I'll certainly cooperate fully."

"Good." She went off to consult with the other officers still at the scene. Thus I found myself standing alone in the glare of the patrol car lamps, revolving red on top, flashing red, white, and yellow in front and back. Malone finished conferring with the patrolmen and she got in her vehicle and left—without a further word for yours truly, though she did throw a mild glare my way before departing.

A couple of minutes later, the other two cops got in their patrol cars and departed.

I suddenly noticed that the February Friday evening had turned very cold. I shivered, not only from the plunging temperature but with fear for my client and her child, and I suppose also with dismay that I felt *really* alone out here in the dark.

Johnny is in the hospital. Reuben and I are pissed at each other. My one current backup is Hap who's spending his days watching Marvin Montgomery.

Which reminded me that I should call him and tell him Johnny's in trouble. He should be home from the day's surveillance by now. I'd let him call Geraldine, Johnny's wife, if the authorities hadn't already notified her. Montgomery might have to go unwatched for a while. And I should have insisted that Samantha Quiller go to the hotel. Goddamn, I should have *made* her go!

Talk about depressing.

Which brought me back to Johnny. That was what I had to do right after calling Hap: Go to the hospital and hope to find him recovering from whatever the hell happened to him out here.

CHAPTER THIRTY-EIGHT

The Providence Portland Medical Center is on Glisan just off Interstate 84. I found my way to an information desk and from there to the appropriate visitor's area where I discovered Hap already anxiously awaiting word from the doctors. He was alone in the waiting area and attempting to get up from the small couch that he filled, but I motioned him to stay put as I crossed the space between us.

"Wow," I said as I came up to him. "How did you get here so quickly?"

"Broke a bunch of laws," he replied shortly. His big jowly face was drawn and pale. Johnny Crew was his lifelong partner and best friend.

"Any word from the doctors yet?"

"Stroke. He had a damned stroke. They don't know yet if it's bad. At least they didn't tell me."

It occurred to me that that was surely the first time I'd ever heard Hap use the word "damn." Unlike Johnny, who can't ask how you are without at least one "fuck" in the sentence, Hap never used curse words. Until now.

"Let's hope it's not bad," I said as I settled into a rickety visitor's chair next to the couch. "At least he's still alive."

The big man waved a meaty hand in the general direction of the double doors that no doubt led to the operating rooms. "Last I heard."

"Gerry on her way?"

"Yeah. I called her soon as you called me and nobody had let her know yet. I offered to go pick her up but she thought somebody should be with Johnny as soon as possible. She was gonna get a cab."

So we waited. Geraldine arrived, breathless and teary, her shoulder-length gray hair in serious disarray. Hap got to his feet and reached down to wrap his arms around her as he once more ran through the little we knew. Then we sat down and waited some more—probably no more than twenty minutes but it seemed like hours.

At last a young doctor came out to tell us that Johnny had had a very mild stroke but was already recovering. They had to do some further tests, but believed he would be fine with a little rest and proper medication. Meanwhile they would let Geraldine go visit with him.

Since they were planning to keep him at least overnight, Hap and I had no reason to wait at the hospital any longer.

He headed home, assuring me that he'd renew the Montgomery surveillance later this morning. I headed home to Stella and Maxine.

CHAPTER THIRTY-NINE

The cats both had a great deal to say to me before I was even through the door, very grumpy indeed concerning their empty food bowls.

It was quarter to eleven by the time I'd filled their bowls and left them munching away in the kitchen.

As I prepared for bed my head was swimming with worries about Samantha Quiller, the safety of Patty Samuels, and the health of my friend Johnny. Meanwhile, Stella and Maxine tumbled around the bedroom trying to cheer me up—or beat each other up, I couldn't be sure which.

I must have finally gotten to sleep at some point because the ringing of the landline phone woke me up.

My bedside clock read 6:28 a.m. and the caller ID on the phone showed an unfamiliar number. Crap. Was it a wrong number, bad news or an insanely early-bird telemarketer? I could only hope for numbers one or three as I reached over and picked up the receiver.

But of course....

"Let's hear it for the big bad detective protecting the little lady and her kid." My mysterious female caller again, sounding both sinister and smug this time.

That bounced me upright in a hurry. "Who are you and what do you want?"

"I got what I want," she said. "I got the kid. You can have the bitch back, if you want her."

"Where...." That was all I managed to get out before she cut the connection.

What the hell? Think. Did she give me anything? The number on the caller ID. That was my only hope. Could she really be that dumb—or me that lucky? I jotted it down and dialed Mike Whitehall's number. He's often in this early.

But not today. The phone rang repeatedly, then went to voice-mail. No point in leaving a message. I dialed the Police Bureau switchboard and asked for Detective Sergeant Malone. Maybe she was on duty. I needed help from somewhere, right now. The cops had faster access to such information than Eleanor, though I'd try her next if this failed.

"Malone." Thank goodness.

"This is Clint McCall. I need you to find the address for a phone number I have here."

"Good morning to you too and what the hell gave you the impression I was your assistant PI?"

"Please. Not to sound like bad TV, but it's a matter of life and death. Really."

"Hmmm. That makes it a police matter, then."

Oops. I didn't want the cops, especially led by someone I neither knew nor trusted, barging into whatever scene it was ahead of me.

"It *might* be a police matter, eventually," I said as carefully as I could. "Right now it's something I need to check out. You've got my word I'll call you back right away if it turns out to be anything."

"So I do your work for you and then you call me again if you think I'm needed for some further chore, is that it?"

This was not going well. I began to calculate how long it would take Eleanor after I rousted her out of bed—if she was even in her own bed. One more try: "Trust me on this. Please."

I must have sounded desperate enough for her to take pity. "Give me the damned number."

She came back with an address on Washington only about ten blocks from my house. An apartment number in a multi-unit building.

"Thanks," I said. "Believe me, I'll call you if there's anything there."

"You do that," she snapped and hung up on me.

I threw on some clothes, clipped the Smith and Wesson to my belt, and hurried out to my car. What were the odds that the call would just happen to come from a location so close to mine? Everything about it shouted set-up. But what kind of set-up? A trap or a taunt?

Since I had chosen not to ask for backup, I guess I was betting on the latter.

The weather was cold but clear and the traffic was light. I made the ten blocks in six minutes flat, adrenaline flow increasing with every block. Three-story nondescript apartment building. There was a buzzer by the front door, but security had already been compromised; the door opened easily when I tried it.

The apartment number was on this floor, probably about halfway back. I pulled my gun and stepped into the well-lit and empty hallway that seemed to be filled with danger and foreboding. I proceeded slowly.

I stopped in front of the apartment door and looked once more to my right, to my left. No one in sight. No sound beyond my own breathing. Somehow the utter emptiness of the corridor added weight to the burden of gloom that I couldn't seem to shake.

I tried the knob. Unlocked. Not good. Gun at the ready, I cautiously pushed the door open and stepped just inside. A rush of warm air and stench assailed my nostrils.

Death had gotten here ahead of me.

CHAPTER FORTY

Shit, piss, and a faint whiff of putrescence. The stark combination of odors was unmistakable. Somewhere within this overheated, dimly lit apartment something was dead. I could only hope it wasn't human.

I hoped with all my heart it wasn't who I feared it might be.

I drew my gun and took a step further inside, pushing the door flat against the wall to my right to make certain no one was concealed behind it. The *thunk* of the knob hitting the wall fell heavily into a silence broken only by a low hum from the direction of the open kitchen doorway across the room. Sounded like a refrigerator trying to stay cool.

And no wonder it was having to work hard; the air felt like someone had turned the thermostat as high as it would go. Morning sunlight glowed faintly through drawn shades in the modest living room. The furniture seemed well-cared-for but a little shabby: several plush chairs with side tables and small frilly lamps, along with a big overstuffed sofa angled across the left rear corner, a skinny floor lamp standing behind it. A diminutive dining table was to the right of the sofa with four plain wooden chairs tucked into it. A couple of five-shelf bookcases contained no books but rather stacks of CDs or DVDs along with a variety of knickknacks. The walls were decorated with what looked like generic motel art. Besides the open kitchen doorway, I could see one other interior door and it was closed. Probably a bedroom.

No dead animals or people in this room.

I cautiously crossed the carpet toward the kitchen.

The entire room was visible from the doorway. I could see the normal appliances, none too modern. Cabinets. The counter was bare as was the small, centered table. The smell was stronger here, but nothing suspicious otherwise.

I stepped a few paces to my right, opened the bedroom door, and looked inside.

She was on the bed—and it appeared she'd probably been there for a number of hours. An almost overwhelming sense of despair seized my chest and shortened my breath.

There appeared to be no point in checking her pulse, but I was about to step to the side of the bed to do it anyway. Suddenly I heard a slight noise behind me in the living room, a whisper of motion. The hairs on the back of my neck stood at attention and a chill darted down my spine.

Crap. There'd been no one in the corridor, no one visible in the living room. I'd thought that space next to the floor lamp behind the big couch was too small for someone to have been crouched back there. Maybe I was wrong. I'd missed something and I was an idiot.

My body was tensing to turn when I heard a familiar voice, not more than four feet from my back.

"Goodbye, Clint."

I'd just lost my bet that it wasn't a trap.

In a situation like this, you have to assume that the person behind you is armed and about to pull the trigger—and that's certainly what her voice sounded like. In other words, you've got no damned choice but to make a move regardless of how unlikely you are to succeed.

I executed what must have been the fastest straight back kick of my life, reaching for my own gun at the same time, at which point the world exploded. My upper body twisted to the right and down as I kicked with my left leg, so the bullet hit me in either the upper left arm or the shoulder. I couldn't tell which, just that there was a sudden and sharp pain.

The move also brought my head around so I was looking down my outstretched right leg at a female, long black ponytail and tall thin build, staggering back toward the middle of the living room, the gun in her hand currently waving toward the ceiling as she tried to regain her balance.

I hadn't felt my foot make solid contact, what with being shot and all, but obviously it had. It is good to be lucky.

Her gun was already coming down again as I registered all this, so I let my right, supporting, leg buckle—which it wanted to do anyway—and I went to the floor as I snapped off a couple of shots in her direction. I heard at least one shot in return, at which point I landed on my wounded left side and everything went absolutely white for a moment.

I must have continued to convulsively pull the trigger because when my head cleared a few seconds later my gun was empty and my assailant was gone. Apparently she'd dived out the door into the corridor in the face of my wild fusillade.

I could see that I was lying on my left side but I wasn't sure I could feel the floor underneath me. This is one of the more un-pleasant uncertainties, believe me. Had I been shot again? Was I partially paralyzed? Dying?

I'm not sure how long I lay there considering the delightful possibilities, but it was probably a much shorter time than it seemed. Then, when I saw a shadow out in the corridor, I discovered I could move after all.

Not that I could exactly jump to my feet and assume a firing stance yet. I could reach back to the bedroom doorframe and pull myself in that direction, but I'd only managed a couple of feet when I saw a handgun slowly come into view from the corridor.

CHAPTER FORTY-ONE

I'd barely had time to jerk myself backward another six inches and wonder if my assailant had returned to finish the job when Detective Sergeant Malone took a giant step into the doorway. She stood for a moment in the classic stance, the one I couldn't manage right now, with gun extended in both hands, surveying the room.

Her eyes came to rest on me and the gun lowered slightly. "Anyone in the other rooms?"

"No one alive," I gasped out.

She took a step back, glanced down the corridor both ways, and then holstered her weapon. She told someone out of sight, probably more than one person, that she was a police officer, the situation was under control, and they should return to their apartments. Then she called for backup, paramedics and the medical examiner as she crossed the room toward me. I expected her to kneel down and check me out but instead she stepped past me to first look in the kitchen, then the bedroom, and finally the bathroom.

"Can't take my word for it?" I croaked. Even a little lightheaded and in pain, I wasn't going to concede that I hadn't looked in that bathroom.

"Never hurts to check," she said as she finally crouched beside me. She scrutinized my left shoulder. "Anything besides this?"

"I don't know for sure. For a while it felt like I'd been shot everywhere."

She did a quick but more thorough exam. "I think that's it," she said briskly. "Barely a scratch." She stood up. "You'll live."

"Gee. Glad to hear it."

"What happened here?"

"What are *you* doing here?"

"I asked first."

"That's my client in the bedroom. Samantha Quiller. I think whoever killed her has her two-year-old daughter, Kinsey."

That got the detective sergeant's attention. Her eyes widened. "We've got a kid snatched?"

"I think so," I said and couldn't help adding a little groan. Unfortunately the numbness was beginning to pass. Scratch or not, the sucker was hurting.

Malone relayed the info about a possible kidnapping to dispatch, then gave me a gimlet eye. "So you came looking for your client and got ambushed."

"Yes, I missed her somewhere in here and she got behind me." I hated to admit it.

"She? Ambushed by a woman, then."

I ignored the fact that she sounded slightly smug about that. Maybe it was my imagination, anyway. "Did you see any blood in the doorway?" I inquired.

She glanced back in that direction. "Nope. Were you hoping you'd hit her?"

"Damned right."

At that moment there was a major commotion in the hallway as backup and EMTs arrived. "We'll talk more soon," Malone said as she stepped back to make room. She'd never answered my question about what she was doing here.

CHAPTER FORTY-TWO

The next couple of hours were a drug-supported blur of medical field procedures, ambulance transportation, and hospital emergency room treatment. The bullet, it turned out, had been a through-and-through of my upper left arm, practically a graze—but not exactly a scratch—with no other wounds besides extensive bruising where I'd hit the floor. My head was just clearing again and my arm beginning to ache when a nurse finally told me I was free to go.

Veronica and Colleen were in the waiting room. As always, they made quite a contrast--Veronica's soft flowing curves against my daughter's prickly angles.

Colleen practically leapt across the room, obviously intending to grab me in a big hug, and then pulled up short as she focused on the injured arm. She offered the arm a series of light, jittery touches. "Dad, are you all right? Mike said you were shot!"

I hugged her close with my right arm. "It's not bad, just a flesh wound." I raised the other arm carefully to demonstrate that it was movable. It really didn't hurt much yet, but the drugs were only beginning to wear off.

Veronica joined us and touched me lightly on my good arm. "I thought she shouldn't be here by herself. You know, in case.... You're really okay?"

"It's fine, really. I'll be a hundred percent in no time. Thanks for being here for Colleen."

And about that time, Mike Whitehall walked in.

"You feeling any better?" he asked me as he came up to us.

"It's nothing. A minor flesh wound." Which was already starting to hurt like a son of a bitch. But why complain. "The scene wrapped up?"

"Just about. You need to come down to the Center for a formal statement, of course." Police headquarters was located in the Justice Center downtown.

I wondered about the way he'd phrased that. "You are the lead on the shooting, aren't you?"

He shook his head, looking a little sour. "Not this time. I was on another call when it came in. Danny Haller's got it."

I knew Detective Haller vaguely: a middle-aged rotund and balding cop plodding toward retirement, by all accounts. I could have wished for better. "But you're going to track it, too, right?"

"Best I can, sure."

"For instance, do they know yet when and how Mrs. Quiller died?"

Colleen interrupted at that point. "I don't think Veronica and I need to hear those details right now. Dad, you have to take better care of yourself. Really."

"I will. You guys take care, too." I watched them walk away, then turned back to Mike.

"The ME's preliminary is a single shot to the heart," he said, "large caliber weapon. Probably no more than six hours."

"There in the apartment?"

"Looks like."

"Nobody heard anything?"

"Apparently not. Must have used a silencer. A very good one."

"Any word on her daughter?" I asked.

"Not yet. Malone is on that."

"Malone. I hadn't met her before you tagged her about Quiller and the kid. Why did you?"

"She's a tough, smart cop. Doesn't let it go. She seemed like the right fit. No surprise you haven't met her before. Your missing person cases don't usually overlap with ours and she likes to work alone."

"No partner?"

"Several, actually, but none right now."

"Okay. What's her first name?" That last came out on pure impulse. I had no idea why I gave a damn.

"Devon. Devon Malone."

Hmmm. Nice name. And now that I was on top of my impulses, I was *not* going to ask if she was single. Plus, Mike was looking at me a little funny. Time to change the subject.

"She's working with Haller, then?"

He looked, if anything, even less pleased. "Not really, but she's on the missing kid. That's her bailiwick."

Just so she was still involved; I was glad of that, though I wasn't sure why. "The shooter turned up the heat to accelerate decomp," I said, thinking back to the sweltering, odiferous rooms. "She wanted me to smell it before she took me out."

That got my friend's attention. "She? Don't tell me you know who did it."

"I don't have a name, not even a description, but I was at that apartment because I got a call from an unknown female who said she had the kid. Malone got me the address from the Caller ID— which I guess is why *she* was at the apartment."

"Malone got it for you?"

"Yeah. You were out in the field that time, too."

"Well, shit." We started walking again. "You've got no idea who this female caller is?"

"Not a clue, although it wasn't the first time I'd heard from her." I filled Mike in on the previous call and its apparent connection to the original mystery of Quiller's dead husband supposedly being sighted.

"Do we know whose apartment it was?" I asked as Mike and I headed for his car.

"According to the landlord, it was rented two weeks ago by a woman named Carol Gordon. Nobody by that name—or any other name—matches the personal info provided. Driver's license and

Social Security number both fake, ditto previous address and so on. We don't have much of a description, either: white, late twenties or early thirties, maybe five ten, long dark hair. He only saw her once and she was wearing a parka with hood plus sunglasses." He glanced at me across the roof of his car. "Could be your mystery woman."

"And the shooter. For all the good that does us," I muttered as I got in.

Samantha Quiller hired me because she thought she'd seen her late husband. Now she was murdered and her two-year-old daughter was missing. Coincidence? Unrelated? Not a chance in hell.

So now all I had to do was find a dead man who walks around downtown Portland and a mystery woman who kidnaps two-year-olds.

Well, that and keep my ex-wife and her friend Patty safe. Oh, and fulfill my obligation to Ray Witkowsky who was my one and only paying client at the moment.

All of which I'd remembered by the time I finished giving my statement at the Justice Center—not least because I'd checked my voicemail during a bathroom break to discover messages waiting from Colleen, Sarah, and Hap Harbaugh. I had yet to listen to any of them, fearing what I might hear.

No pressure.

CHAPTER FORTY-THREE

It was early afternoon when I got free. Giving a statement to Detective Danny Haller had not been fun. He seemed skeptical about the idea that I'd been lured to the apartment. He was unhappy when I mentioned that I hoped he would keep Whitehall in the loop—and downright contemptuous when I mentioned Devon Malone. He referred to her as "the missing persons chick."

In other words, I would not be cooperating with the useless asshole any more than I absolutely had to.

Standing in a light sprinkle on the street outside police headquarters, my shoulder now feeling sore and itchy more than really painful, I thought again about those waiting voicemails and decided I'd listen to Hap first. His was the only message with the remotest possibility of being good news, and I could certainly have used some right about now. On the other hand, with my current streak of luck it would probably turn out that Marvin Montgomery had just died of an acute bad back.

Hap's message was actually promising though not very informative: "Call me. I got your guy."

The voicemail was time-stamped forty-five minutes ago. I pressed call-back as I headed down the sidewalk toward my car. Hap picked up on the first ring.

"Clint?"

"Yeah. What have you got?"

"I got pictures. I'm gettin' more pictures right now."

That sounded good, indeed. "Where are you? What's Montgomery doing?"

"I'm down the street from his apartment building. He's changing a couple of tires. I got him jacking up the car, crouched down removing lug nuts, carryin' heavy tires, and not lookin' like he's got any back problems at all. Pretty spry for a disabled guy, if you ask me. Lots more spry than me, anyway."

Meanwhile I'd reached my own car and decided I'd better drive over to Montgomery's place and confirm all this. There was no way I wanted to be spending time on Marvin Montgomery right now, but maybe I wouldn't have to spend much more.

"You say he's fixing a flat tire?" I asked as I got in and started up the Outback. "On the street in front of his place?"

"*Two* flat tires, actually."

"How'd he get two flat tires?" I had a suspicion what the answer would be.

"He might have had a little help. I was gettin' tired of sitting so much, so I took a little walk around his car when I first got here and now he's got two flat tires. Which he is fixing. And I have pictures."

I had to laugh. Not entirely professional, for sure, but apparently it worked and it did explain why Montgomery would still be at it after nearly an hour. And if Hap had good photos, that would wrap it up. I pressed harder on the accelerator.

It took just a few minutes to reach Montgomery's apartment building at Broadway and Jackson. He was loading two flat tires into a car trunk as I drove by.

I spotted Hap's car just down the block. His head and a camera were poking out the driver's side window. Obviously Marvin Montgomery was not one of the more observant people around. I pulled over to the curb, hopped out of my car and into the passenger side of Hap's.

He looked over at me with a grin, clicked off one more shot, and passed me the camera. "Here you go, Clint."

I hit the camera's review button and tried to focus on the tiny images. I could see that Hap had done a good job. There were several shots of Montgomery carrying two full-size spares to the sidewalk. He was obviously having no trouble with their weight or bulk.

"This is great, Hap. Can I borrow the camera or do you want to email the pics to me?"

"I don't like to mess with that techie stuff. Take the camera. I don't need it for anything else right now."

"You'll have it back by tomorrow sometime."

I started to open the passenger side door when Hap reached over and stayed my exit with one of his massive hands on my arm. "Johnny called you yet?" he asked.

That surprised me. "Johnny? No. Is he even up to calling anybody?"

"He says he's feeling fine. In fact, he's insisting that he just fell asleep."

"Bullshit. That's not what the hospital said."

"Well, that's what Johnny wants to believe. He really does seem to be pretty well recovered—and he was going to call you to apologize."

"For what?"

"Going to sleep."

"Oh, for God's sake. Well, I don't look forward to that call, but I guess I'll forgive him if that's what he wants."

"You're a good guy, Clint."

"Aren't we all."

I finally extricated myself from the car and stood on the sidewalk. It was raining a little harder now and I savored the rain bathing my face. At least I had one worry off my mind.

Marvin Montgomery, meanwhile, slouched wet and forlorn in front of his apartment building, apparently taking a break after all his well-documented work. He never did notice me standing there staring at him.

CHAPTER FORTY-FOUR

It was right at two o'clock when I got to the office. I checked my voicemail and deleted five media inquiries about my involvement in the possible kidnapping of a baby; I knew Alison Roberts wouldn't give up, but she was gone for the moment. It took exactly an hour to wrap up the Montgomery case: photos printed out, final report written, and copies made. I delivered the report, photos, and my bill to Ray Witkowsky's office across the hall. *Something* was finally done.

Back in my own office again, I poured a third cup of coffee and allowed myself to contemplate the death of Samantha Quiller and the fate of her baby daughter. Whether or not I bore any blame for what had happened, I certainly had some responsibility for what was going to happen: namely, the recovery of the kid and the discovery of her mother's killer.

My mysterious caller had said she was watching me. Was she still, now that she had Kinsey Quiller? Probably not. She'd sounded pretty self-satisfied in her last call. Reuben had heard there was a female, almost certainly that same caller, out to kill me. Would she still be trying? Maybe, if I kept stirring the pot, if I could keep her uneasy. One could only hope so. Currently another attempt on my life was my best bet at finding the bitch.

I'd been watching the traffic on Stark as I developed this latest thrilling plan. My eyes wandered from the street level up to the windows in the building across the street. Lots of good locations for a shooter. I pulled the shade on my window and decided it was time to move along.

If I actually wanted somebody to attempt an attack then I should be out and about as much as possible (assuming they didn't have access to the building across the street). First, I'd go see how Sarah and Patty were doing at the hotel.

Their room was on the twelfth floor of the downtown Embassy Suites, just a couple of blocks over from my office on Second. I stopped at the bottom of my building's stairs, contemplating my options. The rain had stopped and there was even a little sun peering through the clouds. I could easily walk over to the hotel. On the other hand, it would be difficult to pursue a drive-by attacker on foot (assuming she missed). Plus there was the consideration that my left side hurt enough just standing here, much less trying to run. I headed across Third Avenue to get my car.

I parked less than four minutes later in one of the visitor spots at the hotel. Better safe than sorry. I hadn't seen anyone following me, but then again there hadn't been much chance to see anyone.

I took the elevator from the parking garage to the twelfth floor, strode down the hall to their room, and rapped on the door. There was a fairly long pause, during which I supposed that someone was checking me out through the peephole.

The chain rattled and Patty Samuels opened the door. "Mr. McCall," she said. She looked oddly uncomfortable and I got a prickly feeling on the back of my neck.

"Someone besides Sarah in there with you?" I asked very quietly.

"Yes."

I started to reach for my gun.

"Your daughter."

I forgot the gun and thought about fleeing. Then about wringing Colleen's neck. Then about kicking myself. All within about a second-and-a-half. "Oh," I said. "Well."

"Yes indeed." She stepped aside so I could enter. I didn't like the combination of sympathy and anticipation on her face, though I could certainly understand it. It occurred to me as I stepped inside that I still hadn't listened to the voicemails from Sarah and Colleen; I probably should have. I also should have cautioned Sarah not to contact our daughter yet. And maybe I should have gone ahead and told Colleen when I had the chance....

You accumulate that many shoulds in such a short time and there's bound to be trouble.

Which was waiting for me right inside.

CHAPTER FORTY-FIVE

It was a two-room suite plus bath, the living area nicely furnished with a comfortable couch and chairs, table, small desk, big TV. My ex-wife sat on the couch looking at me with a barely suppressed grin. My daughter sat on the forward three inches of one of the chairs looking at me with totally unsuppressed rage.

"You shouldn't be here," I said to Colleen. My brain had started to work again and I was beginning to get more than a little pissed myself.

"I shouldn't.... What the...? Goddamn it!" she sputtered as her face got even more red. Sarah's expression soured meanwhile and it appeared she was about to jump into the conversation.

I held up both palms out. "Wait!"

They identically bit their lips and glared.

"I assume you called her," I said to Sarah.

"Of course I called her! You said she was terribly worried...."

"And it's my fault," I interrupted, "for not explaining why you shouldn't do that."

"Why in the hell shouldn't I?"

"Brad Winters knows Colleen is your daughter. If he has followed you to Portland, who's he going to follow now that he's here?"

Sarah sat back, eyes wide. "Well, I...."

"Nobody's following me," Colleen broke in.

I focused on her. "And you know that how?"

"Well, I...."

So then they were both sitting there, wide-eyed and stumped but still clearly pissed.

Patty Samuels spoke up from the corner of the room where she'd established herself as far from the conflict as possible. "Colleen said you'd been shot."

I carefully shrugged my good shoulder. "That's true. No permanent damage."

After a fairly long pause Sarah offered, "Glad to hear it." She didn't specify whether she was referring to the lack of permanent damage or my getting shot in the first place.

One more survey of the three faces—Colleen's angry, Patty's uneasy, and Sarah's grim—convinced me that I might as well move on.

"What does Brad Winters look like?" I asked Sarah.

"Why?"

"I want to check around the lobby and in front of the hotel on my way out to see if I spot him."

"Oh. Well, he's about six feet tall, in good shape for a guy in his mid-forties I guess, dark hair, moustache. Looks a little like Clark Gable, actually."

"Clark Gable?"

She squirmed a little on the couch. "Yes."

"Okay. Sounds like he'd be pretty easy to spot." I looked at Colleen. "I'd like you to stay here at least until I've confirmed that Winters isn't standing around in plain sight."

"All right," she muttered.

"You have your cell phone?"

"Yes."

"I'll call you as soon as I've cleared the hotel. Keep an eye out for someone on your tail—and I'd appreciate it if you steer clear of your mother and Patty for the next day or so. I'm sorry I didn't tell you I'd found her. I was afraid it would endanger both of you." *As it in fact has*, I didn't add.

"All right," she muttered again. Which was apparently about as much forgiveness as I was going to get right now.

Instead of taking the elevator back down to the parking garage, I got out at the lobby level and stood in front of the closed doors scanning the area. Somewhat to my surprise I spotted Frank

147

Samuels and a Clark-Gable-looking companion almost immediately. They were standing beside a large fake potted plant about twenty feet to my left, talking intently to one another. They hadn't seen me yet.

They should have been keeping an eye on the elevator doors, but they were amateurs after all.

I sauntered in that direction.

I made it to within eight feet of them before I caught Frank Samuels' eye. "You!" he said, demonstrating a certain lack of originality.

The man I assumed was Brad Winters swung in my direction. "Who?"

"You guys should consider taking that act on the road," I said as I stepped a few feet closer. "You rhyme and everything."

"What the fuck are you doing here?" rasped Samuels.

"That's not the question," I said. "The question is, how fast can you two leave?"

"Who is this asshole?" Winters—I was still assuming—asked his friend as they went shoulder to shoulder opposing me. And, speaking of shoulders, I was beginning to wonder if provoking a fight was my best option at this moment. Two against one isn't that bad if the one is well-trained, but not so great if he's also one-handed.

What the hell. I took a step back and swept my jacket just far enough aside to reveal the Smith and Wesson. "I am the guy with a gun who wants you to leave. Now."

They looked at the gun. They looked at each other, then back at me. Their expressions rapidly changed from hostile to dubious, but Samuels gave it one more try. "You ain't got no right."

"Maybe not, but what I do have is a gun and the willingness to use it. You are both pathetic fucks who like to hit women and, believe me, I'd be more than happy to put you down. If you aren't gone in fifteen seconds, that's exactly what I'm going to do."

They looked at each other again. "Fucker's crazy," muttered Samuels. "We better go." He glared at me. "For now."

"Come see me any time," I said. "But not here. Tick tock."

They bought my bluff and headed for the front door. I watched them exit, then went to the front desk to ask to talk to hotel security. He or she was not going to be happy to hear that there were a couple of endangered persons upstairs, but at this point I needed all the help I could get.

CHAPTER FORTY-SIX

By the time I left the hotel my shoulder was throbbing and my head wasn't far behind. I needed more drugs and some sleep. Time to go home.

It was just past five when I pulled into my driveway. Stella and Maxine greeted me at the door, almost as if they knew I'd been in trouble, but then made straight for the kitchen to assure me that they expected dinner anyway.

I carefully shed my jacket and holster, dumped some dry food in the cat bowls, poured a can of pea soup (with ham bits) into a pot and put it on the stove, took a couple more pain pills, then slumped onto the couch to await hot soup and pain relief.

It was remarkable, considering how many bullets had been thrown in my direction over the years, that I'd never been shot before. Equally remarkable was how damned much it hurt. I've sustained all the normal martial arts injuries, multiple times, and none of them had achieved this level of discomfort. Nor had any of them required bandages that prevented me from scratching a terrible itch. All in all, it was enough to suggest that I should avoid getting shot in the future.

At least I could rest easy about the immediate safety of Patty Samuels and Sarah. The head of hotel security, a beefy retired cop named Carl Sandusky, had assured me he'd bring in one of his off-duty guys solely to keep an eye on the room. He'd also assured me that hotel management wasn't going to endure the added expense longer than check-out time tomorrow, so I still needed a quick resolution to the problem. If I could think of one.

I'd remembered to call Colleen, as promised, while I was driving home. Hopefully she was on the way back to her own apartment by now.

Good thing I'd set a timer on that soup because I'd almost dozed off by the time it dinged. I sat at the kitchen table and spooned it up without much appetite. The fact that I'd never stirred the soup didn't seem to have done it any harm. The ham made it a little clumpy, but so what.

Sleepy or not, shot or not, it was too damned early to go to bed. I decided to settle back down on the couch and pretend to stay awake while I attempted to digest my unstirred dinner. Stella and Maxine joined me, curling up one on each side. It should have been a cozy, peaceful scene but it wasn't.

I had lost a client—not as in the client was dissatisfied and fired me, but as in the client was dead. I could picture Samantha Quiller clearly as I'd first seen her, standing in my office doorway wearing a scarf and wool coat, looking over the room as if to decide whether to venture further inside. Crap. Maybe she shouldn't have.

She'd asked for my help because she thought she'd seen her dead husband downtown. Now she'd joined her dead husband—if he really was dead—and her two-year-old Kinsey was missing. I thought I knew the voice of the woman who'd killed her and kidnapped her child; I'd had a glimpse of my attacker's appearance, who was surely the same woman. But I had no idea who the woman was, why she'd taken the kid, where they were, or any other damn thing. I still didn't know who, if anyone, Mrs. Quiller had seen downtown and that was my job in the first place. I didn't know if the reappearing husband and the disappearing child were even related. I'd have been willing to bet they *were*, however, taking the dim view of coincidence that I do.

The phone's ring jolted me wider awake and reminded me that the pain pills hadn't reached my head yet. Plus, now I had a slightly upset stomach. Fortunately I could reach the phone from the couch.

"This is Clint."

"Clint, this is Johnny and I'm a smelly piece of shit."

That certainly gave me pause. "Oh," I said finally, "is that, like, some kind of AA thing?"

"AA? What the fuck?"

"You know. Hi, I'm Clint and I'm an alcoholic?"

"Fuck me. I let a woman get killed and lose her kid and you're making a joke?"

So much for that little sally. "I'm trying to convey that you shouldn't feel guilty, Johnny. You didn't *let* anything happen. You had a damned stroke."

"I fucking did not. I dozed off, goddamn it, and I'm sorry about that."

Okay. Hap was right. Johnny was going to insist on the going to sleep bit. "So...are you wide awake now? Do you feel better?"

"I feel fine, except guilty as shit. I don't want to ever hear anything about a fucking stroke again and I want to help find the kid."

"You should probably rest up a little more. I don't have any ideas about what to do to find the kid, anyway."

"Maybe you and me and Hap...."

I interrupted him. "Could I speak to Gerry?"

"What? Why?"

"I just need to ask her something. Is she there?" I would have been very surprised if the answer had been no.

"Sure. Okay. But then we need to talk some more."

I heard a couple of phone fumbles and then Gerry's voice. "Clint? You're not buying any of this man's crap, are you?"

I laughed. "Just wanted to make sure that you weren't."

"Don't you worry. My dumbass husband is staying right here."

I could hear Johnny sputtering in the background. "Thanks, Gerry."

"Fell asleep, my white Irish ass," she said, and hung up. I had a hunch that last was not directed at me.

I finally dropped off to sleep on the couch, surrounded by cats, steeped in regret, and filled with uncertainty.

CHAPTER FORTY-SEVEN

Sometime around two in the morning I awoke just enough to stagger off to the bathroom and then my bed. Six hours after that I woke up again, my shoulder hurting a little less and my head clear.

Along with my head, one other thing had become clear during the night. No matter how many regrets I had about Samantha Quiller or how much urgency I felt about finding her daughter, the first item on my agenda had to be ensuring the safety of my ex-wife, her friend Patty, and not least my own daughter.

Law enforcement was not going to be of any help on that one, but there were other kinds of enforcement that might do the trick. Since it was only a little after eight, I would have to wait at least three hours before talking to Reuben. He wasn't going to be happy to hear from me again so soon, even if I gave him some time to sleep in.

I have a regular routine in the morning. I get up, go to the bathroom, and then do zazen—which is the Japanese word for sitting meditation. I have a special cushion, called a zafu, on the floor in a corner of my bedroom and I sit there cross-legged, meditating for twenty or thirty minutes. Maxine always sits with me, snugged up against my left side, a white noise machine set on "purr." I don't know why. Maybe she converted to Buddhism at some point when I wasn't looking.

Normally zazen means clearing my mind as best I can, letting the thoughts come and go without "attaching" to any of them. This morning, that didn't work. This morning I spent the time convincing myself that it really was a good idea to go back to Reuben Keys so soon. Or at least might be, depending on his answer to a question and who he was willing to work with.

Then I fed the cats, took a shower, fed myself, and checked in with Sarah at the hotel to make sure she and Patty had had a quiet night. They had. I warned them that they were going to have to check out today but that I was working on some ideas toward a resolution of their problem.

It being Sunday morning, I called Mike Whitehall at home; there was nothing new on the Quiller homicide. I left Devon Malone a voicemail at the Justice Center, asking if anything new had come up on the Quiller kidnapping. Probably not, and probably I wouldn't even get confirmation of that until tomorrow.

I got to Reuben's apartment building a little past eleven. It was a gloomy, damp February-in-Portland day and I swear there was actual fog swirling lightly around the second floor balcony in front of his door. I pounded on said door, certain that it was not going to be easy to rouse him.

No kidding. It took several minutes and when he finally jerked the door open he was wearing just boxers and a sleeveless tee—and carrying his Magnum, which was pointed straight at my nose.

"I been in bed less than four hours and you gonna be in the ground a lot longer than that if you don't have a fuckin' good reason to be here right now."

I reached up and casually pushed the weapon aside. "Didn't your mother ever tell you not to point a loaded gun at another person?"

He lowered the gun to his side and shrugged. "Hell, my mother's the one who taught me to blow their fuckin' heads off. What *do* you want, McCall? You want to get on my ass some more about bein' late? How is the old man?"

"He's back home already and claiming he just fell asleep. I think he'll be fine. I hope so. And, no, I'm not here to get on your ass— but I do have a question."

"What?"

"Why were you late?"

155

"I told you, I had business."

"That's what you said in front of the detective. I want more of an answer."

He scowled and I thought he was going to refuse, which would have ended *our* business right there, but then his shoulders relaxed and he took a breath. "One of my girls got beat up, bad, and I had to deal with it."

"A customer?"

"Yeah, big ass old white boy refused to pay and then beat the shit out of her. I had to take her to emergency and then I had to find him."

"Did you?"

"Yeah, I did."

CHAPTER FORTY-EIGHT

And that was all I wanted to ask about that. After a moment, I plunged ahead. "I've got some ladies in danger who need our help. One of them is my daughter."

Reuben had never met Colleen. I try—not always successfully—to keep her at a distance from the less savory aspects of my profession and Reuben definitely qualified. He knew about her, though, from our occasional small talk.

He stepped back and gestured an invitation with the Magnum. "Why didn't you say so? Come on in. I'm always up for helping ladies in distress."

It appeared the maid had not stopped by since my last visit—only three days ago? Reuben's small living room and even tinier kitchen were still littered with every manner of detritus and the air reeked of stale French fries this time, again with an underlying fragrance of marijuana—the perfect combo to make you hungry and nauseated at the same time.

He motioned me toward a relatively clean spot on his couch and plopped onto the overstuffed chair, setting the Magnum on a rickety side table. "What's the story?"

I laid it out for him, along the way assuring him that Sarah was not the female who'd been trying to kill me.

"So," he finally summed up after I finished, "we got these two fake-macho fuck-wimps to scare off and that's all. Shouldn't be too hard."

"I don't want to accumulate any assault charges along the way," I said. "We need to do it strictly with manpower and intimidation. Think we could get your guy Amani to come with us?"

"Fuck," said Reuben.

Amani Drake was a relatively recent arrival that Reuben some-times used as his own muscle. Amani had been a pro football player for a little while, in the Canadian League, and was six-six or so, weighing at least three hundred pounds—not all of it fat by any means—with a belligerent attitude to top it off. Not one of the brighter criminals around but if you were looking to intimidate, Amani Drake was a good option.

"I don't like to use him for business that ain't my own," Reuben went on. "You and me can handle this, sounds like."

"I want to scare these guys, not fight with them," I responded. "For that purpose, you and Amani together will be better than just you. On the other hand, if they do fight I want to win in a hurry. All that's going to be easier if we have somebody Amani's size along; you know that. Give him a call. Of course I'll pay him the same as you."

"More for me. I'm your regular backup."

Oh well. I was not in a mood to argue Reuben's fee or status. "Okay," I said. "More for you. And all the credit. Call him."

He agreed. I was out the door and about to head down to my car when he made a noise like clearing his throat. I turned back to see him standing in his doorway looking almost awkward.

"Something else?" I asked.

"Tell the old detective guy I'm sorry I was late. I hope you find the kid all right."

I nodded. "I will, and we will. Let me know when you've con-firmed Amani. Then we'll set a time and place for our conference with Frank Samuels and Brad Winters."

As I descended the stairs to street level I was pleased, on the whole. Reuben and Amani are both extremely good at looking dan-gerous—and not bad at the being, either.

159

CHAPTER FORTY-NINE

Having nowhere better to go, I drove downtown to my office. The building was otherwise empty; the bookstore downstairs was closed on Sundays and ditto the other offices on the second floor. I stood at my window for a minute looking over the building across the street and decided not to pull the shade this time; all the offices over there would also be closed for the day and it was very unlikely that someone could get inside to take a potshot at me. The daylight was dreary enough without cutting it back even more.

I'd been sitting at my desk for about twenty minutes, going over notes on the Quiller case for what felt like the twentieth time, when the phone rang. I picked it up without even checking the caller ID, assuming it would be Reuben. I was surprised to hear Devon Malone's voice.

"McCall?"

"Detective Sergeant Malone. Working on a Sunday?"

"Yeah, with nothing to show for it so far. The feds tell me they have zip as well. How about you?"

"Nothing here. I actually have another case I have to take care of before I can be of much help on the Quiller kid. How about we meet up late this afternoon to compare notes?"

She snorted. "We're on the clock here; you know what usually happens within the first twenty-four hours of a child abduction."

"I don't think our abductor is a pedophile. I'm betting she wants Kinsey alive, though I couldn't tell you why yet."

"Well, I hope to hell you're right. The Home Run at four? That's right across from your office, isn't it?"

"It is—and that sounds fine to me. See you then."

She hung up without replying, which I took to be agreement. I also noted that she knew where my office was. Apparently she'd done a little asking around as well. A thought not to be pursued at the moment, especially since my phone was ringing again.

This time it *was* Reuben. He had Amani Drake on board, so I said they should meet me beside the main garage entrance of the Embassy Suites at quarter to one, one o'clock being the last possible check-out time. Then I called Sarah and Patty to tell them to check out at one. All this was based on my estimate that Brad Winters and Frank Samuels were 1) dumb enough to ignore my warning about staying away, 2) smart enough to figure the women might leave after discovering their location was known, and 3) dumb enough to be watching for them out in the open.

It was almost quarter after twelve now, so I just had time to stop at the Home Run for a quick burger and soft drink before walking over to meet Reuben and Amani at the Embassy Suites.

Besides instructing Sarah and Patty to check out at one, I'd specified that they should exit the lobby into the parking garage rather than out the front entrance. I did take a moment to glance into the lobby before going on around to the garage entrance and was relieved to catch a glimpse of Frank Samuels sitting off in a corner, his attention focused on the bank of elevators. Where there was Frank there would be Brad. I was in business.

It struck me when I saw Reuben and Amani lounging just inside the garage entrance that we were lucky it was early Sunday afternoon. If there had been many hotel guests in or out over the last few minutes, surely one of them would have reported these two to hotel security.

Reuben had chosen pastel blue pants, shirt and jacket for our adventure, his scarred black face only more menacing in contrast. Drake loomed beside him in a more traditional outfit of black pants and tee shirt, both of which appeared to actually fit. I wondered where the man got his clothes; maybe there was an online Gargantuan and Tall Store.

I greeted them, reassured myself that neither one had a weapon, and cautioned them both—Reuben for the second time—that I was not looking for anyone to add an assault charge to his sheet. We were talking strictly about intimidation here. Amani frowned deeply at this last announcement and I realized my error: using a word with more than two syllables. "We want to scare the shit out of them," I clarified for his benefit. After a few seconds of his wheels turning as fast as they could, Amani grinned in comprehension and we were ready to go.

I knew Sarah and Patty would be coming down in the elevator and I was certain Brad and Frank would be happy to see that, figuring that the parking garage was the perfect place to ambush "the girls" and teach them a lesson. The elevator was located about halfway back in the garage on our right. I stationed Reuben and Amani in the shadows on either side of the elevator doors and took up a position in front of them myself.

At seven minutes after one the doors opened to disgorge the two women.

"Where are you parked?" I asked as they approached.

Patty looked around for a second and then gestured off to her right. "Down there near the end."

"Good. Go get in the car and wait for me."

Sarah frowned. "Are you going to take them on by yourself?"

"Not by myself." I pointed back toward the elevator.

They turned and gaped at my two helpers.

"Oh," Sarah said.

"Jesus," Patty said.

They scurried off to my left, toward Patty's car.

Meanwhile the elevator had gone back up to the lobby and was on its way down again. Before I could set my attention on the doors I noticed that there was one other person in the garage—or, rather, standing very still just inside the street entrance about thirty feet to my right, staring in my direction. Average-looking guy, light-colored hair, sharp features.... I frowned, trying to pull my attention back to the imminent confrontation. The man looked familiar. Where had I seen him before? Not with Samuels or Winters....

The elevator pinged and the doors started to open. I could see that the two men I'd expected were inside but nevertheless my gaze jerked away, toward the garage entrance, and for a moment my whole body went cold.

I suddenly knew where I'd seen the guy before. In a photo, in my office, the photo that Samantha Quiller had brought along when she first stopped by.

George Quiller was standing there staring at me.

CHAPTER FIFTY

I have never in my life had a harder time turning my attention back to muscle-bound cretins approaching with murder in their eyes. The urge for self-preservation provided enough impetus, but barely.

By the time I did get focused on Samuels and Winters they had paused about six feet away, quivering with outrage. Winters was carrying a leather-covered billy club and Samuels was wearing brass knuckles. Apparently they'd planned a good old-fashioned "lesson" for the ladies. (They also, apparently, watched a lot of '50s noir movies.) My guess was that the current pause would be a short one if I didn't draw a weapon or otherwise do something to distract them.

"This is the last time you're going to get in my way," Samuels said through gritted teeth. "Patty is my wife and I've got a right...." His foot was lifting to take that next step even as he spoke.

I held up an empty hand, palm out. "You and your dumbass buddy had better take a look to either side before you expound any further on your rights."

With perfect timing, Reuben and Amani moved up into their peripheral vision, one on each side.

Frank Samuels took in Reuben's pastel blue attire and his heavily scarred face with its wonderfully evil smile. "Fuck," he said.

Bradley Winters, meanwhile, had tilted his head all the way back in order to look up at Amani's menacing frown. "Oh shit," he said.

"You guys could use some vocabulary building but still that sums up your current situation pretty well," I said. "And here's the thing about those rights: they're wrong."

The two men had moved so close together that their shoulders might have been glued to one another. Samuels couldn't seem to take his eyes off Reuben. Winters was either more brave or more stupid. He pulled his gaze away from Amani and glared again at me. "What the fuck? You think just because you bring two nig...ack!"

I had no idea Amani could move so fast, but it explained what little success he'd had in pro football. Winters didn't even have a chance to finish the word before he found himself nose to extremely large and black nose, hanging from his jacket collar clutched in a gigantic fist, feet about eighteen inches off the ground.

"Little white fucks don't call me nigger," Amani rumbled very softly. "Other niggers can call me nigger, but you don't get to do it. You do it again and I'll pound your head clear down through your asshole."

Winters hung there staring into Amani's flat gaze for what seemed a very long time. "Okay," he said finally. At which point Amani carefully set him back on his feet.

It seemed to me that we'd reached just about the right level of intimidation, so I acted to re-take control of the meeting.

"I brought my two friends along," I said, "to provide a reality check about what 'tough' means. You pathetic idiots think you're tough? You came down here to beat up two women, which is about your speed. Try it again, bother either Patty or Sarah in any way whatsoever, and we'll have one more visit—which you will enjoy a lot less than this one. Believe me when I tell you that there'll be no need for us to get together after that. Are you understanding me here? Do you need any further clarification? Am I using words that are too big for you?"

Samuels stood glaring sullenly at me for a couple of seconds while Winters kept darting panicky glances at Amani. "Patty is my goddamned wife," Samuels finally grated. The man obviously was having a hard time letting go.

"Which does *not* give you the right to threaten her, hit her, or frighten her in any way. Maybe you really are too dumb to understand that. So understand this: If you *do* threaten, hit or frighten her

167

again, we three will beat the ever-loving crap out of you. Is that clear enough?"

He dragged his glare away from me to glance from side to side at my two companions. "Yes," he muttered with a bitter-looking twist to his mouth. Winters, meanwhile, still didn't seem to be aware of much besides the extremely large black man looming over him. I had a feeling he was letting go just fine.

"Speak up. I didn't hear you."

"Yes!" they practically shouted in unison.

"Good. Now I suggest the two of you turn around and get back in the elevator. Oh, and have a really lousy day."

They turned, eased carefully between Reuben and Amani, then had to wait a minute for the elevator while the three of us stood watching them. They didn't look back at us, but the tension in their bodies said they knew we were there.

The elevator doors finally opened, the two men got in, and they were gone.

CHAPTER FIFTY-ONE

The figure in the garage entrance that I'd taken to be George Quiller was also gone. I resisted the urge to trot over and see if he was still in sight on the street. I had a strong hunch he wouldn't be.

Instead I shook hands with my two helpers, expressed my thanks, and handed each of them a hundred dollar bill; then, when Amani had turned away, I slipped Reuben an extra fifty as promised. They headed directly for the street rather than taking the elevator. I almost shouted after them to let me know if they saw an average-looking white guy with light-colored hair and sharp features. Then I let it go. For now.

I turned back toward where Sarah and Patty were waiting by their car at the far end of the cavernous space.

Patty stepped forward as I approached. "What happened? What did you say?"

"I'm hoping I scared them off for good—with a little help from my friends."

"That would be wonderful!" She grinned at Sarah as she moved back to her side.

Sarah didn't return the grin. She was looking at me with an expression that was hard to interpret, even though I remembered seeing it fairly often before our divorce. Perplexity? Disappointment?

"Those men," she finally said. "They're really friends of yours?" The tone of that question I *could* interpret: You wouldn't have been palling around with any scary lowlifes like that when I married you. Which is why we aren't married anymore.

All of which I already knew well enough. "Friends might be overstating it," I replied. "Associates, let's say."

"Okay." Softly, as if it were anything but.

"At least I'm confident that Winters will be leaving you alone in the future, Sarah. He clearly took the threat very seriously." I turned back to Patty. "I'm not so sure about Frank. I want to think so, but I'm not positive. Plus, you're married to the man—which is a problem Sarah doesn't have with Brad Winters." Or me.

Her answering smile was without any humor at all. "It's a problem I don't plan to have for very long."

"Ah. Well, if you're planning to return to your house I'd recommend a good lawyer and an even better restraining order, as soon as possible."

She affirmed that those were her intentions, both the return to the house and the restraining order. Then, with a hearty goodbye from Patty and a somewhat pro forma thank you from Sarah, the two women got in the car. As they drove out of the parking garage, I was already thinking about what my next step should be.

CHAPTER FIFTY-TWO

One-thirty now. I was supposed to meet Devon Malone at four. Two-and-a-half hours. Find the baby? Identify the kidnapper? Not likely. I decided my best bet was to take a leisurely, circuitous route back to the office and keep an eagle eye out for George Quiller or whoever the hell it was I'd seen. The odds that a Quiller look-alike just *happened* to be standing there a half-hour ago were absolutely zero. If he was watching me, maybe I'd get a chance to watch him back.

I managed to spend almost an hour meandering back to the corner of Third and Stark. The businesses were mostly closed and the sidewalks empty, leading me to believe that most Portland residents were smarter (and warmer) than me. All I accomplished was near-frostbite of my nose; the temperature was just above freezing with a strong February wind dropping the chill factor well below.

The very first item on my office to-do list was turning up the thermostat.

The second was checking for voice and email. Only one of the former, a man asking for an appointment to talk about his wife; it didn't sound like he'd mistaken me for a therapist. I saved the message, hoping that he'd still have his problem when I had some time. Lots of email, all spam. Nothing relevant to dead clients or kidnapped children.

No use checking down the hall to see if Eleanor was in her office. She didn't start working on weekends until very late in the tax season.

So I spent nearly an hour making notes on index cards and shuffling them around my desk, trying to see some connection or lead that had eluded me so far. If one was there, it continued to elude me. At five minutes to four, I brought the cards together into a stack and dropped them into my desk drawer. I turned down the thermostat, locked the office door behind me, and headed across the street to the Home Run.

Devon Malone was already there. She'd chosen the corner table that viewed the fewest number of TV sets. (It was possible to see as many as seven at once if you positioned yourself correctly.) Apparently a woman who doesn't like distractions.

She'd seen me the second I entered the place. She didn't smile as I approached, looking just as business-like as the first time I'd seen her in front of Samantha Quiller's house. She wore the snug-fitting blue jeans and black leather jacket that was apparently her normal uniform. No doubt she kept the jacket on to cover her weapon, which was the same reason I'd be keeping mine on.

Restaurant patrons tend to become seriously uneasy when the people at the next table are armed, at least in this city. I didn't want to ruin anyone's digestion.

"McCall," she said as I sat down.

"Malone," I replied dutifully.

Menus had already been left on the table and she picked one up. "What's good here?"

"The hamburgers, the French fries, and the soft drinks."

"Gee, you really go for the haute cuisine, huh."

"I get mushrooms on my burgers if that counts."

"I suppose it will have to do." She put the menu down and fixed me with a steady gaze. I noticed for the first time that her eyes were closer to gray than blue. "So," she said. "Now that you've had a few more hours to think about it, why do you believe the kidnapper is not a pedophile?"

So much for witty banter.

I shrugged, still not having a really good answer. "Partly gut feeling. Partly that she doesn't fit the profile. Basically, the whole business strikes me as way too weird to be a simple case of pedophilia."

173

Malone almost smirked. "Pedophilia, of course, being perfectly normal."

"Humph," I responded. "You know that's not what I meant. The unidentified female first calls to try to confirm that I'm working for Samantha Quiller, then later leaves a message assuring me that George Quiller is dead and warning me to drop the case. Finally she calls to taunt me and says that she got what she wanted, presumably Kinsey Quiller. That's not a pedophile. That's somebody with an agenda specific to the Quiller family."

A young waitress interrupted to take our orders. Malone followed my advice, ordered a burger, fries and soft drink. I was careful to not forget the mushrooms on my burger.

The detective sergeant focused in again as soon as the waitress departed with the menus. "Any ideas what that agenda might be?"

"Other than acquiring the child, you mean? No, I don't. You don't buy my hunch, reasoning, whatever you want to call it, that the kidnapper isn't a pedophile?"

She sat back and surveyed the restaurant, then looked at me. "Actually I do. Or, like I said before, I sure as hell *hope* you're right because we're about out of time otherwise."

We spent the next half-hour chewing over both our burgers and every minor detail that I could add to what I'd already told Malone about the Quiller case and its main characters. The detective sergeant ate steadily, displaying an excellent appetite for a woman with such a slender figure.

She downed her final French fry and pursed her lips. "You can't be sure the guy you saw earlier today was George Quiller—especially since you *are* sure the man is dead. We aren't talking ghosts here, are we?"

I looked at my own empty plate and shook my head. "No. Of course not. But I tell you, he looked exactly like the photo Samantha Quiller showed me. Exactly."

"What was that description again?"

Sigh. "Six foot, maybe six-two," I told my plate, "light-colored hair cut fairly close, sharp features, somewhat prominent nose...."

"What was he wearing today?"

Something in her voice brought my attention back to her face. "Gray slacks, brown leather jacket...." She was not looking at me. She was staring past me toward the entrance.

"Like that guy?" she asked.

I turned and looked and there he was, standing just inside the door. He saw me at the same time I saw him. I jumped to my feet, almost knocking over my chair, ready to charge after him this time.

But he didn't run. He waved, like we were old buddies. And started across the room in my direction.

"Is that the guy?" came Malone's voice from behind me.

"Yes."

"Doesn't look like a ghost to me. Think he's dangerous?"

"I have no fucking idea," I said as the man who looked like George Quiller came closer and held out his hand as if to shake. I was just glad I had a witness.

CHAPTER FIFTY-THREE

He stopped and stood there with his hand out. What could I do? I stood up myself and shook hands with him. I suppose it was a relief to find that his hand was corporeal.

"My name is James," he said. "I'm George's twin brother."

Let's hear it for Occam's razor. Yet again the simplest explanation turns out to be the correct one.

"Clint McCall—but I suppose you know that already." I indicated my dinner companion. "This is Detective Sergeant Devon Malone."

His eyes widened and his body tensed. He was clearly not thrilled to learn he'd just introduced himself to a cop.

"Hi there, James," Malone greeted him dryly. "Is the last name Quiller?"

"Uh," he said, and looked to me like he was thinking about running again.

I pulled out a chair, planted a hand on his shoulder, and shoved him down onto the seat. "Join us for a bite to eat, James. Believe me, it will be more fun than getting tackled halfway to the door."

Apparently he agreed, since he retained his seat as I took my own.

Malone rephrased her question. "So you're James Quiller?"

He looked at her, then at me, back at her. Still coping with the whole police officer idea, I supposed. Finally: "James Orkney. My brother was Carl Orkney, really; Witness Protection gave him—us —the name George Quiller."

"Us? You were both in witness protection?" I asked. "With the same name?"

"No. Well. Sort of."

That certainly clarified matters.

Malone leaned in, giving him her I'm-a-badass-cop look. "Did you have anything to do with the kidnapping of Kinsey Quiller? Do you know where she is?" Nothing like cutting to the chase, I always say.

His face lost some color and he shook his head. "No. I don't know. That's the truth."

I jumped in. "What don't you know? What Malone here is talking about—or where the baby is? You'd better start making some sense."

More color drained away. His mouth opened, closed, opened again. Finally: "Where the little girl is. That's what I don't know. Where she is."

"So who took her?" Malone and I asked practically in unison.

"Crystal. Crystal took her. I didn't know she was going to do that."

Malone leaned even further in. "Who the fuck is Crystal?"

I put out a hand to restrain her before she climbed over the table. "Maybe," I said to James, "you'd better begin near the beginning—but make it a very short story." I had a feeling that if he launched into an epic narrative he wouldn't live to finish it.

At that moment, with less than exquisite timing, our perky waitress showed up with a menu for the newest member of our party. She handed it to him and he looked at it as if it were some sort of alien artifact. "Can I get you something to drink?" she asked.

"Uh...." he responded.

"We don't need anything right now," Malone announced firmly as she laid her shield on the table in front of the waitress.

The waitress let out a tiny gasp. "Yes, ma'am." She grabbed the menu out of his hand and fled on her way to serve others.

He watched her go and I snapped my fingers to bring his attention back to us. "The story," I said. "Now."

Gathering himself, he launched into it. "Carl and I were in witness protection. Well, he was—but we traded off now and again."

"Traded off?" I repeated.

"Sometimes he was George Quiller and sometimes I was. Most of the time he was."

Malone looked very dubious. "The feds let you get away with that?"

Orkney—if that was really his name—shrugged. "They didn't know. They thought there was just the one of us. Our parents were really old-fashioned hippies, way off the grid. No paper, you know? No records. The marshals didn't know we were twins. So sometimes we'd trade out."

I suddenly caught the implications, remembering a husband who seemed schizophrenic. "So...most of the time your brother Carl was George Quiller but once in a while you would take his place—and his bed. Right?"

He nodded, looking a little smug. "Right. You got it. We'd always shared girls. Didn't see any reason to stop."

Now I was looking skeptical. "And Samantha Quiller couldn't tell the difference?"

He shrugged. "Well, sure. She noticed some differences, but our look is really just the same. She noticed mostly stuff like I wanted to have sex more than he did. I guess she chalked it up to moods. You're not going to think your husband is suddenly somebody else, are you?"

Malone spoke up. "So you and Carl have both been living here in Portland?"

"No. We're from Chicago and I still live there. I'd just come to visit now and then for a few days. Not so much lately."

"Why is that?" I asked.

"Carl was going a little crazy, I think. Last time I was George, he didn't want to come back. We had to kind of threaten him into it. And he was drinking way too much. We were getting scared he'd blow the whole thing."

"We?" Again, Malone and I said it practically simultaneously.

"Crystal and me."

Bingo, we finally got where we were going.

CHAPTER FIFTY-FOUR

"Tell us about Crystal," I said.

His eyes darted around the room as if he were suddenly wondering how he got here—or possibly worrying that the aforementioned Crystal might be nearby.

"Crystal's my lady," he said finally.

Malone leaned into him again. "And she's got the baby? Where is she?"

"I don't *know* where she is. I wish I did."

Again I restrained Malone from climbing down his throat. "What's Crystal's full name?" I asked, figuring that if we got enough background info we wouldn't have to spend the rest of the day dragging details out of this idiot.

"Crystal Glass."

Oh, yeah. Right. That's going to be on her birth certificate for sure.

"Why did she take the baby?" I asked as patiently as I could, trying to set a good example for Malone.

Orkney sat back, palms out to either side. "You got me. I didn't know she wanted a baby. She never told *me* she wanted a baby. I don't know what the fuck she's doing now."

Malone meanwhile was practically twitching in her seat. "Who is this bitch?" she grated.

"Yes," I agreed calmly, "tell us more about Crystal."

He lowered his hands, looked from one of us to the other, and took a deep breath. "She's a hit man."

Yikes. This was a development.

"A.... You mean she's a professional killer?" I asked.

"Yeah. Or hit person. That's what she says I ought to call her. Hit *person*. Can you believe that shit?"

182

Malone's twitching was even more pronounced. "Kinsey Quiller is with a woman who kills people for a living?" she inquired softly.

"Yeah," Orkney agreed as if this were a common occurrence back in Chicago where he comes from. "She's really good, too. Lots of people think she's the best in the Midwest."

"Oh," I said. "That's great. We wouldn't want the baby to be with a fucking incompetent killer."

He looked hurt. "Well, I'm just saying."

Malone suddenly sat up straight. "Is it *your* baby?"

I hadn't even thought of that, but of course I knew immediately why she was asking.

Orkney apparently didn't. He went completely white this time. "Mine? No, it's not mine. Why do you think it's mine?"

"You had sex with Samantha Quiller just like your brother did," she replied reasonably. "It could be yours."

"We didn't trade off *that* much--and I always used protection. She and Carl maybe wanted a kid. I didn't want one." He stopped, seemed to lose focus for a moment. "Maybe that was the problem," he said finally.

The waitress had begun to give us the eye—from a respectful distance—and I was beginning to think we should probably take this conversation over to my office, but I didn't want to break the momentum quite yet.

"What do you mean?" I asked.

"Crystal," he said, then paused.

"What about her?" The detective sergeant was twitching again. "Come on, damn it!"

"Well, Crystal came with me this time to help me find out who killed Carl—and to watch my back. I know he's been dead a long time but it kept bugging me and I finally had to come check it out even though Crystal kept telling me it was too dangerous." Another pause, like he was working it through. "She hadn't been here before.

She hadn't seen Samantha and the baby. I think maybe it pushed her female buttons, you know?"

"Her female buttons?" Malone again.

"Crystal never had any family. Maybe...." He faded off.

Meanwhile, the waitress was apparently becoming desperate, since she was on the verge of hovering. I motioned her over and asked for the check, which she already had in her hand. I gave it right back to her with my credit card and she hurried off toward the cash register.

"Let's finish this in my office," I said to the other two—then focused on Orkney. "We need to know *everything* you know about Crystal Glass. Every detail. Something in there is going to help us find out where she is now."

"And," added Malone, "if you don't remember enough details we'll finish it in *my* office. You wouldn't want that, would you?"

He shook his head, shuddered a little. "No. I'll tell you everything I can. I didn't come here to kill anybody or steal any babies. I just wanted to find out who killed my brother."

The waitress was coming back with my card. "Speaking of which, you get anything on that?" I asked Orkney.

He hesitated while I filled out the slip and signed it. The hesitation seemed to be more than just waiting for the waitress to leave.

"No," he said as we all three got up from the table. "Nothing for sure. I got an idea, but.... I don't know. I don't like it."

"That'll be something else to share when we get across the street," I said. We headed for the front door, Orkney walking just ahead of me and Malone and not looking all that eager to share.

We came out into a chilly light rain and for some reason—maybe I always do this, but usually have no occasion to remember it—I glanced up at my building. I caught a glimpse of motion on the roof and my adrenaline was just starting to flood when I heard a faint *phuut* from that direction. Almost simultaneously I heard an even fainter gasp from Orkney and he started to fall toward the sidewalk.

"Gun!" I screamed and Malone and I dived behind the nearest parked car. I tried to catch Orkney and bring him with us, but he was already down.

Malone had her weapon out first and poked her head above the hood of the car as I was drawing mine.

"Anything?" I asked her, figuring that as long as she was already exposed I might as well wait to hear her report.

She squinted through the drizzle up at the roof line. "Nothing," she finally said.

We both looked back at Orkney lying on the sidewalk. He was way past needing a paramedic. There was blood everywhere and I could see a piece of his skull lying up against the front door of The Home Run.

So much for sharing.

CHAPTER FIFTY-FIVE

Malone dealt with the first officers to arrive on the scene. Communication cop-to-cop is always so much more efficient.

The staff and patrons of the Home Run had to be escorted through the kitchen and out the back since there was evidence splattered up against the front door. They were lucky. I was going to be seeing that bloody piece of scalp every time I approached this entrance for some time to come. My favorite lunch spot might have to do without my trade until the image started to fade.

No sign of the shooter. He or she—I was betting on a she—had fired from the roof of my building and then apparently leapt the small gap to the next roof over on Stark and taken the fire escape to the ground. Not that there were any witnesses to verify my speculation.

The rest of that Sunday evening was taken up with more responding officers, medics, news vans, the medical examiner, homicide detectives (including Mike Whitehall), a variety of calls from friends and family as the local news broadcasts picked up live feeds from the scene, and finally statements given at the Justice Center.

It was a very big news story, of course. Reuben Keys called from his vehicle, no doubt in the course of keeping an eye on the girls he had working the Sunday night shift. I guess he heard the news on his car radio.

Several of my fellow black belts and even a few of my past students called to make sure I was okay. Hap and Johnny both called, of course.

Colleen saw it on TV and called from Patty's house, sounding more pleased about the chance to catch up with her mother than about my continued well-being. I didn't even bother to remind her that I'd asked her to steer clear of Sarah and Patty for a few days. Obviously she was going to do what she was going to do.

And I certainly wasn't going to worry about Colleen's affection being drawn away from me by the return of her mother. No sir, not me. I wasn't going to worry about that for a second. My daughter could see as well as I did that her mother had been callously indifferent to our fear and concern over the four years she was out of touch. Well, she should anyway.

And that was all the not-thinking-about-that I was going to do today.

I more or less staggered into my house just after midnight, managed to get the cats fed, and fell into bed without thinking further about anything.

I slept in until around eight, when Stella and Maxine began pouncing on various parts of my anatomy to let me know it was a new day (not to mention breakfast time).

I got to the office at nine thirty, hoping to find at least one message—from Malone, Mike Whitehall, or whoever—providing more information about the Orkney brothers, Crystal Glass, or even the whereabouts of Kinsey Quiller.

No such luck. There was a voicemail from a potential client, one Sylvia Quackenbush who suspected that her husband Carl was delving into bushes other than Quacken. I saved the message as I had others, in the hope that I'd be out from under my current investigation before they'd hired another P.I. There was no way I had time to tail a straying spouse right now.

My "current investigation...." Right. Like all I had to do was pull out my note cards and spend the morning confirming who had killed my client, literally blown the brains out of the man who could have been my primary witness, and kidnapped a young child. Then maybe I would spend the afternoon finding the killer and the kid. Then tomorrow morning I'd call Mrs. Quackenbush. Clint McCall to the rescue!

No problem.

CHAPTER FIFTY-SIX

Maybe one problem: I didn't *have* any note cards that would aid me in accomplishing any of those things. I didn't have shit besides a dead client, a dead witness, and a lot of dead ends.

Fortunately, I was rescued from terminal depression by a knock on my office door. It opened before I could respond and Eleanor Ivory poked her head in. She glanced around, probably to confirm I was alone, and then swept into the room.

"My God, I just heard about the shooting on the morning news," she said as she crossed the open space and dropped into one of my visitor chairs. She set her bag on the floor beside it. "Right across the street! Are you okay?"

Her silver-blonde hair was pulled back in a ponytail and she was wearing a light brown skirt and white peasant blouse; the blouse was cut low enough to distract male clients from their tax problems.

"I wish I only had tax problems," I muttered aloud before my brain caught up with my mouth.

"What?"

"Nothing. I'm okay. She hit the guy she was shooting at—which, fortunately, wasn't me."

"She? You've got women shooting at you now?"

"The shooter hasn't been positively identified, but I'm pretty sure it was a woman. The same woman who killed my client and kidnapped her child."

Eleanor grimaced. "I heard about that, too. The client. I am so sorry."

"Yeah."

"So you figured out what was going on with the dead husband?"

"He's dead, all right. The man Samantha Quiller saw was his twin, of whom apparently there was never any record. Not that I actually figured it out; the twin showed up and explained it all—or started to, before he got his head blown off."

"Ah, so that's who...."

"Yep. Across the street yesterday evening."

Eleanor looked off to her right as if she could see it all through the walls of the building, then turned back to me. "What are you going to do now?"

"Find the bad guy, er, girl, and rescue the baby. What else?"

She shrugged. "Do you know yet if Colleen really saw her mother that day?"

It took me a moment. That seemed like another lifetime already. "Yeah, I found Sarah. We've talked." Eleanor leaned forward and opened her mouth. I plunged ahead. "It's too long a story for now. I have to concentrate on finding the kid."

She closed her mouth and sat back. "Is there anything I can do?"

I thought about that for a minute. I knew that Devon Malone was already using every resource available to law enforcement to discover all she could about Crystal Glass and James Orkney. Even with all her research and hacking skills, Eleanor would be unlikely to find out more.

So, what would I be looking at if I didn't have a missing child to worry about? Ah.

"Find out everything you can about two local men named Frank Samuels and Bradley Winters. Samuels lives here now. Winters has been traveling around; he may or may not have a current local address. If you have to choose, focus on Samuels."

Eleanor frowned. "You think one of them might have the kid?"

190

"No, no, this goes back to Sarah and why she's in town. Winters has been harassing her and Samuels has been abusing his wife who's a good friend of hers. I *think* I've resolved both problems, but just in case I wouldn't mind having some more ammunition."

"Oh, yeah, I remember. One of your wife's friends was...Patty Samuels, right? Okay." She dug a piece of paper out of her bag and wrote down the names. Then she retained her hold on the bag and stood up.

"Time for me to get to work. I hope you find the baby soon."

"Me too."

CHAPTER FIFTY-SEVEN

I hung around the office for only a few minutes more after Eleanor left. Yesterday evening Malone and I had made a date for lunch in the expectation that by noon today she'd have more information. I wasn't prepared to sit swiveling in my office chair until it was time to go find out, so I decided to take a walk. Maybe someone would try to contact me, or shoot me, or some damn thing that might lead to a clue if I were out and about.

Or, then again, maybe not.

The Italian restaurant where I had arranged to meet Malone was only four blocks over on Yamhill, but I had more than an hour to kill before noon. I started walking in the other direction, planning to circle around beyond Pioneer Courthouse Square and back to Bergamo's.

The ambience was a typical gray and cold February morning in the Pacific Northwest. According to the weather site I checked at the office, it was snowing to the east in the Columbia Gorge. Not here in Portland, thank goodness. It rarely snows in Portland—and therefore almost always brings the city to a stop when it does.

Both the streets and sidewalks were heavily trafficked, about usual for late Monday morning. Not very many people sitting around the square, though. Too chilly.

I felt hyper-alert as I trod the city sidewalks, trying to check out the cars, people and buildings all at once. The possibility of a bullet, or any other kind of attack for that matter, sharpens the senses wonderfully.

But apparently there was nothing to see and no one to fear. Not this morning, anyway. I arrived safe and sound at the front entrance to Bergamo's Italian Cuisine just five minutes before noon.

Bergamo's is well known for its good service and especially for its excellent spaghetti. Management, on the other hand, clearly makes no effort to be unique in décor. The tables were round, covered in red tablecloths with little red glass candleholders, and seated four. The floor was black and white checked linoleum and the polished wooden walls carried large photos and paintings of Italian scenes. What you saw was what you got.

What I saw as I glanced around the already crowded dining area was Detective Sergeant Malone sitting at a table off in the corner to my right. Not only punctual, but early. Maybe she had some new info.

She was sipping from a glass of water as I approached. "I already ordered," she was saying before I even got seated. "We're having spaghetti with garden salad."

"Ookay," I said as I picked up my cloth napkin and unfolded it into my lap. "That sounds good, if somewhat bossy. With a nice red wine?"

"No alcohol. I'm on duty."

I immediately motioned to the nearest waiter. "Ordering my lunch is one thing," I told Malone. "Denying me wine is another." The waiter came up and I ordered a glass of house burgundy.

She unfolded her own napkin. "I suppose you private guys are never really on duty."

"Au contraire," I replied. "Never really *off*. Besides, a modicum of wine enhances my investigative abilities."

Her eyebrows went up. "Au contraire? Modicum? Did you get a vocabulary injection since I last saw you?"

"I always talk fancy when lunching with an attractive woman in a good restaurant."

"Humph" was her only reply to that, which was disappointing. I just knew she had to be rolling her eyes in spirit, at least, but she was wasn't going to banter back. All business, this woman, at least on this occasion.

193

My wine arrived about then and I lifted my glass to Malone before taking my first sip. "So," I said as I set the glass down, "what's new?"

She reached down into what must have been either a bag or a briefcase beside her chair and pulled out a tattered notebook. Not a PDA, not a laptop, nothing that required a battery. A flip notebook of paper sheets, half of them coming loose from the wire binders. My kind of woman.

She flipped it open. "I guess our buddy James was telling the truth about their one-for-two scam. There's only one sheet, for Carl Orkney, which I guess combines the unlawful activities of the two twin brothers in several different jurisdictions. I wonder how Carl got nominated? Probably the first one arrested. Anyway, it's all petty stuff—joyriding, break-ins, purse snatching, a couple of indecent exposures.... Between them they managed to be one average low-life scumbag."

She flipped to another page. "Crystal Glass, now, is a different story. Born Theresa Mertz, known most of her life as Tanya Marie Glass, her first arrest was at the age of eight. Suspicion of killing her mother." Malone glanced up with a grim smile at my gasp. "Yeah." Back to the page. "Father unknown and already long gone by then. No trial. Insufficient evidence. She was suspected in six more killings by the time she was eighteen, which—considering that she *never* left sufficient evidence—means there were probably more."

She closed the notebook and glared across the table at me. "Which also means she's not the girl you want either stalking your ass or taking care of your client's baby."

"No shit," I replied, a little vaguely. For the last couple of Malone's sentences, I'd been experiencing a sudden disquiet—and not only because of what I was hearing. Something had changed in our environment. I'd noticed something unconsciously that hadn't yet come to the fore. Hopefully it was not the glint of restaurant lighting on a gun barrel. I started to scan the surrounding tables and quickly caught sight of my new problem about halfway across the room over Malone's left shoulder.

It was not a gun. It was worse than that. Alison Roberts was sitting there giving me a big shit-eating grin.

"Oh crap," I said to Malone.

CHAPTER FIFTY-EIGHT

My lunch companion glanced wildly around. "What? What?"

"Keep your weapon holstered," I said. "It's just my least favorite TV reporter sitting over there, giving us the evil eye."

This time Malone followed my gaze and twisted around to look back at Alison Roberts. "The skinny kid with shoulder-length black hair, spiffy suit and huge handbag who looks like she's really happy to see me?" she asked.

"That's the one."

Malone turned toward me and put her hands palm-down on the table. "Crap," she agreed.

"Give me a minute." I pushed back my seat and rose. Alison's grin grew even broader as I crossed to her table. "What a coincidence," I said when I got there.

"More luck than coincidence," she replied as she offered me a seat. "I was driving by when I saw you about to come in here. Seemed like a good place for lunch, so here I am."

Bad luck, maybe. At least she hadn't been following me around downtown while I thought I was so alert. Now that she was here, though, I had to deal with it.

"I don't have anything new for you," I announced preemptively.

Alison looked past me toward my table. "She's new," she said.

"That's Detective Sergeant Devon Malone of missing persons. We're comparing notes on the Quiller case."

"Ah yes. I was covering a story on the coast yesterday or I would have seen you then. Dead mother. Missing baby. And I was right about the father, wasn't I? It was a false identity."

The fake identity had not been in any of the published reports and I wasn't about to admit it. "You'll have your exclusive as I promised," I said carefully, "when the time comes. Along with any credit that you deserve."

I didn't think her grin could get any wider. I was wrong. "It had better be soon," she said. "Anything else I can do to help in the meantime?"

I gave that a moment's thought. Well, why not? She had a whole different set of sources than law enforcement. "I'll give you three more names to check out," I said. "See if you come up with any local hits in the last, say, two years. Crystal Glass. Tanya Marie Glass. Theresa Mertz. All the same person."

She wrote down the names. "Sounds like a person of interest indeed."

"When the time comes," I repeated. "I'm going back to my lunch now."

"Enjoy." She glanced past me again. "She's a looker."

"She's a police detective. Have a nice lunch." I returned to my seat opposite Malone, who was clearly feeling less than patient.

Her expression as I resumed my seat was downright dour. "You two seemed pretty cozy for a 'least favorite' person. She going to be a problem? I want to control the media on this."

"Alison is, at times like this, my least favorite journalist; as a person, she's a friend of mine. Sort of. And, no, as long as I keep promising her an exclusive she won't be a problem. She might even be able to help."

Malone's expression went from dour to sour. "So you get to promise the exclusives on police investigations now?"

"No," I said patiently after taking a sip of wine. "I get to promise exclusives on *my* investigations. You can provide the department's version of the story to whomever you want, whenever you want."

"Whomever." She said it exactly like "humph." There I go talking fancy again.

Our spaghetti and salad arrived at that moment and we were both silent as the waitress arranged the plates. When she asked if we needed anything else, I said no. Malone continued grimacing.

"All right," I said as I settled my cloth napkin in my lap. "Let's get back to the business at hand. Have you tracked down where Orkney was staying?"

She forked a clump of salad. "Motel way out on Burnside." Put it in her mouth and began chewing. I sampled my own salad while I waited for the detective sergeant to decide if she was going to keep talking.

"We found a digital camera in the room," she went on as she twirled up some spaghetti strands. "Just one set of fingerprints on it. Not his. Crystal Glass."

"Ah," I said as I tackled my own spaghetti. "So she was staying with him."

Malone shrugged as she chewed thoughtfully. "She was there at some point. Can't tell if she was a live-in." Drink of water. "You know, the Orkney boys must have gone through lots of pairs of gloves. All those crimes and only Carl's fingerprints ever showed up, on that first arrest—though I'm assuming the second set of fresh prints in the motel room belong to James."

"On the other hand," I said, "usually nobody bothers to lift prints on crap crimes like they were doing in Chicago."

"True."

"The camera? Any images on the memory card?"

She smiled slyly as she helped herself to more salad. "Oh yeah. Pictures of a young child, about two years old I'd say. Candids, taken with a telephoto looks like."

"Kinsey Quiller."

"No question, since her mother is in some of the shots."

"How many pictures? Anything besides the girl and her mother?"

"Close to a hundred, and no, nothing else. Very few include Mrs. Quiller. Most are tightly focused on Kinsey. I'd say we're talking obsession."

I sat back with a frown. "Why? Why would a professional killer from Chicago be so interested in this little girl?"

Malone shrugged. "Don't ask me. It's the child of her lover's twin brother—or, hell, maybe it's James' child; we don't know he was telling the truth about always using protection. Whatever James came here for, it sure looks like Crystal either came for the kid or quickly decided that's what she wanted. The dates on the photos go back to around a week before your client saw James downtown and thought he was George."

"I suppose you checked that the camera's internal clock was set for the correct date."

"Of course."

"Of course." I twirled up another strand of spaghetti. "So: if we can figure out why she wants the kid, maybe that will tell us where she has her."

Malone pointed her fork at me; a little piece of salad dangled from one of the tines. "That's the difference between private eyes and real cops. You follow the speculation while I follow the evidence."

I thrust my spaghetti-stained fork right back at her. "And we'll see who gets there first."

She flicked the salad shred off her fork with her tongue and washed it down with the last of her water. "I don't give a shit as long as one of us gets there," she said as she set the glass down and motioned to the waitress that we wanted the check. She'd eaten only about half of her meal and apparently expected me to quickly finish mine.

Alison Roberts was on her cell phone as we left. She winked at us. I didn't wink back. I'm pretty sure the detective sergeant didn't, either.

CHAPTER FIFTY-NINE

Malone had driven to the restaurant, so we parted company and I headed back toward my office on foot—again keeping an eye out for anyone who appeared to be following and again seeing no sign of surveillance.

Otherwise I was focused on what to do when I got back to my desk—and, as of a block away, I'd come up with nothing but to check messages and mail. Malone was right: I could speculate endlessly about why Crystal Glass wanted Kinsey Quiller, but it would do me no good without any evidence leading toward an answer. It was all very frustrating.

And it turned out I should have been looking somewhere besides behind me. As I reached Stark and started to cross Third with the signal, I did note that traffic had lightened up and there weren't even any vehicles waiting on me at the crosswalk. What I didn't notice was the dark sedan a few car lengths to my left until its engine suddenly roared.

I just had time to register the grill of the vehicle rocketing toward my hip. There was no hope of making it across the street. I caught my forward momentum and leapt backward toward the sidewalk. The sedan actually clipped the sole of my right shoe in the air and spun me off balance so that I landed on my belly on the curb.

I immediately rolled over and sat up but my attacker had already made a high-speed right onto Stark and was halfway down the block. Taking advantage of that damned light traffic, he or she screeched around the corner onto Fourth and was gone.

I sat for a minute, catching my breath, hoping to hear a siren from that direction. (The sedan had, after all, broken any number of traffic laws just blocks from the main police station.) But, no, as usual there was no cop when you needed one.

In fact, no cop ever appeared—not even just happening to drive by. There had been other pedestrians, but I guess none of the witnesses felt my little contretemps was worth a call to 911. Maybe they figured that since I could stand up I could make the call myself if I wanted to.

I did not want to. I'd had enough publicity about attempts on my life lately, plus there was nothing the police could do without a plate number and I'd gotten only a partial, the first two letters. Meanwhile any other potential witnesses (none of whom would likely have looked at the plate anyway) had moved on. I didn't even have the make and model other than it was a dark blue late model sedan. Not like the old days when you could identify a 1981 Ford Granada, say, at a glance. Now you have multiple makes using the same model or at least the same chassis.

I did have one thing, though, as I finally successfully crossed the street and took the stairs up to my office: I had the growing suspicion that more than one person wanted me dead this week. If that car was driven by a professional killer from Chicago, I'd eat my P.I. license. An attempted hit and run in downtown Portland three blocks from the Justice Center shouted amateur hour very loudly.

By the time I settled behind my desk I was vividly experiencing not only a sore gut but also the scrapes on my hands, knees and chin from landing on that curb. Plus my shoulder was hurting again where I'd been shot. I felt—and probably looked—like I'd just finished an all-day sparring session. If I'd been honest with myself, I might have thought something about being too old for this shit...but I find it best to be *dis*honest about things like that.

The phone rang. It was Reuben Keys. "You ever heard of a group called 'Mothers Against Clint McCall'?" he asked.

"No, I can't say that I have," I replied, already with a hunch where this was going.

"Well, I hear that cunt who's out to kill you has got a little kid. Killer mom. That's somethin' you don't see every day."

Bingo. Maybe. "*Who* did you hear it from? Who saw her? When? Where? I need everything you've got, Reuben."

"One of my girls got to talkin' to her at the Gent's Lounge on Columbia, near the airport. I guess killer cunt was pretty stoned and feelin' like she needed to share with another woman. Truth to tell, words wasn't all she wanted to share. My girl made some good money off the bitch."

"Glad to hear it, but how do we know this is the woman you heard about before?"

"All the sharing included your name, along with thoughts about wanting to kill your ass, and some shit about havin' to get back to the baby she'd left in her room. I had the word out with all my ladies to let me know if your name came up like that and so here I am with the info."

"Anything about where that room was?"

"Nope. Sorry. What's goin' on, McCall?"

"I haven't kept you up to date on my client with the kid. She's been killed and her baby kidnapped. One guess who did it."

"Killer cunt? That ain't good."

"No, that ain't good. Your girl get anything else?"

"I'm sorry, man. That's it."

"Well, it's way better than nothing. I appreciate it."

"No problem. I'll have my girls keep listening." He hung up.

I guess I'd been hoping for a little recuperation time at my desk, but it wasn't to be. Now I had a place to check out, The Gentleman's Lounge, and a good chance that Crystal Glass was holed up nearby. I also had a new fear. Maybe she didn't *intend* to hurt Kinsey Quiller, but the result could be just as bad if she was leaving the child alone in a motel room while she went out drinking and screwing around. She probably didn't have the kid with her when she was shooting people, either. Or, if the kid *wasn't* alone, I shuddered to think what kind of "babysitter" might be on duty.

203

Time to wrap up my aches and pains and take them on the road.

CHAPTER SIXTY

The Gentleman's Lounge featured dim lighting, three pool tables, a bar, and about a dozen small round tables with straight-backed wooden chairs. Toward the back there was a stage edged around by more seating for the guys who wanted to see the strippers up close.

The place was not exactly jumping at this time of day. There was an overweight middle-aged bartender and one customer at the bar. Two others nursed drinks at the stage as they watched desultory pole-dancing by a skinny blonde who'd yet to remove either top or bottom.

The bartender grunted in my direction when I took a stool, but didn't actually move. I didn't say anything so he was finally forced to turn his big bald head in my direction. "What'll you have?"

I opened my ID and placed it on the bar. "A beer and some information," I said.

He sidled over to me and squinted down at the ID. "Private cop." He looked up. "What kinda beer?"

"Whatever's on tap."

He grabbed a mug and filled it. "There ain't no information on tap," he announced as he set it in front of me. I was surprised he managed to make a witticism; he looked like he hadn't laughed since he was two. He certainly delivered his little joke with an extremely straight face.

I ignored it anyway. "Were you working the bar last night?" I dropped a twenty-dollar bill beside the ID.

He squinted down again and scooped it up. "Yeah. So?"

"I'm sure you had some whores dropping by—and I understand that one of them picked up a woman, about five-ten, thin but muscular, long black hair probably pulled back in a ponytail. Ladies usually leave with guys, so I thought you might have noticed." Another twenty hit the bar.

This time he just looked at it. I added another bill. He picked them both up. "I mighta seen somethin' like that, but I don't know nothin' about it."

I was willing to go to a hundred but no more, so I traded the last two twenties for the fact that one of the girls working now—not the one currently on stage—had also been here last night and she had been "circulating" a lot. So she might have heard or seen something more than my well-to-do bartender friend. I moved over to one of the tables while he went backstage to tell her she had a visitor.

Upon closer inspection the blonde on stage appeared to be using the pole to hold herself up rather than for dancing. I wasn't sure she was going to have the energy to strip. She was either very sleepy or very doped up already. I could only hope the dancer backstage was in better shape.

A short, almost plump brunette wearing a shiny blue silk wrap bustled out with the bartender who pointed in my direction. She hurried over and plopped down in the chair opposite mine. At least she had a fair amount of energy.

"I'm Brandy." Aren't they all. "Sid says you want to talk to me about somethin' that happened last night."

I gave her the same line about the whore and the female client.

She looked at me and then deliberately scanned the tabletop. "Sid says you got money."

Damn Sid and his big mouth. Fortunately I had some more twenties and it turned out that Brandy did indeed remember Reuben's girl and her female client. She'd been keeping a pretty close eye on them, apparently because she viewed Reuben's girl as competition. I gathered that Brandy enjoyed collecting more than dancing tips from the customers. Anyway, she said she'd watched them go out to a car in the parking lot and get in the back seat. She had no details about what had happened there, other than that it took about half-an-hour.

All of which made me very glad I'd done this follow-up, since Reuben had somehow failed to either find out or mention that his girl had seen Crystal's car. Brandy certainly had seen it and gave me a good description. Late-'90s Honda sedan, probably an Accord, dark green with a rental plate. She didn't get the number—that would have been asking too much—but she did remember that the license plate frame said Hertz.

I left Brandy happily sorting through the small pile of twenties she had accumulated. My best bet, I decided, was to check the nearest Hertz rental—which would be the airport—before I started checking nearby motels.

CHAPTER SIXTY-ONE

The parking situation at the airport was so bad that I might as well have walked from the Gentleman's Lounge. It took about fifteen minutes to find a spot in the long-term parking overflow lot and then another ten to make my way from there to the terminal. When I finally got to the Hertz rental desk, however, there was only one person ahead of me and he was nearly finished with his transaction.

When he was done I stepped smartly up to the desk and laid my open ID in front of the clerk, a young brunette wearing glasses and a bored expression. She glanced at the ID and reached for a rental form. "We don't have many vehicles left this afternoon," she began, "so you may not be able to get exactly what you're looking for."

"That won't be a problem since I'm not looking for a vehicle," I said, and pointed significantly at the ID.

This time she actually looked at it, then up at me with a small frown. "Yes?"

"I'm looking for a woman who recently rented a late-model green Honda."

She picked up the ID this time and inspected it closely, apparently deciding that it carried the same weight as a badge. "That's pretty vague," she said as she handed me the ID. "How recent?"

Not about to disabuse her of her misapprehension, I plunged ahead. "The last forty-eight hours." This was half guess and half hope, of course. If Crystal Glass had been driving the same vehicle since she arrived in the area there'd be no hope of retrieving the information from this young lady's records. If she was frequently changing vehicles, I had a chance.

"Well, let me see," she said as she started tapping away on the keyboard. She didn't sound optimistic. After a moment she stopped and looked at the screen. "There is a green 2007 Honda Accord out right now, rented on Saturday afternoon."

"Excellent. And the name on the rental agreement?"

"Carol Gross."

"Address?"

"A box number in Chicago."

I was certain already, but might as well tie it down if possible. "Were you working Saturday and, if so, do you remember anything about her appearance?"

"I was working that afternoon, but I'm not sure.... A young woman, tall, thin, black hair? I think that was her."

No question, that was her. "Did she provide a local address?"

Again, scanning the screen. "No, apparently she didn't know where she'd be staying yet."

Or at least she didn't want you to know. "What's the plate number on your vehicle?" I pulled out my notebook

She read it off to me and I noted it down. "Okay," I said, "thanks very much."

"Always happy to cooperate with the law."

And I'm always happy to be mistaken for the law. I left the clerk to enjoy her civic virtue and headed for my car, hitting speed-dial for Devon Malone as I left the terminal, open notebook in my other hand.

She picked up on the first ring. "Malone."

"This is Clint. I've got a description of the rental car I think Crystal Glass is driving right now." I gave her the make and model, then read off the plate number.

"That's excellent. I'll put out a BOLO right away. With any luck we'll have this bitch off the street and the kid back home by this evening."

"I hope you're right, but don't forget that she's a pro. We'll need a lot of luck. Meanwhile, I'm going to be checking motels around the airport."

"That's fine. Stay in touch." She hung up. No doubt the BOLO would be broadcast within a couple of minutes. I felt a surge of optimism as I got in the Subaru and pulled out of the lot.

CHAPTER SIXTY-TWO

Three hours later, not so much. I had touched base with every motel within a dozen blocks of the airport and as far as I could discover none of them had Crystal Glass or any alias I was aware of as a guest. I'd heard no further word from Malone, so the car had not been seen either.

Late afternoon. I debated whether to go back to the office or on home. I decided to hit the office one more time. Going home felt too much like giving up.

I was hyper-alert crossing Third from my downtown parking lot this time, but no one attempted to shoot or run me down. I checked my mailbox at the bottom of the stairs, which I'd forgotten to do earlier in the day. Ten junk mails and two checks from clients. Five to one was better than the average day, so I felt somewhat cheery as I unlocked my office door.

I hung up my jacket, stashed the Smith and Wesson in the top right drawer, pulled down the shade on my window, and settled in my swivel chair. No new phone messages. I just sat there for a minute. So no new leads. What to do?

For lack of anything else, I pulled up my client spreadsheets and entered the two payments. I was filling out a deposit slip when the phone rang. Caller ID said it was from the Pen and Pastry. Colleen? Veronica? I picked up. "McCall."

"Clint, we need to talk."

It was Veronica Fortune. "Okay," I said cautiously. She sounded *very* serious. "I don't have anything going on here. I can be there in twenty minutes."

"No, I don't want to talk here. I'll meet you at your house."

"All right, see you there in twenty." My house, after all, was just around the corner from Veronica's café.

"Talk to you then," she said, and hung up.

I had not asked her what she wanted to talk about, but most likely she had further concerns about my daughter. Veronica had, in many ways, been serving as a surrogate mother since Sarah left and I had no problem with that. I'd see what she had to say in a few minutes.

My trek back across the street to retrieve the Subaru was again uneventful. I kept one eye on the rear view mirror as I drove to my house, choosing to focus otherwise on the upcoming talk with Veronica and the talk that I planned to have with Colleen—regardless of what Veronica had to say—if she was still hanging out with Sarah.

Of course my daughter was old enough that she didn't have to do what Daddy said, but still I felt it was too dangerous with no assurance that Frank Samuels, at least, was going to leave them alone. And, I said again to myself, that's the only reason I want Colleen away from her mother. I almost believed it.

I was actually glad to arrive home and see Veronica already sitting on the front step. She gave me a little wave as I pulled into the driveway but no smile.

As I got out of the car I automatically did a quick survey of my surroundings and had closed the door and re-focused on Veronica before it registered that a green sedan was approaching from up the street.

My blood literally ran cold as I looked at it again and saw it was a late model Honda, now only about a hundred feet away. I heard it accelerate as I took off around the front of the Subaru and yelled at Veronica.

"Get down! Get down! Gun!" I screamed as I tried to get to her before the Honda got to us.

Respectable best-selling author and café owner that she is, my long-time friend also has more than ample experience on the streets—and she still has the old instincts. She was diving for the grass at the same time I dived for her.

214

I think I was in the air when I heard a series of pops and the tinkling of glass. It was over by the time I realized I was on the ground beside Veronica. I raised my head and saw the Honda barge through the cross traffic on Hawthorne to head west toward downtown.

Even as I turned to Veronica to make sure she was all right, I felt rage surging through my body. Crystal Glass was going to pay a high price for bringing the war to my home.

CHAPTER SIXTY-THREE

I reached over to put my hand on Veronica's back. She was still face down in the grass, unmoving.

"You okay?"

"I think so," came the muffled response.

"Let's get inside."

I helped her up and saw as we turned toward the house that one of the front windows had been blown out. Immediate image of Stella and Maxine hit by flying glass. I urged Veronica toward the front door even as I promised myself that if the cats were hurt that high price would go even higher.

The first thing I saw inside was that indeed the floor was covered with glass. No dead or injured cats in evidence, however. No blood.

I got Veronica to a chair. She was still pretty shaken up, but seemed otherwise unharmed. As I got her a glass of water, approaching sirens told me that at least one of my neighbors had already called the cops. I really wanted to check on the two feline sisters before my house was invaded by a bunch of adrenaline-charged police officers who were going to frighten them even more. And there was nothing I could do about that, even if I found them unharmed.

Veronica assured me she was fine with me taking time to search for the cats. My best bet, I thought, was to look under the bed. That was their typical scared-shitless refuge. I hurried into my bedroom, grabbed the little flashlight I keep on the side table, and got down on my knees.

And there they were, huddled tightly together in the far corner. Both had their eyes wide open, neither appeared injured, no blood was in evidence on the floor around them, and they weren't crying.

Check, check, check and check. Hang in there, girls. Time to go deal with the first responders.

I was losing count of how often in recent days I'd been surrounded by cops interviewing me about a shooting incident. It was beginning to piss me off.

First I talked to a couple of uniformed officers, neither of whom I knew, then a detective that I'd at least met before, and finally Mike Whitehall showed up. And of course there were the media in the street in front of the house. All four local stations, including my buddy cum nemesis Alison Roberts with her cameraman. If this kept up I was going to make the national news pretty soon. There were probably already bloggers keeping track of the attempts on my life. Another fifteen minutes of fame. Happy day.

It was, in fact, early evening by the time I rid myself of law enforcement and media and found a big piece of heavy cardboard to cover the shattered pane. I figured that Veronica and I had twenty minutes at most before the local news broadcasts broke the story and my phone started ringing.

She was sitting sideways on the living room couch and I chose a nearby chair. I leaned toward her, bracing my elbows on my knees.

"How are you feeling?"

"Still a little shaky, but getting there."

"I'm really sorry you got caught in the middle of this."

"It's not the first time I've been around guns being fired."

"I know that. So...do you even want to bother right now with your original reason for coming over?"

She didn't even hesitate. "Yes, I want to bother."

Must be serious, I thought. I was really hoping it wasn't about Colleen again. "Okay."

"It's about Colleen."

"Veronica...."

She raised one hand, palm toward me. "Hear me out. She needs you right now. She's very confused about her mother and I'm afraid she's going to be badly hurt while you're focused on other things."

"Those other things are a dead client and her missing child, Veronica. I can't exactly neglect them. Besides, I told Colleen to stay away from Sarah for now."

"Well, she's not. She was at the café earlier today and I know for a fact that she was planning to go back to wherever her mother is staying. Do you blame her?"

Shit. Colleen, Colleen, we are going to have to have a serious talk of our own real soon.

"I will deal with that," I said, tight-lipped, "but I think we've talked enough for now."

She stood up. "You're probably right. I need to get back to the Pen and Pastry anyway." She stopped at the front door and looked back at me. "Take care of yourself."

"You too."

And she was gone.

CHAPTER SIXTY-FOUR

I don't know how long I sat there looking at that closed front door, trying to control my breathing and sort out the fury, sadness, frustration, and who knows what else that was swirling around my psyche.

I was finally roused by a couple of cats who'd emerged from under the bed apparently very hungry. They plopped down in front of me and began complaining. I looked at my watch. After six. "Past dinner time, isn't it, girls?" I said as I got up and headed for the kitchen. Stella and Maxine were waiting beside their bowls by the time I got to the doorway.

I got them fed, determined that I had no appetite myself, and was heading back to the living room for no particular reason when my cell phone rang. It was Alison Roberts.

"I didn't have a chance to tell you in the middle of all that chaos earlier. I've got something on a variation of those names you gave me," she said. "Not Crystal or Tanya Marie, but how about Tina Glass? She was in town at least once before, about a year ago."

"That could be. How did you find out?"

"One of my informants had an 'encounter' with Tina after they met at a bar. It must have been quite memorable. After all this time he could tell me the date and the place without hesitation. I think he could have given me a minute-by-minute narrative, but I passed on that. Anyway, both the last name and the description matched. He even remembered that she'd mentioned she was from Chicago. I don't think there's much doubt."

"I agree. You've definitely got something there. Any point in my talking to your informant?"

"No, I'm sure I got everything, except the sexual blow-by-blow, as it were. He wouldn't talk to a cop, public or private, anyway."

"Okay. Give me the exact date and place that they met."

The date was early March of the previous year and the place was a sleazy joint near the airport. It was all fitting. I thanked Alison, reassured her once more about that upcoming exclusive, and ended the connection.

So, I thought to myself as I settled on the couch that was still warm from Veronica, it appeared professional assassin Crystal Glass was here in Portland around the time that Carl Orkney AKA George Quiller got himself blown up. Gee, I wondered, could there possibly be some correlation there? Certainly worth consideration—most particularly about *why* she'd be killing Carl. Talking to Malone and me in the restaurant, James had implied they'd been together at least a year or so—and he specifically said Crystal had not been in Portland before. So either she'd lied to him or he'd lied to us. I was betting on the former. Maybe she'd concealed a little trip during which she killed his brother. If so, the *why* could give me a lot of other answers.

How the hell was I supposed to find out, though, unless I got the chance to ask her?

Stella and Maxine joined me on the couch for most of the rest of the evening. They slept pretty much the whole time. I kept intending to think constructively about how to find Crystal Glass and rescue Kinsey Quiller but for the most part I mulled over relationships past and present—Sarah, Veronica, Colleen, Devon Malone.... Whoops. How did that last one get in there?

Time to go to bed and seek some refreshing oblivion.

The cats woke up just long enough to join me in bed. I was so exhausted from thinking about things I didn't want to think about that I fell asleep almost as quickly as they did.

CHAPTER SIXTY-FIVE

I was dreaming. I was somewhere downtown. I knew it was downtown Portland even though I didn't recognize the buildings. I had to get somewhere and I didn't know the way, but I knew that I'd see something familiar if I could just turn the right corner. I couldn't get to the corner, though, because my legs wouldn't work. Not only wouldn't they work, they felt like they were being jabbed by needles.

Damn, those needles were really beginning to hurt—even though I was waking up. What the fuck?

Finally I came around enough to realize that it was the two cats, one on each leg, digging their claws into my bare flesh. What was this now? Attacked by my own pets in the middle of the night? These were the only relationships I thought I could still count on!

I sat up and was trying to push them aside when the faint smell of smoke registered in my nostrils. Uh oh.

The bedroom clock said 5:30 a.m. The odor was too faint for the source to be here in the bedroom with me, so I immediately checked the living room—already thinking that I'd better call 911 because if it was a smoldering wire in the wall or something like that I might not be able to find it anyway. Not until it was too late.

Then I checked the kitchen. There was no problem in the room itself but I could see a flickering glow through the back window and quickly discovered the back door was hot. The fire was on the back porch, already spreading to the outside kitchen wall.

I'd picked up my cell phone from the nightstand before beginning my reconnoiter. I punched 911 while trying to remember where I'd put the cat carrier after the last trip to the vet and hoping I would have time to find the cats after I found the carrier.

I told the dispatcher who I was, where I was, and why I needed the fire department. I did not stay on the phone after she told me to get out of the house immediately because I knew I'd need both hands—and probably my knees and maybe a blanket—to corral Stella and Maxine after I managed to track them down. I was very grateful that the fire and most of the smoke was outside—at least so far.

I didn't have a lot of time, however.

The carrier was in the hall closet. The cats were, thankfully, under the bed where I hoped they would be. Fortunately for all three of us, they were basically paralyzed with fright and didn't try to run when I wriggled under the bed far enough to reach them. I retrieved Maxine first and stuck her in the carrier, then Stella. They didn't even complain about the confinement as they usually did. The timing couldn't have been better; I was beginning to cough and sirens were coming down Hawthorne Street. I grabbed a jacket on the way out the front and was on my sidewalk as the first engine turned the corner.

I resisted the urge to run around back and see how bad it was already. Instead I got the hell out of the way as firemen spilled from the truck and began pulling hose.

The fire was out within minutes. It had burned through a small portion of the back porch and blackened most of the outside back wall, but there was no water damage inside and probably little smoke damage except to my nostrils.

It took only a few more minutes for the lieutenant in charge of the fire crew to tell me he was sure it was arson. I don't know why that surprised me. Maybe because I wasn't really awake yet. After all, there were no electrical wires on the back porch, no flammable material other than the porch itself. And, of course, people were trying to kill me. A fire, even one as inept as this, might have worked if the smoke had gotten to me before the cats did. I was going to have to buy them some special treats.

So who was the arsonist? Like the earlier attempted vehicular homicide, it didn't resonate with the methods of Crystal Glass. This would be the *other* person or persons attempting to kill me. Were the fuckers tag-teaming now?

Be that as it may, the possibility of arson of course meant the police were also called in as well as the arson investigator. It was a small fire, however, likely—as far as the authorities were concerned—no more than a prank. I was happy to let them think that because it reduced the police presence to two patrolmen and the "arson investigation" to about a half-hour.

CHAPTER SIXTY-SIX

I was back on my own by eight a.m. The smell of smoke pervaded the house but it wasn't overwhelming. I hoped that incense would take care of it over the course of a day or two. I set the cat carrier down in the middle of the living room and opened its door. Both cats immediately went back under the bed. Well, I was a little traumatized myself. In the last twelve hours somebody had shot at me in front of my house and set the back of my house on fire. Home was not feeling sweet home at the moment.

The only positive aspect was that the media paid no attention to minor fires, even when they'd been purposely set—and Alison Roberts turned off her police/fire monitor while she slept. Given that it had been about five thirty when the cats woke me up, I was probably safe there.

Cold outside or not, I was opening windows to air out the house when the phone rang. Damn. Maybe Alison got up earlier than I thought she did. But no, it was Colleen—who was up surprisingly early herself.

"Dad, you okay?"

"I'm fine, kiddo. You listen to the fire dispatch now?"

"What? No. Veronica called me a few minutes ago. Woke me up to tell me somebody took another shot at you. What about fire? Was there a fire too? What's going on?"

Me and my big mouth.

"Uh, just a little fire on the back porch. No big deal. And the bullet missed."

"Jeez. You want me to come over? You need to talk? Sounds like it hasn't been a really great twenty-four hours."

"It hasn't, no, but I'm okay. Are you calling me from home?"

"No, I stayed overnight at Patty's house."

That really pissed me off. "Colleen, I told you to give your mother and Patty a little space until we make sure they're safe, okay? You need to listen to me about these things."

"You know, actually I don't." Now *she* was beginning to sound pissed. "I'm legally an adult and I can decide for myself whether to spend time with my mother who's been missing for years and might have been dead. Besides, we saw Patty's husband outside the house just last night and he didn't do anything. Just glared at us, the idiot."

"He was outside the house?"

"Yeah."

"Frank Samuels was lurking outside the house at night and you don't think there's any danger?"

"He wasn't lurking; he was just standing there, across the street. Maybe he wanted to scare us, but he didn't do a very good job." Pause. "It was creepy, though."

Sigh. Some people just don't have a good sense of when they should be seriously frightened. "Would you go look to see if he's there now?"

"Dad."

"Humor me."

"Oh, okay." She put down the phone and returned after a minute or so. "Nobody across the street now. I think we're safe."

"I would still like you to go be in your own place for a while. Couldn't you humor me about that, too?"

"I'll think about it."

Which was better than nothing, I supposed. "Good. Keep a sharp eye out in the meantime."

"Okay, Dad. I don't know how we got off on all this when you're the one getting shot at and potentially burned up and who knows what else. How about *you* keep a sharp eye out?"

"I'll do that. Don't worry."

"Humph. Talk to you soon, anyway."

CHAPTER SIXTY-SEVEN

I put down the phone and looked at Stella and Maxine who had finally come out from under the bed yet again. "You don't need to worry, either," I told them. "I'll stick around for a while and make sure nobody else attacks the house. How about some breakfast?"

The cats liked the breakfast idea very much, though I found my own appetite to be rather stunted by recent events. I managed a little oatmeal, a dried apricot, and some coffee.

I couldn't really guarantee that no one else would attack the house, of course, not without catching whoever was trying to kill me before they caught me. (I wasn't going to admit that to the felines who clearly had taken my word for it and were now chasing each around the living room.) The real problem, of course, was that there appeared to be more than one killer. Catching a killer is tough enough; catching multiple killers who might or might not even be aware of one another was going to be a major challenge.

Not that that constituted my entire list of woes. I was exhausted and sleepy. I felt at least somewhat estranged from my daughter. My ex-wife was not only back in my life but apparently still in need of protection. And so far this morning it was hard to simply get moving around the house.

Almost three unproductive hours later, I had not gotten much further than contemplating how my career as a private investigator was not going as well as it might. Thankfully this latest preoccupation was interrupted by a knock on the front door.

Through the peephole I could see only Hap Harbaugh's massive face looming just outside. For that and a number of other reasons, I was astounded when I opened the door to see Johnny Crew standing there beside him.

"Johnny! What the hell are you doing here?"

My old mentor grimaced at me. "Well, fucking good day to you, too. You gonna ask us in?"

I stepped back. "Sure, sure, but I thought you were supposed to be resting and recovering."

"He bagged that idea as soon as he heard about you getting shot at again," Hap announced unhappily as he took his smaller partner's arm to help him across the threshold.

Johnny shook off the hand. "Don't need no fuckin' help," he muttered as he shambled straight for the couch.

"Right," I muttered right back as Hap and I rolled eyes at each other.

I registered that Hap was looking guilty as well as unhappy. "And how did our stubborn friend hear about me getting shot at again?" I inquired of the big fellow.

"Well, I heard it on the police band and mighta mentioned it to him—just in passing."

"Ah ha."

"I didn't think he'd do this! Don't be mad, Clint. Gerry already says she's gonna kill me."

"All we can do is try to control him now that he's out and about," I said.

"Hey!" yelled Johnny from the couch. "I'm sittin' right here and I ain't got no fuckin' problem with my ears."

Hap and I apologized, though I'm sure neither of us meant it, and I went to the kitchen to get them some coffee while the big man settled into the biggest chair he could find. I was in the kitchen pouring the second cup and wondering what to do with these two when my cell phone rang.

I dug it out of my pocket. "Clint McCall."

"Clint, this is Eleanor. You got a minute?"

Hallelujah, someone who apparently does not own a police and fire scanner. "Yeah, I'm still at the house. What's up?"

"You asked me to do some more checking on those two guys, Winters and Samuels?"

"Yeah."

"Well, I got a big bingo on Samuels. It wasn't easy to put together, but he's got a record going back to when he was twelve, across seven states, under more than twenty aliases."

"Shit."

"So far—and I'm not sure I'm done, mind you—I've come up with about two dozen assault charges and a couple of attempted murders. Only two convictions, on early assaults. Apparently he got very good at disappearing after he's been identified."

"Apparently he also has some severe impulse control issues. No wonder his wife was in such fear of him. Any previous wives, by the way?"

"One that I know of, in Ohio. She was the victim in attempted murder charge number two."

"Yikes."

She chuckled. "That was pretty much my reaction, too. Your friend isn't with him anymore, is she?"

"Not officially, but it sounds like he's still hanging around. I just talked to Colleen and she told me they'd seen Samuels across the street from Patty's house last night."

Very serious again. "Not good. Colleen's in the middle of this?"

"I'm trying to get her out of the middle but, yes, right now she is."

"Really not good."

"I know. Look, Eleanor, I really appreciate all the work you've done on this. Keep at it and let me know anything else you find out."

"It's not like I'm doing it for free, but thanks. I'll be in touch. Meanwhile take care of yourself—and your kid."

"Will do." We hung up.

I picked up the two cups of coffee and went back to the living room. I had an idea now about what to do with Johnny and Hap.

CHAPTER SIXTY-EIGHT

After the coffee and some conversation, they agreed to follow me to Patty Samuels house.

We were both able to park right in front, and of course I scanned the area for Frank Samuels as soon as I got out of the car. Not in sight. By the time the three of us reached the front door, Patty already had it open and was looking a little surprised, especially at Hap.

"I brought along some backup," I explained as she stepped aside to invite us in. "Colleen told me that Frank's been hanging around. This is Johnny Crew and Hap Harbaugh, two retired Portland police detectives who often help me out. Guys, this is Patty Samuels."

I surveyed the living room as they were exchanging hellos. "You remember my ex-wife, Sarah," I said, "and of course you know Colleen." Who is not very good at following her father's advice.

I'd already decided there was no point in telling Patty Samuels right then about her husband's criminal past. She already knew who he was, even without the details. Learning how thoroughly she'd been deceived and how much danger she had been in all along would only depress her at a time when she needed to be up and alert.

Thus the next half-hour was consumed by some initial small-talk, offers of coffee and tea, confirmation that Frank Samuels had been seen across the street last night but not today yet, and pronounced awkwardness between me and my daughter.

At one point I followed her into the kitchen when she excused herself for a coffee refill. She looked back at me standing in the doorway and opened her mouth a couple of times before getting any words out.

"I'm not going to apologize."

"I didn't expect you to."

"But you expect me to do what you tell me to do."

I sighed. "You're a grown woman, Colleen. I can only hope that you'll do what I think is best."

"Humph."

On the whole, this exchange did not lessen the awkwardness. We returned to the living room, where I finally convinced everyone concerned that it would be best if Johnny and Hap focused on protecting these three women rather than me.

I drove from Patty Samuels' house to the office with one eye on the rearview mirror, my mind seething with various distractions and dissatisfactions. Nothing of significance appeared in the mirror or the mind. Nobody shot at me, attempted to run me down, or threw a Molotov cocktail at me as I crossed the street from the parking lot to my building.

Having arrived safely in my office, I hung up my coat, started the coffeemaker, stashed my Smith and Wesson in the drawer and stood for a minute behind my desk looking out at the street. No threats in sight. No movement in any of the windows of the building across the way. I could be properly cautious and pull the shade but the day was dreary enough already. I needed what daylight I could get. Fuck 'em if they managed to get a good sniper's perch over there again.

CHAPTER SIXTY-NINE

I sat down at the desk and tried to concentrate. I had to find Crystal before she harmed me or the baby. (It would have been more noble to put the baby first, but no one is going to get rescued by a dead detective.)

I wished I could have talked to Samantha Quiller, or especially James Orkney, about my latest theory that Crystal might have been his brother's killer. What I really wished, of course, was that I'd been able to keep them both alive.

Time to force myself back onto a more productive train of thought.

What about the attacker behind door number two? I remained convinced that the attempted hit-and-run and the bumbling arson were not the work of Crystal Glass. She was more professional than that, though it had to be said—if all this speculation was correct—that her efforts were failing as well. There was an element of hurry or desperation in her attempts, if indeed they were hers. It didn't fit with her previous unblemished record of success and that was yet to be explained.

Actually, I was pretty sure I had my answer about who was lurking behind that second door: Frank Samuels. Apparently Brad Winters had taken my warning to heart, but good old Frank wasn't smart enough to go away. It was a good bet that he wasn't stalking only his ex-wife; no question he had reason to be extremely pissed at me as well. Plus, I estimated that his level of competence matched the two ineffectual attempts on my life. *Ipso facto*. Or, *ergo*. Or whatever the hell Latinate term applied.

Maybe with Hap and Johnny watching over the women, Frank would decide to give me another try. Now that I thought I knew who I was dealing with, I looked forward to it.

Still it was all, every bit of it, fucking speculation.

I called Eleanor Ivory and told her to see if she could find anything on a "Tina Glass." I left a voicemail for Devon Malone summarizing the newest info I'd gotten from Alison Roberts and asking her to do the same. I was tempted to add my theory about Crystal killing Orkney/Quiller but decided I'd wait to see if Malone put it together the same way.

Finally I went over to the Home Run for lunch, determined to think about absolutely nothing for an hour except enjoying my burger and fries while watching whatever sporting events were being broadcast.

An hour later I was safely back in the office after successfully emptying my mind of all but food and golf. (Televised golf is uniquely suited for mind-emptying. Golfer swings, ball flies through air, ball bounces and rolls on grass.... Time after time. That's it.)

I was just opening my drawer to retrieve the Smith and Wesson and go tackle the world again when there was quick knock on my door and it opened. In came Johnny Crew along with Colleen, Sarah and Patty.

This couldn't be good.

CHAPTER SEVENTY

Johnny looked like he was already worn out and the three women looked worried. They weren't holding him up but they all three looked like they wanted to. He came slowly, almost shuffling, across the room and lowered himself into one of my chairs. He grimaced and motioned back at the women now gathered behind his chair. "I brought the ladies downtown to get a restraining order on Samuels. They wanted to stop by. Don't ask me why."

I could make a good guess as to why, but I looked inquiringly at them all anyway. Nobody said anything. Johnny had settled in his chair with arms crossed; it didn't look like he was going to say anything more for a while.

"Were you able to get the restraining order?" I finally asked.

"Yes," Colleen answered.

"Do you think it will do any good?" Patty asked.

I reached back and pulled my window shade down. "It should," I answered. "It depends on how determined he is to bother you." Or do you harm, I thought but didn't say. It wouldn't hurt, I was thinking further, for somebody like me or Hap to punch the bastard's lights out on behalf of his wife.

I looked at them some more. "Where's Hap?"

Johnny dropped his arms. "He's tailing Samuels. The motherf...guy showed up again out front and then took off when Hap started after him. We'd already decided that one of us should stay on him this time—and that we'd get the restraining order."

"That all sounds good." I ran my eyes over the faces of the three women yet again. They were all looking uneasy, though only Sarah looked away from me. Colleen had probably told her all about my objections to their spending time together. "So, what can I do for you?" I asked the room in general.

238

My daughter finally bit the bullet. "Now that there's a restraining order, we don't think we need Johnny and Hap to protect us anymore." She gnawed on her lip for a second. "They're kind of cramping our style, actually."

All of which was bullshit and everyone in the room knew it. They desperately wanted to get Johnny off the hook before he collapsed on them. Meanwhile his arms were back firmly crossed against his chest. If his chin had jutted out any further it would have poked me in the eye.

"Fine with me," I said. Really it wasn't, but I understood how they felt and I had no idea how I could keep Hap on the job without mortally offending Johnny.

Johnny, of course, called it right away: "Bullshit."

"The clients determine the coverage. You know that."

"Bullshit."

"Johnny, I understand...."

He was leaning forward now, face mottled, hands trembling. I'd never seen my old friend look quite so old. "You understand fucking nothing! Hap and me started our agency after we left the department because we don't retire. We hired on with you after we closed our agency because we don't retire. *I* don't retire. You want to me to watch your back, you want me to watch out for these ladies? I can do that. You want me to sit home and rot? No fuckin' way!"

I was failing completely to come up with a good response when the phone rescued me. "Hold that thought," I said to Johnny and picked up the handset. "Clint McCall."

"Clint, it's Hap." Oh good. Maybe he could help talk some sense into his partner.

"Johnny and his three charges are here in my office," I said right away. "Maybe you could stop by and help us resolve a couple of issues."

239

"I'll be stoppin' by, all right—because Frank Samuels just parked downtown and is headed toward your office on foot."

CHAPTER SEVENTY-ONE

"Shit. Really? Where is he now?"

"A block east on Stark. I'm still in my car. Can't find a darn parking place. He's walkin' fast."

"Thanks, Hap. Keep him covered even if you have to block traffic."

"Okay."

I hung up. "Frank is on his way here," I announced as I pulled my holstered Smith and Wesson from the drawer and stood up.

Patty Samuels let out a little gasp and the other two women gripped her arms. Johnny started hauling himself up out of the chair as I came around the desk. I paused to put my hand on his shoulder and gently hold him down. "The ladies need you here."

He glared up at me. "They said just a fuckin' minute ago that they don't need me at all."

I glared right back. "I don't expect Samuels to get past me and Hap, but somebody has to be here in case he does. You know that."

He re-crossed his arms and looked away from me. "I don't know fuckin' anything anymore."

There wasn't much to say to that—not in the few seconds I had available right then. I briefly locked eyes with my daughter. "Take care of yourself," hers said to me. "Take care of Johnny," mine said to her. I left the women gathering around the old grump, clearly intending to take on the daunting task of cheering him up. My part would have to come later.

By the time I got down the stairs onto the sidewalk and looked to my right, Samuels was nearly at the corner. Hap must have found a parking spot or simply abandoned his car; he was lumbering along the other side of Stark about a block behind.

As Samuels stopped for the light he saw me turning toward him and did an abrupt about-face of his own. I don't know if he saw Hap or not but he quickly ducked between the two buildings beyond my parking lot. I started to run, hoping the light would turn in my favor and, remarkably, it did.

I pulled up just short of the opening into which he'd disappeared. It was too narrow to be an alley, but I knew from walking past it many times that it served little purpose beyond collecting windblown trash. There were probably doors to both buildings somewhere in there but they were almost certainly locked. If so, Samuels was in a dead end.

I waved to Hap to make sure he saw me and then peeked around the corner. There indeed was my quarry, standing at the far end against a blank wall, looking pissed. His hands were empty of weapons so I stepped into the clear.

"Maybe you don't know it yet," I said as I started toward him at an even pace, "but your wife just got a restraining order against you. That means you can't legally approach or contact her from now on."

"Fuck you." As articulate as ever.

"Not even if you buy me dinner first," I said, and stopped about five feet from him.

Apparently he wasn't prepared to stretch his vocabulary any further. *"Fuck you!"* he shouted as he pulled back his jacket and went for a pistol that was stuck in his waistband.

I didn't want to shoot the dumbass unless I absolutely had to. You're taught in any decent martial arts training that hand-to-hand techniques are not very smart against a gun. There's only one kick that might work and, if it doesn't, you're shot. However, this was a complete amateur we were talking about and one that wasn't too swift in any sense of the word.

So I left the Smith and Wesson in its holster and took one step forward. My right foot was coming up at the same time his right hand was. I got there first, solidly contacting the weapon before it was leveled and sending it bouncing off the granite wall to my left.

He howled with what sounded like a combination of pain, frustration, and fury as he threw himself at me and tried to punch me in the face. Again, the poor guy didn't make it. I caught his wrist and let his momentum carry him past me as I twisted his arm down and behind his back. The howl this time was all pain as I brought the arm up sharply and slammed him into the right-hand wall.

"You're breakin' my fuckin' arm!" he screamed.

I leaned in close to his ear and spoke softly. "Not yet. But we're going to have a little talk now and if I'm not happy about your participation in our chat I *will* break your fuckin' arm." I gave it a little extra pressure. "You understand me?"

"Yes! What the fuck do you mean, *chat*? What do you want?"

I stayed right there by his ear. "Did you try to run me down yesterday?"

"No! Fuck no! I don't know what you're talkin' about."

A little more pressure. "Remember what happens if I'm not happy." I glanced to my right and saw Hap literally filling the entrance to the alleyway. No one would be bothering us as long as he was there. I did a quick survey of the upper walls on either side. No windows. I had plenty of time and no witnesses besides my backup. So...a little *more* pressure. I could feel that the elbow joint was about to go.

So could Samuels, I guess. "Okay! Okay! I tried to run you down. Let me go!"

"And you set my back porch on fire last night, right?"

"Yeah, okay! I did that too! Let me go!"

I eased off a little. "I don't think so," I said. "I promised not to break your arm. I didn't promise to let you go. You just confessed to arson and attempted murder, dumbshit. Fortunately we're only seven blocks from police headquarters. It's an easy walk." I jerked him away from the wall and pointed him toward Hap. "We'll be there in no time."

I had Hap pick up Samuels' weapon for me and I dropped it in my jacket pocket, noting to my captive that that gave me *two* guns I could shoot him with if he tried to run. His right arm firmly in my grip, I escorted him in the direction of the Justice Center, leaving Hap to report the latest developments to Johnny, Patty, Sarah and Colleen.

Samuels offered no trouble along the way, though he did babble a lot about how illegal it was for me to bring him in this way and how he'd be out within a few minutes of getting a lawyer. I let him have his illusions.

Alas for Frank Samuels, "citizen's arrest" isn't something just made up by movie and TV writers. Private investigators would have a hell of a time some days if it weren't a genuine, legal option.

Oregon law, for instance, states clearly that I have the right to arrest anyone who commits a crime in my presence if I have probable cause to believe the arrested person committed the crime. Both the arson and the attempted murder were certainly committed in my presence and a confession is more than adequate for probable cause. As to whether said confession was coerced, I preferred to think of it as "encouraged." Besides, state statutes do permit a private citizen to use physical force when confronted by an armed aggressor.

Still, it took a while to get everything sorted out after we reached police headquarters. A citizen's arrest may be legal, but it isn't every day that a guy comes in carrying two guns and claiming he has a criminal in custody. It didn't help that the cop on duty at the front desk had somehow never heard of me.

To my relief, both Mike Whitehall and Devon Malone were in the building. Between the two of them, my bona fides were soon established, Samuels' gun taken into evidence, and his person taken off to one of the cells upstairs. Then I had to spend some time upstairs—different floor—giving a rather lengthy statement.

CHAPTER SEVENTY-TWO

It was late afternoon by the time I returned to my office. I hadn't had a chance to check in from the Justice Center and didn't know what Johnny and the others had been doing in the meantime or where they might have gone.

I was still a few feet away from my office door when I was pretty sure I had both answers: I smelled hot and fresh pizza from within.

And there they all were, gathered around my desk which was currently serving as a food counter. It looked like they'd gotten two large, which meant one for Hap and one for Johnny, Sarah, Patty, and Colleen. I found myself hoping that there was at least one piece left for me. I'd burned a lot of calories since lunch.

"The guys didn't think we should leave your office unlocked and unattended," Sarah explained as I came over to join them, "and we all got hungry. Hope you don't mind."

"That's fine," I said. What *I* hoped was that nobody had dripped pizza sauce on any of my electronics.

Of course everybody wanted to know what happened to Samuels. I managed to snag a fair-sized slice of pepperoni and a few additional crumbs of crust while I brought them up to date.

They were all relieved but Patty wasn't ready to relax yet. "You mean the police just took your word for it that Frank tried to run you down and burn your house?"

"Well, yes and no," I replied. "I'm a licensed P.I. with a good reputation, so they're certainly willing to take him into custody on my word, but they'll now do their own investigation. Given your husband's intelligence level, I have no doubt they'll find plenty of corroborating evidence."

She grimaced. "Don't call him my husband."

"Okay." Obviously she was planning to alter her marital status as quickly as possible.

I had to spend another half-hour reassuring her and all concerned that Frank would surely be staying in jail. Patty even insisted on talking to the detective in charge of the case, a guy named Lou Rizzo that I didn't know well, to get assurances from *him* that they believed me and were keeping her husband in custody while investigating further.

Finally I had everyone calm and feeling relatively secure, at which point the three women decided they'd go back to Patty's and have a drink or three. I exchanged a look with my daughter as they left, but we didn't say anything except "so long." I had no further reason to caution her about being around her mother and Patty, of course; I could only hope we'd soon be saying goodbye to the distance between us as well.

I suggested to Johnny and Hap that they come over to my house for a strategy session. We didn't really need one at this point, but I was thinking that if we got Johnny sufficiently tired Geraldine might be able to keep him in bed after Hap took him home.

Hap and Johnny followed me out to the Hawthorne District in Hap's car and pulled into the driveway behind me. First thing on exiting my Subaru, of course, I surveyed the street. No one on foot, no vehicles approaching, no apparent threat of any kind.

We headed for my front door and, for whatever reason, my karma to live longer I suppose, I lost my grip on my key ring as I reached the front step. I heard the first shot just as I leaned over; I felt splinters from the doorframe pepper the back of my neck.

I reached for my gun and started to twist sideways when I was slammed clear off my sidewalk by Hap. By the time I rolled and came up with my weapon out, he and Johnny were both returning fire at the upper story of the house across the street. We were sitting ducks and there was no place to run.

Well, there was one.

I heard Hap grunt and saw Johnny go down as I snapped off a single shot of my own and then charged toward the street. The only hope was to get to her before she killed all three of us.

.

CHAPTER SEVENTY-THREE

I got off one more shot in the general direction of the house's second floor as I sprinted across the street and up the front sidewalk. It was an older house, a little shabby, and the front door looked like it might be breakable.

I certainly hoped so, because I didn't plan to slow down.

There was only a single step up to a small, square concrete landing in front of the door, which at least gave me a straight shot at it. I led with my right shoulder, hoping against hope that the door would give way first. And also aware that you have to have a very strong neck to slam a door that hard and not bounce your skull off it.

It gave way, all right. In fact the impact blew it off both hinges as well as out of the locking mechanism. The door ended up flat on the floor in the middle of a small dark living room. Having a lot more momentum than the door, I tumbled head over heels and came up on my feet at the far end of the room—not even woozy.

I quickly took in my surroundings. The house was absolutely quiet now, no gunfire or any other noise. Off to my left a stairway led upward. The sole resident of the house, an old man I'd often seen out in his front yard but had never gotten to know, was slumped in a recliner to my right. His throat had been rather spectacularly cut.

I trod lightly up the stairs as quickly as caution would allow, alert to the slightest movement or sound above. The likeliest explanation for the sudden silence was that Crystal Glass—as I assumed —was waiting to ambush me.

Other than an occasional soft complaint from the steps under my feet, I heard no noise or motion. I reached the second floor without incident. The hallway was empty and still. I calculated that the door immediately to my right should open into the room from which the shooter had been firing. I stepped quickly across the hall-way, put my back against the wall, pushed off and kicked the door open. Cold winter air poured in through the wide open window. No one in sight. I checked behind the door through the crack, stepped through the doorway, and found the rest of the room to be empty as well.

Blood spattered the floor near the open window and several tiny drops led back toward where I was standing. One of us had scored a hit, though it didn't look very bad. Damn it.

I crossed the floor to look down at my front yard. Johnny still sprawled in the grass, Hap kneeling over him. As it seemed I had so often lately, I heard sirens approaching in the distance.

I couldn't worry about Johnny Crew quite yet, however, be-cause there were other rooms on this floor and the animal I hunted was hurt. I went back out into the hallway and saw more barely dis-cernible drops of blood.

I followed them down the hall to a doorway on the other side, then to a second open window providing access onto a back porch roof that sloped down toward the ground. I had a clear field of vi-sion beyond the edges of the roof. Wounded or not, the shooter was gone.

I holstered my gun and headed home. Now was the time to worry about Johnny.

CHAPTER SEVENTY-FOUR

In the time it took me to get back downstairs and out the door, two patrol cars had pulled up in front of my house. A paramedic van was coming around the corner as I trotted across the street. I told the first patrolman I encountered who I was and that there was a dead body in the house behind me. After a quick confirmation of my identity, he took off in that direction and I went over to where Hap was on his knees beside Johnny. I saw as I approached that the big man was holding a cloth of some kind against our friend's right calf. Then I noticed he was grinning down at him. Sheer astonishment brought me to a halt four or five feet from them.

"Hap?"

He looked up at me. "It's not bad," he said. "Caught him in the lower leg. Not much more than a graze."

Johnny reached up and punched him in the arm. "Well, it still hurts like a motherfucking son of a bitch, thank you very much!"

I was incredibly relieved to hear the strength of his voice.

Hap, who apparently hadn't even noticed he'd been punched, gently placed his free hand on Johnny's shoulder. "Take it easy there, buddy. It might not be bad, but you're still recovering from a stroke. You need to stay calm."

"You stay calm the next time you get fucking shot! And I did not have a whatever. I fucking dozed off!"

"How about you?" I asked the big man. "I thought it sounded like you were hit, too." Hap shook his head and looked up at me. "Nah, I'm okay." He must have grunted like that when he saw Johnny go down, I thought.

"Did you get the shooter?" he asked.

By that time the paramedics were out of their vehicle and at Johnny's side. Hap stepped away to join me in watching them work on him. There was no urgency in their motions or voices, so that was reassuring.

"No," I finally answered Hap. "I didn't get the shooter. She got out a back window before I made it to the second floor." The paramedics had wrapped the leg wound and were transferring Johnny to a stretcher. "She killed the old man who owned the house. Cut his throat. We'll get her, Hap. We'll get her for all this."

"A woman," he said very quietly. He too was focused on the paramedics. "A woman killed him," even more quietly. A second ambulance had pulled up in the meantime, along with several more patrol cars and an unmarked. "We never shot a woman, neither of us. Never did."

"One of us hit her," I said. "There was a blood trail."

He gave me a wry glance. "I hope it was Johnny." About that time two newly arrived paramedics, a man and a woman, were heading into the building across the street to confirm the death.

Johnny was still complaining as they carted him off to the hospital accompanied by Hap in the paramedic's van. There was nothing I wanted more to do than follow along myself, nothing I wanted less to do than deal with another few hours of police questioning, media attention, and concerned calls from family and friends; I had had way too much of all that lately.

CHAPTER SEVENTY-FIVE

It was well past six p.m. before I found myself alone inside my house. I called the hospital and learned that they'd already treated Johnny's wound but were not releasing him yet—no doubt because of his age and the fact that he'd so recently "dozed off."

My own condition was fairly critical. First I'd failed to protect Samantha Quiller and James Orkney. Now Johnny was wounded and the old man across the street, the neighbor I'd once waved at but never spoken to, was dead. Bet he didn't know he was waving back to the guy who was going to get him killed.

Morton Kinghoffer. That was his name, according to the cops. Sorry, Mort.

I was brought out of my funk by Maxine shoving her head against my right leg as Stella pressed against my left. They probably were wondering why I was just standing in the middle of the living room. I crouched down and put a gentle hand on each of them.

"I know, girls," I said. "I'm stuck here feeling sorry for myself when I should be doing something productive like getting you some dinner." I stood up. "And doing a hell of a lot more than that." We all headed for the kitchen.

Ten minutes later I was out front getting in my car. Needless to say, I covered the distance between my front door and the driver's side door in record time. No bullets flew. I started the engine and backed out into the street. There wasn't much I could do after seven in the evening besides be there for Johnny and Hap. I could at least do that.

Driving to the hospital, I focused on my breathing. I've known for a long time that one of the best ways to deal with worry, regret, fear, or any other kind of tension was to simply sit quietly and concentrate on your breathing in and out. It's what I try to do every morning; no harm doing it during the day as well.

I'd already wallowed more than enough in regret and guilt, and clearly I was in no shape to make creative new plans about how to get to Crystal Glass before she killed anybody else, especially me. I well knew that the only reason I was alive at this moment was because I'd dropped my keys; that kind of luck wasn't going to last. If she got another shot, I'd be dead.

And if I didn't get my act together, still more people might die.

I needed to see my friends, get some rest, eat something (which I'd failed to do when I fed the cats), restore my strength, collect my wits, and then deal with Crystal Glass. Meanwhile I would breathe.

The hospital parking lot, even this late in the evening, was almost full. The waiting room on Johnny's floor, on the other hand, contained only his wife Geraldine and my daughter Colleen.

I was extremely pleased to see that Gerry wasn't entirely alone and not surprised that it was Colleen keeping her company; her "Aunt Gerry" must have called her for comfort. (Johnny and Hap had been Colleen's "uncles" for many years.) I did find it sad that there was no one else. Back when my two old friends had been active Portland police detectives, the waiting room would have overflowed into the hall with uniformed and plainclothes cops waiting for word after a shooting like this, minor as it was. Too long ago, apparently, for anyone else to remember.

Colleen had been sitting with her arm around Geraldine's slumped shoulders. She jumped up and came over as soon as she saw me standing in the doorway.

"Dad! You okay?"

"I wasn't hit." We were both whispering. I'm not sure why except that everybody whispers in a hospital waiting room. "How's Johnny? And where's Hap?"

"Hap's down the hall in the bathroom. They say Uncle Johnny's pretty good, but they're running some tests to follow up on the stroke, I think."

256

I looked past her shoulder at Geraldine, who was leaning forward, elbows on knees and head cradled in her hands. She was wearing an old housedress and slippers. An overcoat was piled on the seat beside her opposite where Colleen had been sitting. She looked every day of her sixty-eight years and then some. "Gerry?"

Colleen glanced back and gave a little shrug. "About how you'd expect." She looked at me. "She was telling me that in all his years as a cop this is the first time he's been shot."

I put my hand on her arm. "I saw the wound. It really was minor. He'll be fine."

And she put her hand on mine. "I hope you're right."

Somehow, the intimacy of our two hands together suddenly brought into focus what a fool I'd been lately concerning my very grown-up daughter. She was doing her best to deal with the return of her mother. I knew that Sarah's disappearance had been one of the most important concerns of her life for the last four years. Now she must be dealing with mixed feelings of relief and betrayal —and I had been no help at all.

"He'll be fine," I said again. "We'll all be fine." I squeezed her hand and went to sit beside Geraldine. As soon as I put my own arm around her shoulders she lifted her head from her hands. "I know God is taking care of Johnny." Her voice was raspy.

I believed more in luck, myself, but.... "You can take comfort in that," I offered. "He wasn't hurt bad, as far as I could tell."

She nodded without really looking at me and repeated my daughter's words: "I hope you're right,"

Speaking of luck, Hap returned at that moment and told us he'd encountered Johnny's doctor in the hallway. The doctor had reaffirmed that the wound was minor, a through-and-through, and that Johnny would probably be released in a few hours.

Gerry clapped her hands and smiled. I was glad for her. God had come through for her. She didn't need to know my opinion of our culture's dominant mythical deity.

Then she sat back and gave a great sigh. "But this won't slow him down, will it? He should retire, really retire. He's an old man." She cocked an eye over at me.

I shrugged. "Hey, there's nothing I can do about it. And you'd better not let him hear you calling him old, either. I don't think he's noticed."

Her lips quirked but then firmed up again. "You could stop using him for jobs," she said.

That was too much for Hap, who'd been seated quietly in a chair nearby since returning. "Gerry, we need those jobs. It's a little extra money and it keeps the blood flowing, you know. It's why Johnny *isn't* old."

"Yeah, well," she said dryly, "I hope not to hear about any other blood flowing in the future."

"We'll all do our best," I reassured her.

I stayed with the three of them for maybe another half-hour. A couple of other people, relatives or friends of an accident victim, I gathered, joined us in the interim. It didn't sound like there was going to be any more news before Johnny was released, so I headed home to get some rest. I was hoping that tomorrow would be a very busy day.

CHAPTER SEVENTY-SIX

My cell phone rang as I crossed the parking lot to my car. I kept walking as I dug it out of my pocket and punched the "talk" button. Then stopped dead when I heard the voice.

"You're a lucky man, McCall."

I'd heard that voice on my phone before, the "mystery woman" who called most recently last Thursday to warn me off the Quiller investigation—a mystery no more, of course. I spun around quickly, looking in all directions, but I knew it was pointless. If she were nearby and had me in sight, I'd be dead already.

I didn't know why the hell Crystal Glass would be calling me at this point, but I'd take anything I could get. I stood very still in the dark, in the cold breeze flowing across the parking lot, as if moving might lose my contact with her. "So far so good," I said with what I thought was remarkable calm.

She actually chuckled. "Next time will be as far as you get. I guarantee it."

Which was enough talking about me. "You have Kinsey? How is she?" I asked.

"The baby's good. I'm going to call her Tanya. Fuck this Kinsey shit. Tanya's what Jimmy and I decided on and that's what I'll call her even after you fucked everything up. That's why you're gonna die. Because you fucked everything up." No laughter in that voice now.

"James told me he didn't know you were going to kill Samantha Quiller and take the baby."

"James told you. James *said*. Jimmy shouldn't have been talking to you at all! Of course he didn't know." Her voice was going up half a register with every sentence. "It was supposed to be a surprise! Instead you made me *kill him*."

"I made...."

"You *fuck*! You fucker! This was going to be *our* baby, the baby we always talked about. Now I'm gonna be a fucking single mother because of you!"

Okay, we had moved entirely into crazy country now. And this woman had an infant in her care. I had to keep her on the phone until I got some kind of break. The one nice thing about complete nutcases is that they often make mistakes.

"Why Kinsey?...sorry, I meant to say Tanya. There are a lot of babies out there that need homes."

"Because it was Jimmy's baby, you stupid fuck! You think his pansy-ass brother could have made a kid? I know it was Jimmy's and there was no way that bitch should keep it. Jimmy is mine and his baby should be mine." There was a long pause as her breath sounded as if it caught in her throat. "He *was* mine. It's your fault, you motherfucker." There was another sound during that pause besides her breathing. A train whistle. Very close-by wherever she was. I looked at my watch. Ten twenty-two. Maybe her mistake was simply in making the call.

"How are you feeling?" I asked. "I saw blood up in that room. You were hit."

"I'm about to get fixed up, you shit. I'm a lot better off than those two old fucks you were with. How are *they*, huh?"

Hmmm. Present-tense. About to get fixed up right now. With any luck, I had enough to move on. "They're better off than you're going to be," I said and disconnected the phone.

Keep her angry and not thinking straight—though that latter didn't sound like it would be a problem. I trotted toward my car as I punched in another number on my phone.

Forget tomorrow. Tonight was going to be very busy.

CHAPTER SEVENTY-SEVEN

Devon Malone had given me all her contact information when we had lunch, including her home phone for emergencies. I figured this qualified—and I hoped she wasn't in bed asleep already as I opened my driver's side door, listening to her phone ringing. I needed her to be in a cooperative mood.

"Malone." She certainly sounded wide awake, if somewhat irritated.

I started the car. "This is Clint McCall. I think I have a good lead on finding Crystal Glass. Could you meet me down at the Justice Center?"

She was silent for a long moment as I pulled out of the hospital parking lot and headed for the freeway, the quickest way to get downtown. "It had better be really good," she said finally. "Twenty minutes." She hung up. A woman of few words at this time of evening.

I would be there in less than ten, so that was fine—even though she hadn't inquired.

It struck me as I entered the stream of traffic on the freeway that this was probably the first time I'd ever called a cop other than my old friend Mike Whitehall to back me up like this. Lots of changes.

In turn, that thought for some reason suddenly reminded me of how much of my fifty-six-year-old body was in pain. Bursting through Mort Kinghoffer's door earlier today had done nothing good for the bullet wound in my left shoulder even though I had hit right-shoulder-first. It seemed that everything else was nearly as sore. Johnny and Hap weren't the only ones not getting any younger.

I took the Fourth Street exit and immediately hit a red light, finding myself sitting alone in the dark at the intersection. No other cars waiting, no cross traffic, a rare occasion even for eleven o'clock at night in this part of Portland. I felt the same unease I had experienced when I stopped in the middle of the dark hospital parking lot. There was no way to avoid moments of vulnerability, though, no guarantees of safety, not with a professional killer on my case. Not even when said killer was stark raving nuts.

All I could depend on was a certain amount of luck to avoid inadvertent exposure and a steady, deadly anger to power me through the confrontation I intended.

I had no trouble finding a parking space near the entrance to the Police Department and was in the lobby chatting with the officer on duty when Malone swept in through the door.

"Upstairs," she said as she blew past me toward the elevator. I followed along, hoping that she did indeed find my new lead to be good.

The elevator doors closed and she punched the button for what I assumed was her floor, then stepped back even with me, eyes on the doors. "I heard there was another shooting at your place."

"Yeah. I didn't think lightning would strike twice. It put a friend of mine in the hospital, back in the hospital actually, and I feel like shit about it. Johnny Crew."

"Ex-cop, right? He and his partner Hap Harbaugh?" It sounded like she'd been following the story pretty closely.

"Long time ago. They set up their own agency after they retired from the force and I apprenticed with them to get my license. Then they decided they were too old to sustain an agency of their own and I started using them as backup."

She glanced over at me. "You think it was your fault Crew got shot?"

264

I thought about Colleen. Veronica. Johnny and Hap weren't the only ones whose lives had been threatened by my work. "There are times that it's very dangerous to be in my vicinity," I said finally.

She gave a soft little snort as the elevator stopped and the doors opened. "I'll be sure to keep my distance then."

"Probably smart," I said as we exited.

She stopped and punched me in the arm. Hard. I managed not to wince as the vibration hit my wounded shoulder. "Lighten up," she said. "I'm just kidding. Everybody in law enforcement, public or private, has to deal with it. The people who care about you make their own choices."

I thought about Sarah. "True enough."

CHAPTER SEVENTY-EIGHT

The Missing Person's squad was on the same large, brightly lit floor as the robbery homicide division. It looked like any small corporate headquarters: fairly roomy cubicles spread around a large open space with floor-to-ceiling plate glass windows looking out over the city. However, the corner to which Devon Malone led me was on the other side of the building from Mike Whitehall's office. (Lieutenants and above rate an office; everyone else gets a cubicle.) I could hear at least one person who sounded like he was on the phone in Robbery Homicide and there were probably one or two more over there. Missing Persons, on the other hand, apparently didn't run a night shift.

Malone's space, I noticed, was one of the least personalized—maybe because she was relatively new to the force. Or maybe it was just her personality. There was a desk, a couple of chairs, pedestal coat rack in the corner. The desktop was bare except for a stack file, inbox, telephone set and the obligatory flat-screen monitor plus keyboard and mouse. No photos, no artwork of any kind, not even any stray files or papers. The one individual note was the swivel chair behind the desk; it was one of those weird ergonomic constructions that look like they'd be impossible to sit on. I wondered if she'd purchased it herself. Those things were expensive and I doubted the department would have put up the money.

We hung our jackets on the metal rack and I took one of the lightly upholstered visitor chairs while she settled onto her seating device. She swung a little from side to side and leaned back. She seemed comfortable enough.

"So," she said. "What's the lead?"

"Crystal Glass called me this evening, just a few minutes before I called you."

"Yeah? She tell you where she was?"

"No, it was mostly to taunt me, I guess—but she did say her injuries were 'being worked on' right then. I heard a train whistle that sounded like it was practically on top of her location. The time was ten twenty-two. Can you get access to a schedule of when trains were coming through town this evening?"

She sat forward with a slight frown and reached for her phone. "I don't know. I doubt that there's just one schedule." She pulled up and looked at her watch instead. "Shit. It's pushing midnight. Who...." She seemed to zone out for a few seconds, then picked up the phone. She gave me a look before bringing the handset to her ear. "Why don't you take a walk and let me see what I can do."

I looked around the big room. "Walk where?"

"Go see if your friend Whitehall is in."

"It's the middle of the night. He's on the day shift."

She held the phone steady and kept looking at me. "Sometimes you aren't too quick. I'm not making this call until you're on the other side of the room. Is that clear enough?"

"Oh, well," I said a little grumpily as I got up. "You could have just said so."

"Pardon my subtlety."

"Who the hell are you calling that I can't listen to your end of the conversation?"

"Somebody who owes me a favor. If he's willing and able to help out, I'll fill you in when I'm done." She motioned me off with her free hand. "Now take a hike."

I took a hike. It turned out I knew one of the night-shift rob- bery homicide detectives slightly and I stood at his cubicle chatting for a couple of minutes while I watched Devon Malone on the phone across the room. Whoever she was talking to seemed to re- quire a lot of gesturing. Finally she hung up and waved me back to her desk. I wished my acquaintance a quiet night and headed for the opposite corner.

"Any luck?" I asked as I re-took my visitor's chair.

She shrugged, a slightly sour expression on her face. "Maybe. My friend works for the National Transportation Safety Board and thinks he can access the local train schedules from his office computer. He's heading over there now."

I glanced at my watch. "At ten after midnight? Must be a really good friend."

Another shrug as she sat back in her chair and looked away. "Used to be."

"Ah ha."

She gave me a glare. "He wouldn't have to be *that* good a friend. Here I am in *my* office at ten after midnight and I don't even like you very much."

"Really? I'm hurt."

"Yeah, well, I got tissues somewhere in the desk here if you feel like having a good cry."

"Thanks, but I think I can cope."

She sat forward. "So you think crazy killer woman called you this evening just to give you a hard time? And what else did she say?"

"Let's see. She said the baby's okay and named Tanya now, it's my fault she had to kill her boyfriend who she believes is the baby's father, and I'm going to die. That about sums it up."

"In other words, she's fucking crazy. Which we already knew."

"And explains why a supposed professional is screwing up in so many ways."

CHAPTER SEVENTY-NINE

Malone put her elbows on the desk, rested her chin in her hands, and looked thoughtful. "That's true, isn't it? Everything we have on this woman says she's a top-flight pro and that's not what we're seeing here."

"Not exactly, no. The shooter who never misses keeps missing. When she ambushed me in the apartment, she actually said something to let me know she was there before she fired. And now she maybe gives her location away—we can hope—by calling me up just to rant about the injustice of her situation."

I got an appraising look. "So far you're a very lucky guy, Mc-Call."

"That's just what she said."

"But I bet she wasn't as happy about it."

I had to grin. "My continued existence makes you happy?"

The look turned sour again. "I'm happy to avoid paperwork whenever I can." She dropped her hands to the desk edge and actually pushed her chair a little further away from me. "On a more serious note," she said, "we've still got a baby out there being cared for by a homicidal maniac."

That wiped the grin off my face, bringing back images of Johnny in the hospital and Kinsey Quiller the last time I'd seen her. My momentary good spirits were once again subsumed by simmering rage. "If Crystal Glass hurts that baby, I'm going to kill her," I said grimly—surprising even myself.

Malone's eyebrows went up as well. "Gee, I suppose you're aware that threatening to murder someone is itself a crime. And voicing said threat to an officer of the Portland PD is so stupid that it *ought* to be a crime."

I got myself under control. "You're right. Forget I said anything about it."

"Okay—but if you do end up killing her she'd better be trying to kill you at the same time."

I shrugged. "Well, given her track record so far, that shouldn't be a problem."

She looked like she wanted to say something more but her phone rang at that moment. She looked at the caller ID. "There's my guy."

"That was quick."

"He lives near his office," she replied as she picked up the handset.

I gathered from the ensuing conversation and the extensive notes taken by Malone that her contact was successful. She verified as much when she hung up.

"As far as my friend can tell, there were three trains passing through Portland and vicinity at ten twenty-two. There were others on the tracks but they shouldn't have been moving—and therefore wouldn't have been blowing their whistles—at that time." She opened a desk drawer and pulled out a Portland area map. "Let's see...." she muttered as she spread it open on her desktop. I came around to look over her shoulder.

She scanned the map and put her finger on a spot south of downtown, across from Ross Island in the Willamette River. "One location was here," she said. "That's an industrial area." She consulted her notes and the finger moved north to a spot near where Interstate 405 crossed the river. "Industrial," she said again. "And the third..." The finger swung way off to the northwest. "...was out here by the airport, where Lombard Street parallels the Union Pacific line. More of a commercial area."

"It could be any one of those three," I said.

She sat back and looked up at me. "We'll just have to check out all three. Not that I have a good clue what we'll be looking for."

I got a sudden inspiration—that immediately led to a sinking feeling. "I have an idea," I announced a little hesitantly.

272

"That's good. It's one more than I have. What is it?"

"I'm guessing that Crystal didn't go to a hospital, a clinic, or even a reputable doctor—any of whom would feel obligated to report a gunshot wound to you guys. If there's a medic in one of those areas who's in the business of treating wounds without reporting them, I know somebody who could probably point us in the right direction."

"Not one of your more respectable friends, I gather, but somebody you can roust out of bed?"

"Not respectable, no—and not in bed this time of night. We'll have to meet him out on the streets."

"Ah ha." She stood up as I moved back around in front of the desk. "You have his number? Let's go then."

We grabbed our jackets and headed for the elevator as I punched Reuben Keys' number into my cell phone. This was going to be an interesting meeting.

CHAPTER EIGHTY

To describe Reuben as less than thrilled at the idea of meeting a police detective right in the middle of his illegal nocturnal activities would be a massive understatement.

"You out of your fuckin' mind!" was his actual response.

"She's with missing persons, Reuben. She's not going to care about what you're doing." I hoped. "We need your help. There's a baby out there that needs your help."

After a brief pause of heavy breathing: "You better be right about this bitch cop. Meet me at 12th and Ankeny. And don't keep me waitin'."

"Thanks. We'll be just a few minutes. We're leaving the Justice Center now."

"Yeah, that fills me with fuckin' good feelings right there." He broke the connection.

Out of the corner of my eye I'd been watching Malone listen to my end of the conversation. I'd seen no reaction and decided it was better not to ask if she agreed with me that she wouldn't care about Reuben's business. Even if she was willing to let it go, she probably wouldn't want to say so out loud. And, what the hell, I was happy to take my chances with Reuben's potential incarceration.

Neither of us spoke as the elevator doors opened and we walked quickly through the lobby area to the main door. Out on the sidewalk there was an awkward moment as I started to turn left while she started to the right. We stopped and looked at one another.

"My car's this way," she said.

"Reuben's going to feel better if we show up in my car," I replied, "which is this way."

"And I'm supposed to care whether your pimp friend feels good?"

"No, but you're supposed to care whether he feels like coming up with the information we need."

She stood there for another couple of seconds. I would have sworn she was literally vibrating with the desire to have it her way. Then there was an infinitesimal relaxation of her shoulders and she stepped in my direction. "Okay," she said brusquely, "your car. Let's go."

"You won't regret this," I offered.

"Too late."

I could tell that this was going to be a really fun get-together. Ten minutes later, as Devon Malone and Reuben Keys stood practically toe to toe glowering at each other on the corner of 12th and Ankeny, I was sure of it.

The physical contrast between them was almost as extreme as their mutual hostility. Malone with her short brunette hair and trim athletic body stands maybe five six in her boots. Reuben is no taller than me but he's built heavier and seemed to loom much larger. The contrast of his deeply scarred coal-black skin against his brightly colored outfit only added to the intimidation factor.

I was explaining what we needed while Devon tried to show him the map—which he had promptly crumpled against her chest. He wasn't going to help a cop he didn't know, at least not before displaying some testosterone, and she wasn't going to take any shit from a pimp, especially one this big and mean-looking.

I stepped in and put a hand on Malone's shoulder before she drew on him. She shook the hand off even as I spoke. "Okay guys," I said urgently, "let's forget the pissing contest and remember the baby. Malone, stand down. Reuben, take a look at the damn map."

They glared at each other for another moment, then at me. Reuben grudgingly reached out and took the map that Malone reluctantly handed over.

He spread it out on the hood of my Subaru and looked at it. "What am I supposed to tell you?" he asked grumpily.

I pointed to the three spots that Malone had highlighted back at the Justice Center. "We're looking for a doc or a medic that fixes up bullet wounds without reporting them. You know anybody like that in any one of these three locations?"

He leaned over the map and took his time scrutinizing it. Finally he placed a finger on the Lombard Street location near the airport. "There's a guy there," he said. "Name's Needles, I think; that's what they call him, anyway, 'cause he mostly gives people shots. But I've heard he can dig out a bullet if he wants to."

"That's good," I said. "Got an address?"

"Fuck no, I don't have no address. It's a bicycle shop, that's what I heard, near that corner there, Lombard and 47th."

"A bicycle shop?" That was Malone, sounding more than a little skeptical.

Reuben never looked at her. "That's what I hear," he said to me as he shrugged slightly. "Maybe he don't give enough shots to get by."

Malone gathered up the map and I thanked Reuben. We got back into the Outback and headed for the airport. I saw out of the corner of my eye that Malone was checking her watch and I looked at the clock on my dashboard. Quarter to one.

"The bicycle shop won't be open," I said, "but if we're lucky the clinic will be."

"I get that," she responded. "I was just wondering if I'm going to get any sleep tonight."

"Sleep will probably take more luck than we've got."

CHAPTER EIGHTY-ONE

Her only response was another one of her grumpy sounds. That was pretty much it for conversation until we approached the corner of Lombard and 47th. It was a "commercial" neighborhood only by a stretch of the imagination. We were passing what looked like an auto junkyard on our left and fenced off, untended land to our right. I stopped at the deserted intersection and we looked both ways. Unfortunately, there were no streetlights. Nothing much to see but industrial fences and a few shadowy buildings.

"Let's go left," I said at precisely the same moment Malone said, "Let's check to the right." We looked at each other. "We're using your car," she said. "So I win this time." We went right.

And there, about fifty yards down the street, was a shabby little building tucked in next to a storage facility. "Bike Shop," announced the peeling sign above the dirty front windows. I pulled to the curb, shut off the engine, and we sat there giving it the once-over.

"No lights in the front," Malone pointed out, "but I see a glow coming from the back."

"Could be a security light back there," I said.

"Or the clinic."

"Might as well go find out."

We climbed out, eased the car doors shut, and approached the building with guns drawn. The rumble of traffic on a near-by overpass covered any noise we might have made on the gravel under our feet. Unfortunately, it also masked any sounds that might have been coming from inside the shop. We made our way slowly along the side of the building. I was a little surprised that Malone let me go first.

There was a security light, dim, almost burnt-out, on the back of the building—but there was also light streaming from the steel-mesh-covered windows. The windows were about a foot over my head, so it was impossible to see inside.

We crept around the corner. There was a door in the back. I could see as I got closer that it was ajar. I motioned behind me for Malone to stop, then leaned back to whisper in her ear. "Door's open. You want high or low?"

"Low and left."

"You got it." We moved to the door and set ourselves. I kicked it open and went in fast, sweeping my weapon from center to the right as Malone came in behind me at a crouch, sweeping to the left.

There was no reaction to our entry, no one in sight. The room was small and brightly lit, the only furnishing a six-by-three table in the center. It was draped in blood-stained white cloth. The two side walls were covered by shelves that held a meager cache of medical supplies. The door in the back wall that apparently led to the bike shop was tightly closed.

I could smell the blood, antiseptic...and cordite.

Malone must have smelled it too. "Somebody fired a gun in here," she said as she stepped up beside me.

I pointed at the table with my Smith and Wesson. The way the cloth was hanging, there could still be someone hunkered down be-hind it—if they were small enough. A petite female assassin, say. Just then I heard what sounded like a faint groan from that direction. Again Malone went left and I went right.

Behind the table we found not an assassin but another victim. He was a small, almost wizened man twisted into a fetal position on the floor in the middle of a blood pool. The very faint groans were coming from him, so he was still alive. I crouched down to check his vitals while Malone pulled out her cell phone. She called 911 while I determined that his pulse was very faint. His breath was coming in short, faint gasps. I'd seen this too many times; he was going to be dead any minute and there was nothing I could do.

"Tell them to hurry," I said.

"Like that would make a difference," she muttered. "They haven't even answered yet."

Just then they apparently did because she began reeling off our location and the situation. Meanwhile I leaned in close to the old man's face because he seemed to be trying to say something. There might be time to get some information.

"Bitch shot me," he whispered.

Which was not exactly news. "The medics are on the way," I whispered back as hopefully as I could. "The woman who shot you, did she say anything that could help us catch her?"

"It hurts."

From what I could see of his body, it looked like he had two entry wounds in his stomach and at least one exit in his back. I believed him.

"I know. Hang in there. You don't want her to get away with this, do you? Tell me if she said anything."

He took a couple of stronger, ragged breaths, as if thinking it over. "She made a call," he said.

That was something, maybe, unless he was talking about the call she made to me. I could only hope. "Any indication who she was calling?"

"Somebody catatonic."

Well, that wasn't me. "What?"

"She said somebody was catatonic." More ragged breaths. "I think that's what she said. Oh, shit. Doesn't make sense, does it? Maybe something else, something that sounded like.... Fuck, I don't know. Oh, shit...."

Then there were no more breaths, ragged or otherwise.

Malone joined me at his side as I sat back on my heels.

"Dead?"

"Dead."

"He say anything?"

"He said she called somebody who was catatonic—or somebody told her somebody *else* was catatonic or…. Crap, I don't think he had any idea what he was talking about."

"Damn. I hope the baby hasn't gone catatonic."

That put a shiver down my spine as I got to my feet. "There's a cheery thought," I said.

"Anything else?"

"He said it hurt."

She looked down at his twisted, huddled body and let out a long breath through pursed lips. "I imagine so."

CHAPTER EIGHTY-TWO

I finally got home around 4:30 in the morning. I gave the cats a snack to assuage their resentment at being left alone most of the night and then fell into bed. Even with plenty of adrenaline left from the police interviews and all the other activity at the latest crime scene, I fell asleep immediately. My plan was to sleep late. Very late.

So of course the phone woke me up at seven. It was Malone.

"Do you ever sleep?" I muttered plaintively.

"Hey, you rousted me out of bed just last night. Turnabout is very satisfying."

"Glad you're enjoying it," I yawned.

"I was thinking: What are the odds that the baby or anybody else Crystal Glass knows is catatonic?"

I took a moment to get my groggy brain in gear. "Well, not very good. The old man probably misheard her."

"Right. So...what if it's a name? The name of the person she was talking to or maybe the name of a place."

"A name that sounds like 'catatonic'?"

"Why not? Why don't you give your pimp buddy a call and see if he knows of any street names like that?"

I squinted at my bedside clock. 7:08 a.m.

"He probably just got to bed a couple of hours ago. Reuben's not very cooperative when you wake him up."

"I think it's worth a try. It's all we've got right now. Tell him if he cooperates I won't arrest his ass for what he was doing last night."

"I already told him that. You heard me. You're missing persons. He's vice."

"I heard you, but I didn't agree to it. Look, probably half his girls are missing persons in some jurisdiction or another. I'll bet I could close a dozen cases just by rounding them all up."

"He doesn't even run that many girls."

"Whatever. You take my point—and you'd better see that your friend takes it." She hung up.

"He's not...," I said to the dial tone. "Well, I guess he is my friend, now that you mention it," I muttered as I put the handset back in its cradle.

I made myself some coffee and fed the cats before facing the wrath of a rudely awakened Reuben Keys.

He apparently fumbled the phone, dropped it, picked it up, and greeted me exactly as I'd anticipated: "What the fuck?"

"It's McCall. I've got another question...."

"What the fuck time is it?"

"It's seven sixteen." I started to talk fast. "Don't hang up! I've got just one question and Malone is threatening to go after you if you don't cooperate."

"Like I give a shit if that skinny bitch...." Whatever else he had to say degenerated into incomprehensible muttering. But he didn't hang up. Finally: "So what the fuck is the fucking question?"

"Do you know anybody or any place with a name that sounds like 'catatonic'?"

There was a long pause, then: "What the fuck?" Which brought us back around to the beginning.

"You heard me. Catatonic. Think about it."

Another long pause. "Fuck, I don't know. There was this white guy named Clyde had a girl named somethin' like that. Callatonic, maybe? Callaphonic? Yeah, that was it: Callaphonic."

"Clyde? Callaphonic? Are you putting me on?"

"No, man. He called himself Clyde. She called herself Callaphonic. I don't have a fuckin' clue what it means."

"Okay. Where do I find Clyde?"

284

"Shit, how am I supposed to know? He said his last name was Gorman, I think. That's what he said. Clyde Gorman. He was running just a few girls out toward the end of Sandy. I don't even know if he's still in business. He was new, you know, a young guy—and fuckin' white. Ask one of your cop friends."

"I'll do that, thanks. Have a nice sleep."

"Fuck you." He hung up.

I started to punch in Malone's work number, hoping she had called me from the Justice Center. I didn't have much faith in the existence of Clyde or Callaphonic, either one, but it was all we had right now.

CHAPTER EIGHTY-THREE

Malone was in the office and, amazingly, found them both in the database.

"Young Mr. Gorman is currently in the slammer," she told me as I heard her keystrokes in the background. "And...the lady named Callaphonic, real name Serena Rae Knowles, is currently not—though she has been our guest a number of times. I get an address on Burnside."

"Want to meet me there?" I asked.

"You know I do have a life outside of your case, McCall."

"Anything more important than a murdered mother and missing baby?"

Sigh. "I'll see you there." She read off the address and hung up.

I hurriedly dressed, petted Stella and Maxine goodbye, then slowed down enough to survey the street and the houses on the opposite side before trotting out to my vehicle.

The address on Burnside was a shabby two-story apartment building with a yard that had given up long before this winter started. I think the building might originally have been some kind of beige but in the early morning February gloom it looked like it simply had jaundice.

Malone pulled up behind me two minutes later and we both got out of our vehicles.

"It should be on the first floor in back," she said as she joined me at the head of the cracked walkway that led to the front door and then around the side. We followed the concrete trail and found it went from cracked to crumbling by the time we'd gotten around the corner. Then nothing but a little gravel sprinkled over mud in front of the back entrance, a dark-painted wooden door with no nameplate, no doorbell. One small window to the left of the door showed the interior to be dark. I stepped up and rapped loudly on the peeling brown paint.

No response. I tried again. We waited. I banged with my fist. After another moment a light came on inside and I heard what sounded like shuffling on the other side of the door. Then a voice —groggy, raspy, but definitely female.

"Who is it?"

Malone stepped up by my shoulder. "Portland police," she announced. "We need to talk to you."

Much more effective than "Hi, I'm a private detective who needs information." We heard two locks turn, a chain drop, and then the door opened a couple of inches.

A young black woman cautiously peered out at us.

Malone remained in charge. "Serena Rae Knowles?"

"Yeah."

"Can we come in?"

After a pause, the door opened more widely. "I guess."

She was tall, thin, almost cadaverous, with unnaturally red hair done up in cornrows. She was wearing a thin blue bathrobe with apparently not much under it. Her eyes glistened even in the diffuse February daylight. I wondered as I followed Malone through the doorway how long it would be before Serena Rae Knowles overdosed. My bet? No more than a month.

The lighting in the small apartment was even duller than that outside, though not dim enough to conceal the grime and disarray. It looked like one room and a bath. A quick glance around revealed a ratty two-person sofa, a straight-back wooden chair sitting beside a card table in the corner, a small fridge next to a counter that held a hot plate, an unmade single bed on the other side of the room, and many of her possessions simply spread across the floor. No closet or chest of drawers. The door to the tiny john was wide open.

Certainly there was no baby, catatonic or otherwise—though I noticed one side of the sofa was padded with blankets like a small nest.

The young woman didn't invite us to sit down. She simply turned to face us when we all reached the middle of the room. "What do you want?"

"Your street name is Callaphonic?" Malone again.

"Yeah."

I couldn't help myself. "Where did the name come from?"

She shrugged and almost smiled. "It's weird, ain't it? I remembered it from some old mechanical magazine my daddy had when I was little. I always thought it was a cool word, so that's what I called myself."

"What's it mean?"

"I don't know. It just sounds cool."

Malone must have figured that I'd lowered the woman's guard far enough and pointed to the sofa, obviously having also noticed the pile of blankets. "Is that where you kept the baby?"

That wiped away the almost-smile. "What baby?"

"The baby you were taking care of for Crystal Glass."

Serena Rae—I really couldn't bring myself to think of her as Callaphonic, especially since I didn't know what the hell it meant—began to wring her long thin hands together.

"I ain't got no baby."

Malone took a big step forward and went nose to nose with her. "You don't have a baby *now*, but you were taking care of one for Crystal. No use lying to us. We know. Now we need you to tell us when she picked up the baby and where she went with it. Otherwise I arrest you on kidnapping charges and you probably get turned over to the FBI. You want to disappear into a federal prison somewhere, girl? You want to do that? Not much fun in there for a skanky black whore, I bet."

The young woman jerked back. "Hey! Who you callin' skanky?"

Malone took another step to maintain her distance. "The baby, Miss Knowles. Now."

I think being called "Miss Knowles" surprised her even more than "skanky" offended her. Her eyes went wide, she took another step back, and almost laughed. The detective sergeant was doing an excellent job of jerking her around.

"I.... It ain't against the law to babysit."

At which point Malone did smile, letting the younger woman have her space. "That's quite true. Unless you happen to be babysitting for a kidnapper. Let's just say you were babysitting for a friend. You didn't know your friend had kidnapped the baby. Let's just say that you can tell me where your friend went with the damned kid. Let's just say that otherwise your ass is mine."

Back to the hand-wringing. "I didn't! I didn't know. She said it was hers. How was I supposed to know? All I had to do was take care of the kid for a couple of hours. She paid me a hundred bucks! She was here maybe forty-five minutes ago, an hour maybe. I don't know where she took the kid. How would I know that?"

"Was the baby all right?" I asked.

"Sure. Sure the baby was all right. I took good care of it. Gave it the bottle and everything."

I felt relief wash through my system and could see that Malone relaxed slightly as well.

"Why don't we all sit down," I suggested, "and take our time talking about this?" If this woman had a clue—literally speaking—it was going to take us a while to drag it out of her. Might as well be comfortable while we were working on it.

Serena Rae sat on the sofa, on the blanket nest, with Malone next to her. I pulled over the chair so that I was knee-to-knee with her. We commenced to talk.

It took ninety minutes. Our young friend finally got impatient and distracted enough to inadvertently use the pronoun "they" when going over the pick-up of the baby for what must have been the thirty-fifth time. "She wrapped up the kid and they left in a hurry, like I told you already a hundred times," she said in an exasperated tone.

Malone and I both leaned toward her so quickly and simultaneously that the woman must have thought we were about to attack. She jerked away. "What?"

Malone: "You just said 'they.'"

Me: "You never said 'they' before."

Malone: "So who was with her?"

Me: "Was it a boyfriend?"

That last was a stab in the dark on my part, figuring that maybe Crystal had already found a substitute for the recently deceased James Orkney. Serena Rae went wide-eyed and sat back like I'd slapped her for real.

"How the fuck...?"

I could sense Malone tensing up and I reached out to put a hand on her arm. The young woman's reaction was too strong for what I had guessed—so now I had another guess.

"*Your* boyfriend? Is that it? She recruited your boyfriend to help her out?"

"Shit," she said. And we were there.

CHAPTER EIGHTY-FOUR

It was quarter to ten when we left Serena Rae Knowles AKA Callaphonic slumped on her sofa, having assured her that she wouldn't be arrested for kidnapping and that we'd make certain her boyfriend didn't know she had given him up. She believed the kidnapping part; she was dubious about the boyfriend guarantee. For that matter, so was I.

Once Serena Rae decided to spill, we learned that in fact Crystal was now running around with two guys as hired muscle. The boyfriend's name was Diego Calderon and *his* friend was called Starch; Serena Rae didn't have any other name for him. She did give us pretty good descriptions of both men. In fact, she over-shared a bit about Diego; we didn't really need to know the massiveness of his wanker.

So now we had two local goons to look for—a much easier task than locating an assassin from out of town. And a task for Malone rather than me; she had access to many more eyes than I did. (One of the few disadvantages of being a private eye.) She was on her cell phone and had BOLOs out for the two by the time we got back to my car.

She wanted me to drop her back at the Justice Center so she could talk to the gang unit and see if they had info on local hang-outs for Diego or Starch--and, for that matter, if the database had a real name for Starch. Having already spent a good part of the previous night looking over her shoulder at her desk, I decided I'd rather check in at my office. She promised she'd give me a call as soon as she had something.

No one followed me to the parking lot and no one took a shot at me as I crossed the street. I retrieved my mail from the box at the bottom of the steps and trudged up to my office. There was no one in the hallway. I thought about stopping in to see how Eleanor

293

was doing, but just didn't have the energy. I was learning the hard way that I didn't do as well on a couple of hours sleep as I used to. I unlocked the door, turned on the light, hung up my jacket, tossed the mail on my desk, dropped the Smith and Wesson in the drawer, decided to leave the window shade up again, and more or less collapsed into my chair. Apparently the adrenaline surges didn't last as long anymore, either. And all my recent injuries were hurting again.

I actually thought fondly—just for a few seconds—of my old married life before apprenticing with Johnny and Hap, before so many people wanted to injure me and mine. Then I was trying to decide between sorting my mail or taking a nap when there was a knock on the door. I had my hand on the gun when I called to ask who it was. The door opened and Eleanor stuck her head in.

"It's me. You busy?"

"Come on in," I answered as I quietly closed the drawer.

She was wearing a gray pantsuit with pink blouse today, very business-like as befit the beginning of tax season. She settled in one of my visitor chairs. "I couldn't find anything on Tina Glass," she said.

For a moment I was at a complete loss, then I remembered the conversation with Alison Roberts followed by my inquiry to Eleanor.

"Right," I said. "Okay. It was too much to hope that you would."

She held up a finger and grinned slyly. "*But*," she said, "I got something on Tina Crystal."

That set me forward in my chair. "Really?"

"Yep. You said your girl was using a lot of aliases, so I just took a random shot and there she was in the credit card records."

"No kidding. What did you find out?"

294

"In the last three weeks, Tina Crystal has used a credit card multiple times at a fast food place out on Sandy near 57th Avenue. Nothing else, so I can't tell you where she's staying or what she's driving."

I sat back. "I'll be damned. That's fantastic. I already know what she's driving and she's probably staying somewhere close to that restaurant. Hot damn!"

Eleanor practically wriggled with pleasure in her seat. "I told you that those specialized databases would pay off."

"Yes," I agreed with a big grin. "You did. You said that—and you were right."

"So you're going to stop bitching about the bill?"

"As of now—and forever."

"Glad to be of service. By the way, you are looking like crap."

"I don't sleep well when someone kills one of my clients, shoots one of my friends, and tries to burn my house down. Plus there's still a baby out there I have to find."

"Jeez. I can understand that you might be looking a little under the weather. How is Johnny?"

"He's doing okay, considering that he's an old man who was shot on top of having a stroke."

"Jeez, again. Tell him for me to get his butt well. Is there anything else I can do?"

"No, I think you've done a lot and I need to make some calls to start following up."

She pushed herself up out of the chair and started to turn toward the door. "Well, let me know if there is anything else. Take care of yourself. Crystal, Tina, whoever is a very dangerous lady."

"Don't I know it. See you later."

She hadn't even gotten the door closed behind her before I was dialing Malone's office number.

She picked up on the first ring. "I was just about to call you," she said. "I've got something."

"Me too."

"What's yours?"

Just for a second I was tempted to do a I'll-show-you-mine-if.... But no. "I might have at least the neighborhood that Crystal Glass has been staying in."

"Wouldn't happen to be out around 60th and Sandy, would it?"

Crap! Foiled again! "How the hell did you know that?"

"I couldn't find anything on a Starch, but we've got a shitload of info on Diego Calderon and apparently his favorite hangouts are a couple of skuzzy bars right around there."

"And I've got a party who calls herself Tina Crystal using a credit card at a fast food place near 57th and Sandy."

"Glass. Crystal. Good job putting that together."

"You can thank my accountant, actually."

"Really? You can tell me all about your clever accountant during the stakeout."

"That's just what I was thinking. We've got two people and a car to look for."

"Which means we're in business."

"You want to bring Haller in on it?" I was betting I knew the answer.

"That prick? Let's wait until we've got something."

"How about Mike?"

"Not his case. He could get in trouble."

So could you, I didn't say out loud. "How about I pick you up in a half-hour?"

"How about I pick *you* up in an hour, in my personal car? Crystal is likely to recognize yours."

Sometimes you gotta go along to get along. "Sounds fine," I said.

We hung up and I sat back in my chair, grinning at my empty office. We were in business.

CHAPTER EIGHTY-FIVE

Malone's personal car turned out to be an older-model black Jeep Cherokee, which in most parts of the country wouldn't be that great for a stakeout. In the Pacific Northwest, however, it looks like half the vehicles on the street. My Subaru looks like the other half, so we would have been okay either way.

Our first decision was whether we *really* wanted to do a stakeout as such or not. We had two bars and a fast food place as potential targets, after all. They were all within a three-block stretch of Sandy but even parking right in the middle still left you with two spots you couldn't observe very well.

Nevertheless we decided we'd try that for a while. The fast food place, Carl's Chicken Bonanza by name, was the one in the middle and it was nearing lunch time. We wanted Crystal more than we wanted the muscle and this was where she'd used the credit card. So we'd stake it out for a few hours, probably through the early evening, and if she didn't show for either meal we'd hit the two bars in search of the two guys. We figured Malone could run over to the fast food place to get us take-out for lunch and dinner; Crystal wouldn't recognize her even if they collided at the entrance. We would be going Dutch, of course.

We had settled in by eleven thirty, Malone sitting upright and alert in the driver's seat and me more or less relaxed, leaning back in the passenger seat. The "less" came from being perhaps a little too aware of her sitting there. I had an excellent view of her profile as she watched the street. Nice forehead, nose, lips...and the rest wasn't bad either. I could smell a very faint fragrance, like cinnamon, which surprised me, but maybe it was shampoo. Devon Malone hadn't struck me as the perfume type.

I tried to focus on my food hunger rather than any other kind. "Ever tried Carl's Chicken Bonanza?" I asked.

She replied first with a little grunt. "I'm afraid I've not had the pleasure," she continued. "I'm pretty sure it won't *be* a pleasure."

"Well, we have to eat."

She glanced over at me. "You're hungry already?"

I pointed at the clock in the dashboard. "It's just about lunch time. A growing boy needs his nourishment."

Another grunt. "Right. Well, it probably is better to beat the rush since she'd more likely be part of the rush. Give me some money and I'll go get us what I can."

I dug out my wallet and handed over a ten. "I think I'll have chicken," I said.

"I think you're right," she said as she opened her door and slid out.

I *was* right. Carl, however, was not correct in characterizing his chicken as a bonanza; it tasted like it had been cooked yesterday and not very well at that. The fries had apparently been sitting around for a day or so already when the chicken was cooked. The soft drinks were okay.

Our conversation was desultory as we attempted to digest what we'd been able to eat. It was easy to keep track of the lunchtime crowd at Carl's since it never developed. No more than a dozen people stopped in between noon and one. None of them was Crystal Glass.

"She must be staying very near here," I supposed as I tried to suppress a belch. "There's no other explanation."

"Or she has extremely poor taste in chicken."

"I think my explanation is more likely."

"Agreed. If we don't have any luck at dinner time or in the bars, I'll set up a canvas of all the motels in the area. I hate to do that, though, both because it would mean involving Danny Haller and it would have to be uniforms; she'd be in the wind if she saw them coming."

"Maybe we'll get lucky," I said.

Malone chuckled softly.

"Why is that funny?"

"Just a stray thought. Never mind."

I realized that I had a theory about what thought had strayed, but instead of pursuing it I settled back in my seat, an eye on the side mirror and my side of the street.

CHAPTER EIGHTY-SIX

Once lunchtime was over our stakeout perked up somewhat—not because we saw anyone of interest on the street but because our cell phones, particularly Malone's, began to ring. In the old days you had only yourself and perhaps a partner for company during a long surveillance. Now the whole rest of the damned world is in the car with you.

Her calls all seemed to be business, dealing with various other cases she was working on. My two calls during the afternoon were both personal. Colleen checked in to let me know that her mother and Patty Samuels were recovering nicely from the recent threats. Reuben called just to remind me that I owed him for his help so far.

"Colleen is your daughter?" Malone asked after I disconnected from the first call. She had happened to be off her own phone during my conversation.

"How'd you guess?"

"You sounded fatherly."

"Really? I'm not sure that's a good thing."

"Me neither, but there you go. Is Patty another daughter?"

"Patty is a friend of...my daughter's." I hadn't mentioned Sarah on my side of the phone conversation and decided I'd just as soon leave her out of it.

"They've been having trouble? Not that it's any of my business."

"Patty's been having trouble with an ex."

I could see that Malone was grinning, even though her head was turned away toward the fast food place. "You have a sideline advising women about man trouble?"

"This was more like dangerous stalker trouble."

"Ah. And all taken care of, sounded like."

"Yep."

She didn't pursue it any further and she was on a call of her own when I was talking to Reuben. She probably wouldn't have had any questions about him anyway.

We made it through dinner time, Malone again getting our own take-out before the potential rush. I didn't dare use Carl's restroom but we were parked in front of a mom and pop bakery that let me use theirs. An unnecessary precaution, since Crystal Glass again was not among the dozen or so customers who showed up during the standard mealtime.

"Okay," Malone decided a little before seven, "that's it. Let's go prowl those bars and then get the hell out of here. I've got a whole other life I'm supposed to be living."

"Besides work?" I asked as we started to get out of her vehicle.

"Besides your damned work," she told me over the roof as she clicked the locks. "My lieutenant is getting a little pissed that I'm spending so little time on my real cases. He'd be *really* pissed if he knew I was moonlighting with a private eye."

"You've got cases more important than a missing baby?"

"For some strange reason my lieutenant seems to prefer that I handle cases like this using our own department resources. Standard procedure and all that." She took off toward the nearer of the two bars.

"In other words," I said as I took a couple of quick, long strides to catch up, "your lieutenant would be pissed that you're spending time with me."

She glanced over at me. "Yes, he would. For that matter, *I'm* pissed that I'm spending time with you."

CHAPTER EIGHTY-SEVEN

The first bar was dark, grimy and sparsely populated. We didn't see anyone who matched the photo of Diego Calderon that Malone had printed off from her database. The bartender, an old heavyset guy who'd obviously made us as cops the second we walked in the door, didn't know anybody who looked like the photo, didn't know anybody called Starch, and probably couldn't have testified as to what planet his establishment was on.

We headed back past Malone's Jeep to visit the other bar. It was a little more brightly lit and crowded. There was even some live music of sorts, a ragtag band of two guys on guitar and a girl singer. None of them looked older than sixteen and they were playing some sort of alt-rock. Maybe. Not that I really know what alt-rock is. I'd heard Colleen and her friends use the term and whatever this was didn't sound like regular rock.

The bartender was equally heavyset and equally aware that we were cops, but somewhat younger than bartender number one.

There were several mean-looking mid-twenties Hispanic men in the room who could have been Diego Calderon, but weren't. Malone slapped her badge and the photo on the bar in front of the bartender. "Ever seen this guy in here?"

"Never," he responded immediately without even glancing at the photo.

Malone cut her eyes over toward the band. "Gee, that's too bad. I think that means I'll have to go card those kids. If any of them are under-age, you could lose your liquor license—not to mention being up for all the child labor law violations."

Her eyes came back to him as he in turn gazed over at the three band members. I could see him running the calculation: he didn't *know* that any of them were under-age, but he hadn't checked and they sure did *look* young.... He picked up the photo.

"He's been in," he said as he tossed the photo back onto the bar. "Him and his dumb shit buddy."

"When was the last time?"

"I dunno. I don't keep track of everybody's comin' and goin'. Last night, I think."

"They're regulars?"

"Pretty regular, I guess."

"About what time?"

He turned and looked up at the clock on the wall behind him. Seven forty. "I dunno. Around nine, I guess."

Apparently he felt that "guessing" everything he told us made it less like snitching to the cops. Fine with me.

Malone picked up her badge and the photo. "Thanks very much," she said. "Two things. If this guy or his friend come in this evening, we weren't here." She looked over at the band again. "And if those kids are in here again tomorrow night, they'd better be legal."

"Okay," he said. "I'll make sure."

"Good enough."

We left the bar, taking a quick survey of the street as we stepped outside to make sure our quarry wasn't early.

"Diego and Starch," I said. "Sounds like an eighties TV show."

"Humph. Let's move the car up closer and see if we can get them cancelled this evening."

We hurried down the street to Malone's Jeep and she moved it to a spot almost directly across from the bar. We settled down to wait once more.

"Why aren't you?" I tossed out just to provoke some conversation.

"Why aren't I what?"

"Using standard procedure for this case instead of sitting here with me?"

She was quiet for a moment. "I'm not actually neglecting standard procedure. I've used department resources when I could, but it's also been working to use you as a resource. Besides, my lieutenant is a sexist pig. Don't tell him I said so."

"I wouldn't. But, I gotta say, you don't sound like a happy camper."

"How many happy campers do you know?"

"I'm happy."

She offered me something close to an outright sneer. "Right."

We sat quietly for a few moments.

"So I'm a resource," I said.

"Yes, I guess so." Then: "You're a resource," she agreed definitively.

"Sorry about your lieutenant."

"He's not the first. Won't be the last."

My cell phone rang. We hadn't been interrupted by a call since around five, so I was startled. I pulled it out and flipped it open. Veronica's cell number. I was sorely tempted to let it go to voicemail, but it might be something about Colleen. I finally hit the talk button.

"This is Clint."

Silence on the other end.

"Veronica?"

"She can't come to the phone right now." It was that same deep, strong female voice I'd heard in my office and in the hospital parking lot. Crystal Glass.

CHAPTER EIGHTY-EIGHT

My body jerked like I'd been hit. I could sense Malone's sympathetic reaction next to me.

"Fuck!" I said.

Crystal laughed out loud. "Now *that* is one of the few things I'm *not* going to do to Veronica here if you don't get off my back."

"What do you want?" I asked, leaning forward and listening intently. Nothing in the background so far. No train whistles, nothing.

"What I just said. Leave me and Tanya alone. We deserve a life together and I'm tired of you nippin' at my heels like some fuckin' hound dog. You leave us alone and your friend here lives. You *don't* do that and your friend dies. Then I go after your daughter."

"Let me speak to Veronica."

"You don't need to talk to her right now."

"Yes, I do. That's how this works. Proof of life before I agree to anything."

Another little laugh. "Huh. I saw that movie. Okay. Gimme a minute. We'll do it like in the movies. That's fun." I heard her put the phone down hard. It sounded like on a wooden table.

I covered the receiver with my hand and hissed my cell phone number and provider at Malone, assuming she'd already picked up enough from my end of the conversation to know we needed the call traced. I was right. She was asking information for the number of my provider the second I stopped speaking.

Crystal came back on my line. "Heeeere's Veronica!" Doing a little Ed McMahon for me. Having fun, like she said.

"Clint?"

I barely recognized her voice, it was so distorted by tension and terror. "Keep it together, kiddo. We'll get you out of this. Can you tell...?"

"Nooooo," returned Crystal's voice, "she's not going to tell you a thing. Ever. If you don't leave me and Tanya the fuck alone."

"Okay." Anything to keep her on the phone. "How do you want to work this?"

"You'd fucking love it if I gave you a long list of instructions right now, wouldn't you? But I'd rather keep it simple. When *I* believe that you're gone out of our lives, I let the bitch go. Until then she's mine. And don't forget your daughter." She cut the connection.

I snapped my phone closed and looked over at Malone who was still on hers, listening intently to someone. "I know you did," she said after a moment. "Thanks." She closed her phone and looked over at me.

"Crystal, right?"

I nodded. "She's got my friend Veronica now. Could you locate her?"

"She was on a cell phone as well. We got one tower but that's it. Probably fifty square blocks coverage, maybe more. Not nearly good enough."

"What fifty square blocks?"

"We're in the middle of it right now. The tower's about two blocks away. Like I said, it doesn't tell us anything new."

"It tells us we're right to be sitting here."

She gave me a beady look. "And sitting here is going to help exactly how?"

I focused past her out the front windshield at two males coming down the sidewalk on the other side of the street toward the bar. They were both big, wide in the shoulders, with the rolling gait of street fighters, one with a moustache and dark hair hanging to his shoulders, the other with a burr cut that made him look almost bald in the glare from the streetlights. They matched the descriptions of Diego and Starch.

I pointed. "That's how," I said. "I think it's show time."

CHAPTER EIGHTY-NINE

Malone's head whipped around to look and her eyes widened. "Well, damn," she said. "You could be right about that."

We opened our doors as the two men came even with the front of the bar. They may have had the walk, but they apparently didn't have the awareness. They paid no attention as we exited the vehicle.

They were turning to enter the bar and we were two-thirds of the way across the street before they glanced in our direction. One glance was enough; they knew we were trouble and braced themselves to bolt.

Malone and I simultaneously drew our weapons. "Police!" she announced. "Stay put and keep your hands where I can see them."

I watched the two guys calculate the odds; they literally swayed back and forth as they decided if they had a chance at running. Then raised their hands in resignation. They turned to face the façade of the bar as we stepped onto the sidewalk. Not unfamiliar with the drill, obviously.

Malone pulled out her cell phone.

"What are you doing?" I asked.

"Calling for backup."

"Hold off on that," I said. "Let's move this meeting off the public sidewalk first."

She stopped punching numbers and glared. "What?"

I gestured toward the corner of the building with my gun. There was an opening between the bar and the building next door, not really an alley but close enough. "I want to take this around back and have a chat with our friends here before you make any calls."

"Are you shitting me?"

"We take these guys downtown, they lawyer up, and it could be forever before we find out what we need to know. I don't think my friend can wait that long."

"That doesn't mean...."

"Oh yes it does. That's exactly what it means. We need to have a talk with these guys right now, off the grid, off this street." I prodded Diego in the back. "So let's go."

Malone stood, phone in one hand and gun at Starch's back in the other, looking at me as if I'd just arrived from another planet. I stared right back at her. Finally Diego piped up, looking over his shoulder at Malone. "You gotta take me downtown to see my lawyer, cunt. It's the fuckin' law."

There are times when keeping your mouth shut is the best policy. This would have been one of those times for Diego Calderon.

Malone transferred her gaze to Calderon and after a moment slowly nodded her head. "Back of the building it is," she said.

Diego protested all the way around the corner of the building and down the narrow walkway. Starch had yet to say a word, though he kept glancing at his voluble partner with what looked like mild disgust. Guess he didn't approve of volubility.

As for me, by the time we got to the back alleyway with its garbage containers and delivery doors and windows covered with wire mesh and the faint smell of decay I was very close to losing it. My imagination roiled with images of Samantha Quiller dead on that bed and her little daughter the last time I'd seen her in her stroller. Now, of course, I could add what I imagined of Veronica at the mercy of a cold-blooded killer.

I've spent a lot of time on maintaining focus and control, thousands of hours meditating and thousands more training in Taekwondo. Right at the moment the urge to violence was totally defeating the desire for peace.

310

We came around the corner in the alley and I slammed Calderon up against the bare brick wall with my Smith and Wesson jammed into his throat.

"Whoa!" I heard Malone say, but I only had eyes for Diego. His were at half-mast for the moment since his head had hit the wall pretty hard.

"I will say this only once," I said to him so softly it was almost a whisper. "You are going to tell me where to find Crystal Glass, right now, or I will blow your fucking brains all over this wall."

That opened his eyes up again. I guess what he saw told him I wasn't kidding.

"Five blocks," he gasped. "About five blocks east, a little old white house, used to be a massage parlor I think, that's where she is."

I jammed the barrel in harder. "Address?"

He could barely speak and I didn't give a damn. "I don't know!" he squeaked. "Who looks at a fuckin' address? It's on this street. It's the only house with crappy little stores all around. It's next to a big parking lot!"

"There are stores all around *and* it's next to a parking lot?"

"Except for the parking lot!" The squeak hit an even higher register. "There are stores except for the fuckin' parking lot. It's an old fallin' down house. I think it was abandoned and she just moved in. There's a fuckin' yard in front, man, you can't miss it!"

I took a breath and stepped back. As the rest of the world came back into focus, it occurred to me to wonder what Malone had been doing all this time. I glanced over. She and Starch were standing there staring at me with their mouths open. She was still holding her gun on him, but I don't think either one of them was aware of it.

"Now," I said, "would be a good time to call for backup."

311

None of us said a word after she made her call. We just listened for the approaching sirens. She turned Diego and Starch over to the four uniforms who shortly appeared and told them she'd be in soon to do the booking, that they should just put the two guys in a cell in the meantime. No calls until she got there. She didn't say anything about me and none of them asked.

We followed the cops and their detainees back out to the front sidewalk, Diego protesting all the way about police brutality and wanting his lawyer. No one paid him any attention as he and Starch were loaded into the two cruisers, after which they were driven away. Then we were just standing there.

"Would you have stopped me?" I asked finally.

"I don't know," she answered after a long silence. "Probably not, I guess. In for a penny, in for a dollar, or whatever."

"I think it's pound. 'In for a penny, in for a pound.' Old British expression."

"Okay. But then I would have arrested your ass."

"After we got Crystal."

"Yeah, probably after."

"So let's go get Crystal."

CHAPTER NINETY

The first thing we did was make sure we could identify the house Diego had described. It was there on our right, next to the parking lot, just as he said, and fairly well lit by the nearby street-lights. I actually recognized it. Diego was correct that it used to be a "massage parlor"—one that was famously staffed by two elderly ladies rather than the sexy young things one would normally expect.

It was a small bungalow, the white paint flaking off the wood siding and the cluttered front porch sagging. How it had avoided demolition with the commercial district growing up around it was a mystery, especially since time was doing such a good job of tearing it down anyway.

I took all that in at a glance. Neither of us wanted to do more than glance, nor slow down, because there was a very large fellow sitting on the front step eying the traffic going by. Apparently Diego and Starch weren't the only muscle Crystal Glass had recruit-ed.

Malone drove another couple of blocks, pulled around a cor-ner and stopped the car. "You think there's a guy in back as well?"

"How deep is that parking lot next door? Maybe we can get a look."

"Let's check it out."

She made a U-turn and we headed back up Sandy to the park-ing lot entrance where she turned in. The lot extended about fifty feet beyond the back of the house and the land immediately behind the house was undeveloped.

"How did Crystal get your friend?" Malone asked as she steered the car toward the far end of the lot.

"No clue," I said. "She just has her."

"I mean, how did she even know about this Veronica?"

"Ah. Maybe she followed me to the café at one point. Or maybe she just did some research. It's pretty well known that Veronica was my first client and is an old friend, even a kind of surrogate mom for my daughter."

"Hmm. Lucky it wasn't your daughter," Malone said. She pulled into a slot in the far northwest corner of the lot, where we would have the best view we could get of the building's rear entrance.

I shuddered. "No kidding."

"Maybe she's working up to that."

"She's not going to get there."

"Nope."

I focused on where we were parked and noted that this spot put us almost directly underneath one of the bright parking lot lights.

Malone obviously wasn't pleased with our location, either. "If there is somebody keeping watch in back of that house and we stay here more than a couple of minutes, we're going to be made," she muttered. "This lot is not exactly full of cars right now."

I leaned toward her as I looked back at the house. "Let's pretend to make out while I look over the situation," I suggested.

She shrank away from me. "You've got to be kidding."

"Pretending, for Christ's sake, and just for a minute while I scope out the back of the house. We're in the light and it's in the dark. I need some time to see what I can see. I'll just look past you while we hug. I promise not to cop a feel, okay?"

She brought her arms up with obvious reluctance. "You'd better not."

Lucky for us, there was a small window in the upper half of the house's back door. Some kind of filmy curtain covered the glass, but I could see a light on inside. Unluckily for me, I was finding it relatively difficult to focus with Devon Malone's cheek up against mine and her upper body pressing close.

314

I gritted my teeth and did my best to concentrate.

"Well?" inquired Malone into my right ear.

"Ah," I said after a moment. "I can see a shadow through the back curtain. It just moved a little. Another big man, looks like."

She immediately pulled away and shifted the car into reverse. "Okay, so it's covered front and back. Time to get out of here, call it in, and plan the operation."

She flipped her cell phone open with one hand as we pulled out of the parking lot and turned left down Sandy again. I reached across and grabbed it out of her hand.

"What the fuck?" she exclaimed and swerved to the curb. "Give me back the damned phone."

"Let's think about this for a minute," I said.

"Give me back the damned phone."

"What happens when you make this call?"

"For the.... What do you mean, what happens? We get the damned backup and put together a plan, that's what happens. Give me back the fucking phone. I mean it."

She lunged forward and tried to grab it back. I blocked the attempt and gave her a little shove back into her seat.

"Wait!" I said. "Take a breath. I'll let you have your phone after we give this some thought."

She knocked aside the hand that I'd shoved her with. "What's to think about? If I have to arrest you right now, then that's...."

"Just picture it for a minute," I interrupted loudly enough to override her. "Just think about it! We're talking about a kidnapping here, so we get the Feds as well as the local cops. It's a hostage situation, so we get a negotiator. There are at least two armed men and a professional killer inside so we get SWAT. On top of all that we get every media outlet in town because they all monitor the local and federal frequencies. And where are we, you and me, in all that? I'm private, you're missing persons...so we're nowhere. Way out on

the edge of the action, just watching, waiting for the massive fuck-
-up that we know has to happen. Think!"

She sat there looking at me, quivering with adrenaline. I could
see the movie running behind her eyes.

"You make the call," I said, "and everybody in that house dies."

After what seemed like about an hour but probably wasn't
more than thirty seconds, her shoulders slumped slightly.

"Do you know how much trouble I'm going to be in if we
cowboy this thing on our own and it goes south? Or, fuck, even if
it doesn't go south."

"It's not going to go south. We can't let it."

"How are the two of us going to do that?"

I handed her phone back and took out my own. "First of all, *I*
call for backup."

There was a time when that would have meant Johnny Crew
and Hap Harbaugh. It might again, but not today. I was really wishing I had a time machine as I punched in Reuben Keys' cell phone
number. One of these days I was going to have to figure out how
to program a contact list on this damned thing.

I checked my watch while I listened to it ring. A little after nine.
He was probably on the street since it had been dark for several
hours already and the girls would be out in full force despite the
February chill. Sexual need knows no seasons.

CHAPTER NINETY-ONE

He finally answered. "Reuben." Traffic noise in the background. Definitely on the street. He wasn't going to be happy about having his work interrupted but I figured it would be easy enough to talk him around. He fancied himself an action hero rather than a drug-dealing pimp, after all, and he was in fact very good in action if not as a hero.

I explained my current situation as succinctly as I could and asked him to meet us a few blocks down from Crystal's location on Sandy. He bitched and moaned, as I expected—and then agreed, as I also expected.

"I'll bring along Drake if I can find him," he finally said. "See you in thirty."

Meanwhile the temperature in Malone's car had dropped steadily as she realized who I was talking to and listened to the conversation. I hung up and was hit with the iciest stare I'd ever seen in my life.

"We," she began, speaking with exaggerated emphasis, "are going to do this with one of your pimp friends as backup?"

"Two of my pimp friends, actually. Reuben is going to bring along a colleague called Amani Drake, a very big colleague who might come in handy."

She held the stare for another moment and then it was like all the air went out of her. She leaned back in the driver's seat and looked blankly out the front windshield. "I'm fucked," she said.

"Reuben is extremely good in a firefight and Drake is about the size of the Justice Center. We'll be fine."

"Right." She shook herself. "Speaking of the Justice Center, I have to go downtown to do some paper on Diego and Starch."

"Now? Reuben will be meeting us in about a half-hour. We need to get on this."

317

"I told the uniforms I'd follow up. I don't show and somebody is going to radio to ask where I am. It shouldn't take much more than a half-hour to do what's necessary; I'll drop you off where you said you'd meet your guys and get back there as soon as I can."

She was still looking out the front at the street-lighted pavement. I pictured her bursting into the watch commander's office with this wild story about kidnapped females and a nutcase local PI.

"You'll come back alone?" I finally asked.

Now she met my eyes. "I've agreed to an assault on armed men holding hostages with you and two pimps as backup—and you're asking if you can trust me?"

I shrugged. "I wasn't sure you had agreed."

"God help me, I don't know why, but I'll come back alone."

I had told Reuben to meet us in front of a hamburger joint three blocks west and that's where Malone dropped me off. It being a cold February night, I ducked inside to get a cup of coffee. There was no one else in the place and the kid behind the counter looked like he was thinking of closing up, but he said nothing when I sat down at a table in the front window to keep an eye out for my two associates.

Sitting there sipping the hot brew, I found I couldn't lose that image of Devon Malone blowing the whistle on me. No help for it now. Either I'd eventually see her, Reuben, and hopefully Amani out the window or I'd see a whole squadron of cop cars going by toward Crystal's lair. Meanwhile, all I could do was wait.

CHAPTER NINETY-TWO

Twenty-seven minutes later Reuben's colorful pimpmobile pulled up right in front of the window. I assumed Reuben was driving; I couldn't see him at all past Amani Drake in the passenger seat. Having long since finished my coffee, I went out to meet them on the sidewalk.

Drake emerged ponderously from the passenger side as Reuben came into view exiting the driver's side.

"How you doing, Amani?" I inquired.

"Good," he said. A long sentence, by his standards.

"So we're here," Reuben said as he came around the front end of the vehicle. "What now?"

"Malone should be back in a few minutes and then we do some scouting and make a plan."

I had already told Reuben that Malone was part of the team, but his face twisted into a sour look anyway. "Where's the little bitch cop now?"

"Doing some paperwork at the Justice Center."

Both men stood there looking at me for a long moment. "Jesus," said Reuben.

"We already got a couple of Crystal's guys and she had to do the paperwork. She'll be back soon."

"You trust her?"

"Yes," I replied, and I didn't even have my fingers crossed behind my back—though I could feel them twitching.

I turned back toward the fast food entrance. "Let's...." And found myself looking at a CLOSED sign. Apparently the kid behind the counter was not eager for the late-night patronage of two very dangerous-looking black guys. I didn't blame him.

"...sit in your car and wait for Malone," I finished as I continued my turn back to the street.

To my great relief, Malone's car pulled up behind Reuben's just as we were opening the doors. I hadn't been looking forward to spending time in the pimpmobile with a less than hygienic Amani Drake.

The three of us re-gathered on the sidewalk. Malone was looking up at Drake as she joined our circle between me and him. Standing beside him she looked like she was about two feet tall. Finally, still craning her neck to look up at his massive billiard-ball (or maybe more like bowling-ball) head, she said, "Gee."

Said head bent way forward to look down at her. "Hi there, officer," rumbled the big man. Three words. He must have found her incredibly attractive.

She looked at me. "We need to talk," she said.

"Yes," I agreed. "It's too early to do anything now and we need a plan." I glanced around us. "We need a place to talk."

Malone and I both looked back at the CLOSED sign. The kid was still visible, inside cleaning up. "No problem," said Malone. She walked back to the glass door, knocked on it sharply, and slapped her badge against it so the kid could see.

He stopped wiping down the counter, started to shake his head no, registered the badge and frowned mightily. Then came over and unlocked the door. He opened it just enough to look out at Malone. "We're closed," he said.

Malone made a show of looking at her watch. "Are you normally closed at ten o'clock?"

"Sometimes. If we ain't got no customers."

"Well, you've got customers--so I guess you ain't closed."

The kid wasn't happy but he let us in. We chose a table in the back corner, Malone and I opposite Reuben and Amani, and the kid brought over four cups of coffee.

Malone looked at me. "So, what's the plan?"

"We go in the house, take out the bad guys, and rescue the innocent victims."

"Ah. Good plan."

Reuben glared from one of us to the other. "What the fuck? You think this is a fuckin' comedy club? We doin' stand-up now?"

"I just outlined the strategy," I said. "Now we have to talk tactics."

CHAPTER NINETY-THREE

We drank coffee and talked tactics until midnight. The kid even got a few more customers before his evening was over. Reuben put his cell phone on vibrate and gave it to Drake; then we moved out to take our places.

Reuben drove the pimpmobile three blocks closer to the house and Amani Drake set off on foot to go around and approach the back of the house. Malone parked right behind Reuben again. The plan was to give the big guy twenty minutes to get as close to the back door as he could without being spotted. Fortunately, it was a new moon and cloudy to boot; there was little chance he'd be seen if he was careful. No question he'd be careful. Amani Drake had zero book smarts but he'd survived a long time on the street.

Malone and I said very little as we waited. I was entirely focused on the coming action, trying to imagine—and wishing I knew— where Veronica and the baby might be in that small house. Probably not next to either the front or back doors, at least.

Malone said only two things. After about five minutes: "She's going to be on alert. She knows Diego and Starch didn't come back."

"I'm guessing she's more like mildly confused," I replied, "maybe pissed, thinking they flaked out on her. She'd expect the cops to show up if they'd been nabbed."

"Yeah, well," was the dry response, "so would I."

Then after about fifteen minutes: "The story will be we were questioning your informants when we saw Crystal entering the building and believed the baby to be in immediate danger, okay?"

"Sounds good to me," I said. Truthfully it sounded more than a little thin, but I couldn't think of anything better. I reminded myself to ask Malone after all this was over why in the world she was going along with it. I was glad she was, because I sincerely believed a large police presence would get the hostages killed. But I was still curious.

At twenty minutes exactly, I punched Reuben's number into my cell as Malone turned the ignition. Amani answered in a whisper that sounded like a distant rumble. "We're moving," was all I said and snapped the phone shut. Malone flashed her headlights at Reuben and we heard his engine turn over.

He hit his accelerator. Malone waited three seconds and then tore out after him, lights but no siren.

If all was going according to plan, Amani was knocking on the back door of the house as we roared toward the front.

Thirty-five seconds later, Reuben hit his brakes, slewed over to the curb in front of the house, bailed out of the pimpmobile and ran for the front door.

All we needed, we had told ourselves, was ten seconds or less hesitation inside the house.

We were counting on three things. One, at this time of night the people in the house would be bored, tired, and slow to react. Two, they'd be confused by sudden and simultaneous distractions in the front and back of the house. Three, it wouldn't immediately occur to them that either Reuben or Amani had anything to do with a law enforcement operation. Somebody would be seeing a huge thug-looking guy at the back door without being aware that a flamboyantly pimp-looking guy was running toward the front door. It would be just the opposite for whoever was watching the front; plus, he or she should be further confused by an apparent hot pursuit with no siren.

And, yes, that's a hell of a lot of things to count on. If I had believed in a god, I'd have been praying like hell at this point.

Malone cut the lights and screeched to a stop a few yards behind Reuben's vehicle as he slammed his body into the front door of the house. We were out of the car and coming down the sidewalk as the door burst open and he stumbled inside yelling some

324

bullshit about how they had to hide him. I'd heard no shots yet; it was working.

Then Malone and I hit the doorway and there was no more hesitation.

CHAPTER NINETY-FOUR

Reuben apparently decided at that point that he'd done his bit. He was diving for the floor as we came in, leaving the front-room lookout to level his weapon at us. All I registered of the bad guy was a medium-sized blur wearing a ragged black tee shirt and firing a big handgun.

I snapped off one shot just in time to make him miss and then hit him in the chest with two more. Malone meanwhile was covering an open doorway to our left. We pulled up short in the center of the room surrounded by a sudden silence. Gunfire still ringing in my ears, I started to take in other details.

We were in a small, sparsely furnished living room. Everything dusty and musty. There was a closed door in front of us that probably led to the kitchen where Amani would have been coming in. We'd not seen or heard anything of him or the guy he was supposedly taking out, so I had no idea what might be on the other side of that door.

The doorway on our left that Malone had covered opened into a short corridor. My guess was two small bedrooms and a bath. If Crystal, Veronica and the kid were indeed in the house, they were somewhere in there.

We both stood absolutely still. Reuben rolled over far enough to look up at me, but otherwise remained quiet. Aside from some gurgling sounds from the guy I had shot, there were just the faint noises of any older house—creaks and clicks and hums. I thought one of the hums was probably a refrigerator in the kitchen but there was no other sound from beyond that closed door.

Then there *was* a sound from the open doorway.

A knob turning. A door down the hall swinging open. Something like shuffling. Malone and I both stepped back, she to her left to increase her angle on the door, me to my right to decrease it. I could now see about halfway down the dimly lit corridor. A figure jerked into view.

The person was propelled forward another couple of steps and I could see it was Veronica—mouth taped, a gun to her right temple, a hand grasping the opposite shoulder from behind.... She was clutching a blanket-covered bundle to her chest. It had to be Kinsey Quiller.

She was pulled to a halt maybe five feet short of the doorway. By then she could see me and her eyes were wide with recognition and fear. I still couldn't see who controlled her from behind; only the thin bare arm holding the gun and that hand digging into the shoulder.

Then a head peeked out, looking past the gun arm at me.

Crystal Glass's face was thin, but not with the pallor I would have expected; rather, it was a mottled red. Her hair was pitch black and pulled tight in a ponytail of some kind. What struck me most forcibly were her eyes. They were wide and glaring and utterly mad.

"Stay the fuck away from us, McCall. Try to take me and your friend here dies. Tanya dies. Everybody dies. You *hear* me?"

And that voice. It was an hysterical tremolo heading upward into stratospherically crazy.

For a second I didn't know who the hell "Tanya" was and then I remembered she'd renamed Kinsey.

"Take it easy, Crystal," I replied as evenly as I could. "Nobody has to die today."

She pushed Veronica forward a few more steps. Veronica was almost as wide-eyed as Crystal. The baby that she held was quiet. Either Kinsey was drugged or a very sound sleeper. I wasn't even going to think about the third possibility.

Crystal peered past her captives at the guy I'd shot. "Looks like somebody is," she said. He was still struggling to breathe, so maybe not. Then she focused on Reuben. "You, black guy. Are you hurt?"

He didn't answer. "You're not hit, fucker, not unless you're too tough to bleed. Get the fuck up and stand beside McCall."

He did as she said, meanwhile giving me a slant look that promised a slow and painful death from him if we survived otherwise.

Veronica shuffled forward just into the room, pushed by Crystal who was still peeking at us from behind her. Crystal seemed to finally register that two out of three of us were holding weapons. She jerked Veronica to a halt.

"Drop the guns and kick them away," she said. "I'll blow this bitch's head off if you don't."

Malone spoke up, her voice low and intense. "What if I blow her head off instead? Then where are you?"

I'm just thinking to myself, *What the fuck?* when I see Crystal's mouth twitch. A grin has come and gone. "Shoot the hostage?" she says. "I saw that movie, too. You won't do it. Drop the fucking guns."

I guess I hadn't seen the movie.

CHAPTER NINETY-FIVE

Our weapons hit the floor simultaneously. Crystal began pulling Veronica sideways toward the closed kitchen door, her eyes darting around the room as she did so. Meanwhile I'm calculating how quickly I can hit the floor and come up with my Smith and Wesson again if it looks like Crystal's going to get away through the back. At that point, I figured, we might as well risk shooting Veronica because she was going to be dead anyway. I was confident I could snap off a couple of shots without hitting the baby, at least.

They got to the door. Crystal was going to have to let go of Veronica and reach back to turn the knob. The gun against Veronica's temple didn't waver as she did so. The knob turned and she gave the door a good push to swing it open into the kitchen. There was no light on in there, but illumination from the parking lot dimly outlined the empty doorway behind them.

We were going to have to make a move.

She regained her firm grasp of Veronica's shoulder and started pulling her backward. Suddenly the faint glow from the kitchen disappeared, completely blocked out by something that filled the doorway. As far as I knew, there was only one sentient thing in the vicinity that was that big. My body tensed for action. One more step back....

And she took it.

I don't know what it must have felt like to suddenly come up against an unyielding human body that was nearly twice her size. The sound she made as the gun momentarily jerked up and away from Veronica's temple hinted that it must have felt pretty weird. It was somewhere between a grunt and a shriek.

Malone went for the gun as I went for the hostages.

I grabbed Veronica and spun her away from Malone's struggle to hold onto Crystal's gun arm. I pushed woman and baby into a far corner of the room, then turned back to see Crystal trying to throw Malone to the floor as they continued to fight for possession of the weapon.

Meanwhile Amani Drake was still simply standing there in the doorway.

With exquisite timing, the struggle swung Crystal around toward me just as I arrived. A hand strike to the proper neck nerve essentially paralyzed her for the moment and Malone stepped back with the gun in hand, letting her opponent fall to the floor.

"You okay?" I asked Malone.

"Fine," she said and then glowered at Amani. "Why didn't you do something to help?"

He gave it a few seconds consideration. "I don't hit no woman 'less she workin' for me."

Malone gave *that* a few seconds. "Jesus," she finally said, and crouched to handcuff Crystal where she lay.

CHAPTER NINETY-SIX

Malone finally put in the call for backup, as well as medics for the wounded man who was still gurgling along. The guy who'd been at the back door also needed serious medical attention. I got Veronica, who was understandably pretty shaky, to sit down.

Reuben and Amani started fading toward the back door as soon as they heard Malone talking to dispatch. On his way out, Reuben stopped and punched me in the arm. "Next time," he said, "the white folks go in first. You gonna owe me extra big for this one."

"Fair enough," I said.

I turned back to Veronica and gestured at the still-unmoving bundle in her arms. "Is the baby okay?" I asked with a certain amount of dread.

She looked down as she turned back a bit of the blanket to reveal a sleeping face, still thankfully with healthy rosy cheeks. "I think so," she said. "That bitch sedated her to keep her quiet, but I'm pretty sure she's okay otherwise."

"That would be good," I said. "We'll have her checked out as soon as some EMTs get here." I wished that Samantha Quiller could have been here to take the child from Veronica. I wished that Veronica weren't looking so fragile. But Samantha wasn't and Veronica was.

So I turned to Malone instead.

"We did it," I said.

Her look wasn't exactly one of enthusiastic agreement. "Yeah, and I'm feeling so lucky that I think I'll run right downtown and buy a dozen lottery tickets."

"Come on, you know bringing in the troops would have been a disaster. You agreed to that."

"I did. I did agree. God knows why."

"Actually, I was thinking that *I'd* like to know why."

She looked away, apparently thinking it over. "It seemed like a good idea at the time," she said finally.

"You're just full of movie quotes tonight. That was *The Magnificent Seven*, right? What was the other one from?"

"Shoot the hostage? That was from *Speed*." Her mouth twitched into a momentary grin. "I really wanted to be Keanu Reeves in that movie." Then we heard approaching sirens and the grin was gone. "Too bad this isn't a movie."

Within a half-hour the little house was crawling with uniforms, paramedics, and detectives as the street outside filled with media vans.

Malone was still on the scene, surrounded by said detectives, when I was taken down to the Justice Center to give a "statement"—which turned out to be a three-hour interrogation. They couldn't seem to understand how—or why—Malone and I had managed the assault on the house all by ourselves. I could only hope that Malone was also leaving Reuben and Amani out of it; I was going to look like the liar I was if she didn't.

Luckily for me, before the rubber truncheons came out somebody in authority determined that I was one of the good guys. Apparently Malone had supported my story.

By the time I finally stumbled into my house at five in the morning, I was asleep on my feet, the two cats were furious at being left unfed, and my voicemail was up to eight messages. I managed to dump some food in the cat dishes and turn off the ringer on the phone and that was about it. I fell across the bed fully clothed and was immediately lost in dreamless sleep.

CHAPTER NINETY-SEVEN

The next week was remarkably quiet, all things considered.

Kinsey Quiller had gone straight to the hospital from the house on Sandy that night, but she turned out to be unharmed aside from some slight dehydration. Samantha Quiller's sister would raise her in Milwaukee and hopefully the poor little kid was young enough to recover fully from the emotional trauma.

Crystal Glass had gone straight to jail and with any luck at all was going to stay there until she died of a miserable old age. Her henchman apparently had gotten around to breathing again and would survive to join her there.

Alison Roberts was pestering me before I'd gotten nearly enough rest, so I grumpily gave her the promised exclusive and even more grumpily appeared live on camera for her segment that day. I had a terrible premonition that my least favorite TV news person was going to be focusing on me even more in the future.

And, speaking of grumpy, Reuben called to announce that I owed him extra because Amani Drake had decided Portland was too hazardous for his taste and abruptly left town. I guess he preferred being muscle only when confronting women.

I spent my days in the office, catching up on bills and invoices and mail. There were at least two promising new client contacts, neither of which sounded likely to result in shootings nor any other mayhem. I made appointments with both parties and looked forward to combining some boring surveillance of a possibly straying spouse with skip-tracing a deadbeat tenant. Nice, safe multi-tasking was just the ticket right now.

I saw my daughter Colleen for lunch several times, my ex-wife Sarah once before she left town again—this time promising to keep in touch, with Colleen at least—and Veronica as she was released

335

from the hospital with minor injuries and major PTSD from her latest adventure thanks to me.

I spent most of my evenings at the dojang, catching up with my fellow black belts and working through my various injuries. By the end of the week I was actually able to punch almost full force with my left hand. The shoulder would probably be entirely recovered within another week or two. When I would have my head fully back in the game, I wasn't sure.

CHAPTER NINETY-EIGHT

And then there was Devon Malone.

It was the end of the week before I heard from her again. I'd called her both at the Justice Center and at home several times, but gotten no further than voicemail. She hadn't called back. Then, on a Thursday afternoon, she appeared in my office doorway.

I turned away from my PC and invited her to come in. She was dressed as usual in jeans, blouse, leather jacket and boots but she was wearing even less make-up than usual and her hair seemed to have lost its healthy sheen.

She crossed the space between us briskly enough, however, and took a seat in one of my visitor's chairs, her facial expression somewhere between grim and determined.

"How are you?" I asked.

That brought forth a crooked but very brief smile. "Suspended with pay for now," she answered. "After the IA investigation, maybe without pay."

"Shit. I didn't know that. There was nothing in the news. Why didn't you...?"

"Final decision only came down this morning. It'll be in the news soon enough. 'Officer Suspended For Unbelievable Fuck-Up.' That will probably be the headline."

I wanted to get up and put my arm around her, but there was a very clear no-fly zone all around her chair. She looked like she'd vibrate to pieces if she were touched.

"You didn't fuck up. You saved two people and captured a really evil scumbag."

"Which may at least save me from being prosecuted myself. Which I certainly could be, for going vigilante instead of following *any* of the established procedures. Not a fucking one of them. And I don't know why!"

She was leaning forward as if torn between embracing and attacking me, her face twisted with the apparent conflict. Maybe that's exactly where she was. In the meantime I was feeling more than a little helpless, unsure of what she wanted at this moment. I didn't know why she'd done it, either, though I had an inkling...or was it a hope?

"If there's anything I can do...."

"That's what I came for," she interrupted. She took a breath. "To tell you that I don't know why—and that I don't *want* to know why. We did what we did and I'm prepared to deal with the consequences. All I ask of you is that you stop calling. Just leave me the fuck alone."

I sat back in dismay but also in the certainty that there was no point in arguing. So much for the hope. I could practically see the wall shimmering between me and her.

"Sure," I finally said. "I can do that."

"Good." And with that she got up and turned toward the door.

"Take care of yourself," I said.

"Just leave me the fuck alone," she said again without looking back.

She left the office, closing my door quietly behind her.

Everything was quiet. Everything but my imagination. I was pretty sure that one of these days I'd be seeing that woman again.

The End

ABOUT THE AUTHOR

Glenn Harris lives and writes in the middle of the Columbia Gorge National Scenic Area (Hood River, Oregon). Besides creating detective novels and short stories, he serves as staff to the same two cats that live with Clint McCall. His former lives include college English teacher, private K-12 school director, graphic design business owner, weekly newspaper managing editor, corporate manager, and taekwondo instructor.

Keep reading the McCall and Malone mysteries! Stay tuned for *Mortal Vows* and be sure to visit Glenn Harris' website www.glennharris.us where you can subscribe to his free e-mail newsletter to get updates and background of the series!